John Harris was born in 1916. He authored the best-selling *The Sea Shall Not Have Them* and wrote under the pen names of Mark Hebden and Max Hennessy. He was a sailor, airman, journalist, travel courier, cartoonist and history teacher. During the Second World War he served with two air forces and two navies. After turning to full-time writing, Harris wrote adventure stories and created a sequence of crime novels around the quirky fictional character Chief Inspector Pel. A master of war and crime fiction, his enduring fictions are versatile and entertaining.

D0801037

ARMY OF SHADOWS
CHINA SEAS
THE CLAWS OF MERCY
CORPORAL COTTON'S LITTLE WAR
THE CROSS OF LAZZARO
FLAWED BANNER
THE FOX FROM HIS LAIR
A FUNNY PLACE TO HOLD A WAR
GETAWAY
HARKAWAY'S SIXTH COLUMN
A KIND OF COURAGE
LIVE FREE OR DIE!
THE LONELY VOYAGE
THE MERCENARIES
NORTH STRIKE
THE OLD TRADE OF KILLING

PICTURE OF DEFEAT
THE QUICK BOAT MEN
RIDE OUT THE STORM
RIGHT OF REPLY
ROAD TO THE COAST
THE SEA SHALL NOT HAVE THEM
THE SLEEPING MOUNTAIN
SMILING WILLIE AND THE TIGER
SO FAR FROM GOD
THE SPRING OF MALICE
SUNSET AT SHEBA
TAKE OR DESTROY!
THE THIRTY DAYS WAR
THE UNFORGIVING WIND
UP FOR GRABS
VARDY

JOHN HARRIS

SWORDPOINT

A NOVEL OF CASSINO

HOUSE OF STRATUS

This edition published in 2001 by House of Stratus, an imprint of
House of Stratus Ltd, Thirsk Industrial Park, York Road, Thirsk,
North Yorkshire, YO7 3BX, UK.
Also at: House of Stratus Inc., 2 Neptune Road, Poughkeepsie, NY 12601, USA.

www.houseofstratus.com

Typeset, printed and bound by House of Stratus.

A catalogue record for this book is available from the British Library
and the Library of Congress.

ISBN 0-7551-0242-8

'If I had anything like your ability and industry, I think I should concentrate almost entirely on the actualities of war – the effects of tiredness, hunger, fear, lack of sleep, weather, inaccurate information, the time factor and so forth. The principles of strategy and tactics and the logistics of war are really absurdly simple; it is the actualities that make war so complicated...'

A P Wavell to Liddell Hart

Author's Note

It is virtually impossible for the staff who plan a battle and the men who fight it to see it the same way. Indeed, for the men who are doing the shooting and are being shot at, it is usually difficult to understand what is going on except in their own small corner of the affair.

This is the story of a battle seen at one level through the eyes of a battalion and at another through the eyes of the planners. It is not my intention to denigrate the staff. Though the regimental soldier often denounced the staff in no uncertain terms, it was largely ritual, and the intense dislike that existed for the staff in World War I never existed in World War II. Nevertheless, war isn't just numbers. Personalities come into it, and my wish is merely to show how personality can become another of the actualities of war.

All units and characters are fictitious and I have tinkered a little with geography; but, apart from the ending, the battle did take place very much as described, though earlier and with troops which were not British.

I am very much indebted to Fred Majdalany's two books, *Cassino* and *The Monastery,* without which it would be almost impossible to write a clear account of what occurred on and around the Rapido, the Liri and the Garigliano rivers in the early part of 1944. I am also indebted for company, battalion and higher command details to *Charlie Company* by Peter Cochrane, and to Major-General F H Brooke, CB, CBE, DSO.

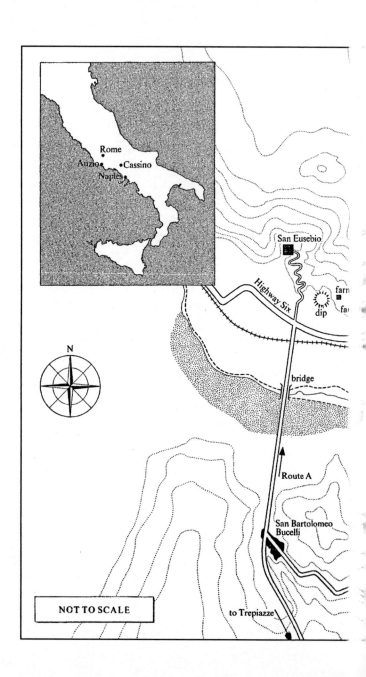

NOT TO SCALE

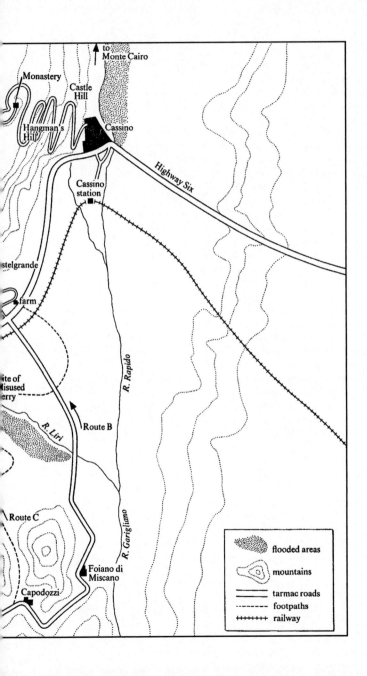

to
Monte Cairo

Monastery

Castle
Hill

Hangman's
Hill

Cassino

Highway Six

Cassino
station

stelgrande

farm

R. Rapido

ite of
disused
erry

R. Liri

Route B

R. Garigliano

Route C

Foiano di
Miscano

Capodozzi

flooded areas

mountains

tarmac roads

footpaths

railway

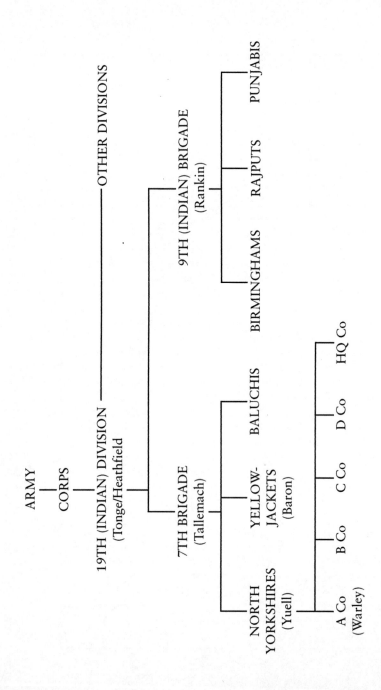

ARMY

CORPS

19TH (INDIAN) DIVISION
(Tonge/Heathfield) —————— OTHER DIVISIONS

7TH BRIGADE
(Tallemach)

9TH (INDIAN) BRIGADE
(Rankin)

NORTH YORKSHIRES (Yuell)

YELLOW-JACKETS (Baron)

BALUCHIS

BIRMINGHAMS

RAJPUTS

PUNJABIS

A Co (Warley)

B Co

C Co

D Co

HQ Co

PART ONE

The Sword

> 'It is the common soldier's blood
> that makes the general a great man.'
> *Eighteenth-century saying*

o n e

The track swung past a tangle of dead mules, wrecked containers and torn panniers, where a heavy stonk from the German batteries had caught a supply column as it had rounded the corner and spread them all over the hillside. Winding away from the craters and the seared stones, it then crossed a wooden footbridge and dropped into a gully scattered with the relics of old battles – steel helmets, ammunition pouches, bits of rifles, bits of machine-guns, bits of boots, bits of clothing – even bits of human beings, because sometimes the helmets held part of a head or the boots part of a foot.

Warmed by a couple of strong whiskies at battalion headquarters, Mark Warley zigzagged through the battered olive groves until they grew sparse and finally disappeared. Then the track began to climb, wet and slippery to his feet because it had never stopped raining for a month. The mud coated his boots and gaiters and lay in grey slashes and smears on his uniform – as it lay in slashes and smears on everything. The downpours had reduced men, machines, roads, mountains and fields to a uniform drabness.

Directly in front of him a great wall of mountain rose about three miles away. It was a view that should have been breathtaking but only made Warley's heart sink as he saw it. It was the strongest part of the German defensive position running across Italy that was known as the Gustav Line, and the highest peak, Monte Cairo, was over 5000 feet high and bleak enough to be quite uninhabitable. Lower down was another peak, and 1500 feet below that the River Rapido, a puny enough stream in normal times but a formidable obstacle to an army with the bulk of the mountain behind. There was something titanic about the scene, frightening in its vastness, sombre under the low cloud and drizzling rain that blurred outlines and gave the slopes a menacing appearance of evil.

In the grey light the peaks looked like cut-outs for a stage presentation. On the one to the west of Monte Cairo, just ahead of the others, was the uneven crumbled shape of a building. The Abbey of Monte Cassino had been founded by Saint Benedict in the sixth century and it overlooked the town of the same name in the valley below where it was known Mark Antony once had a villa. The abbey had been wrecked by the Lombards in the sixth century; by the Saracens in the ninth; by an earthquake in the fourteenth; and finally at the end of that winter of 1943/4, by the Allied troops trying to drive Kesselring's German divisions up the length of Italy. And this time there was little of it left, because in February heavy and medium bombers had dropped hundreds of tons of explosive on it.

Even if there were no Germans in the monastery – and German propaganda insisted there weren't – it had been decided that it had been built as a fortress and, in effect, still was a fortress, with walls 150 feet high and ten feet thick at the base, pierced with slits for the defenders to shoot through. Despite its religious significance, nobody had had the slightest doubt that, in the extremity of defeat, the Germans would occupy it and the only way to prevent that had been to destroy it, and with it, unhappily, the works of art it contained.

Although he was a sensitive man and regretted the artistic loss, Warley felt no regrets whatsoever at the bombing. The monastery had overshadowed his life for too long, and the people in the top echelons of power were growing impatient. The whole Italian campaign – indeed, the whole war and the invasion of Europe – was being held up by it, because it was believed now that the Germans were using the ruins as an observation post for their guns. They dominated the whole plain to the south below them, and there wasn't a single man in the armies around who hadn't realised that they were the key to Rome. When the monastery fell, Rome would fall. Everybody knew it. It was there all the time, overlooking everything they did, everything that went on in the flooded plain and along the Rapido, the Garigliano and the Liri.

To Warley, in the failing light it seemed that ten thousand eyes watched every footstep he took. Far behind him, he could see the flashes of guns, and hear the thump of the German artillery replying and the rush of the shells tearing over his head. He felt curiously detached from the war. A single-minded man, a journalist in York in civilian life and not a particularly important one, he had the ability to forget his past life and the possibilities of the future in order to concentrate solely on the present. It made things very simple. He was a stocky man, young for his rank of major, dark-visaged but typical of the county he came from; strong, tireless, by no means a man of brilliance with the speed to win races, but dogged, stolid; cheerful for most of the time; quick to anger and just as quick to simmer down. To Warley the war was a nuisance; he had plans for the future and the war was simply something that got in the way. His character enabled him to accept it, however, not complaining, waiting patiently until it ended. And he knew it *would* end before too long, because the Germans had been in retreat everywhere since the last months of 'Forty-two.

As he worked his way across a last shell-torn stretch of flat land, the smell of death became increasingly powerful. The cause was a mule, in an advanced state of decomposition. 'Bear right when the mule begins to smell really strong' was the instruction they gave visitors. It was the same smell he'd smelled a hundred times before, whether the dead were four-legged or two-legged, whether British, American, Indian, German or Italian.

Company headquarters were in a wrecked farmhouse that looked as though it had simply been dropped down and forgotten. Meagre grass and infrequent patches of scrub were the only vegetation, because all the trees had long since been blasted by the artillery. It was a desolate area patterned only by the formation of rock and the paths worn by men's boots to where Warley's understrength rifle company was fanned out in a rough semi-circle.

Captain Jago, his second-in-command, was waiting for him, big, rangy and red-haired, the harsh angles of his face caught by the light from a pressure lamp. There was a mug of tea on the box that did duty for a table, and Jago sloshed a measure of rum into it and held it out.

Warley grinned as he took it. 'You'd never believe it, Tony,' he said. 'The Gurkhas are taking over. We're being relieved.'

They moved out that same night. The artillery was stirring things up among the German positions so that the sound of boots and lorry engines wouldn't be heard. Since the firing wasn't particularly violent, most of the men moving back considered that all it would do was make the Herrenvolk suspicious.

Nevertheless, they were glad to go. For the past week they'd been living on food cooked a mile behind the lines and brought up in hot boxes by mules or on the shoulders of Indian porters. They'd shaved and cleaned their teeth in the dregs of their tea and performed their bodily functions into bully-beef tins. They'd lived in stone-built shelters because the ground was too rocky to dig trenches, aware that medical evacuation, if they were hit, constituted an enormous problem. On a wet night you could count yourself lucky to be in a dressing station within a matter of hours and without being dropped by the stretcher bearers.

The army's advance up the spine of Italy had been that of a bull, wearied yet still willing, butting its way head-down into assault after assault. The pattern had rarely changed.

Plains were few and far between and no sooner had one river or mountain barrier been crossed than another had barred the route. They'd battled across the Creti, but behind the Creti was the Agri, and behind the Agri was the Sele, and behind the Sele was the Volturno. As someone had said, there was always 'one more river to cross'. To say nothing of the little towns they'd had to fight for, street by street, house by house, even floor by floor. On one spur of land, so many shells had been dropped the Americans had called it Million Dollar Hill. The whole country, every river, every town, every hill, had shown them how useless machines could be when climate and terrain conspired to make them so.

'Oh, yes,' the current joke ran, 'the Germans are retreating all right. Unfortunately, they're taking the last ridge with 'em.'

They weren't even sure why they were there. Some said it was to distract the Germans while they got the Second Front going in France; others that they were trying to get to Vienna before the Russians.

'Strategically,' Jago had observed more than once, 'Italy might be the soft under-belly of Europe, but physically it's more like a bloody hard backbone.'

Again and again the Germans had held a position until it had become dangerous, then pulled back a mile or so to the next, leaving behind them a trail of minefields, blown bridges and demolished roads. Again and again they had forded streams or assaulted heights in the darkness, to dig themselves in before dawn, leaving the Sappers to remove the debris and repair the damage behind them for the tanks to pass through. But always the Germans, already pulling out to the next place, had frustrated them by raining down artillery and mortar fire on their own recently-vacated strongholds.

Added to all of which, the Italian winter – something they had never known about in the days when their knowledge of the country had consisted of picture postcards, colourful calendars and a quick gallop through 'The Isle Of Capri' – had hit them with all its bitter drenching fury, so that mud made transport virtually useless and the low ceiling grounded the supporting aircraft. Now, here, before Cassino, they had stopped yet again, to lick their wounds, to reorganise and rest, just holding the line. That, in all conscience, had seemed quite enough but in the end it hadn't proved to be, and two major assaults on the German position had already been thrown back with heavy losses.

They had been fighting almost continuously for six months. Wet and frozen, they had known nothing but mud and mountains for weeks, sometimes never seeing the sky or even the next slope for days when the mist and low cloud clung round the hills. And what did they get for their trouble? Complaints from home that they weren't moving fast enough and – as if it weren't enough to know that back home the men training for the Second Front at least had beer and girls to go for – the nickname D-Day Dodgers'.

'Which D-Day do they mean?' Jago had said. 'It's all bloody D-Days out here.'

The Gurkhas appeared as soon as it was dark; small, smiling brown men whose teeth shone in the shadows.

'Tik hai, Johnny,' they called, because the Gurkhas were trusted troops and everybody got on well with them.

'Tik hai,' the little men called back, moving into the positions they vacated.

They accomplished the changeover without casualties, racing against the coming daylight. Eventually they bumped into other battalions which were also being relieved, the returning mule columns jostling against each other in the congestion, all of them with only one idea in their minds – to reach safety.

They passed a ditch crammed with dead animals and smashed vehicles, then branched away from the road and took a mule track. The early morning mist was rising out of the valley, and away to the north it lay heavy by the river where it was thickened by smoke shells. They could just see the outline of Monastery Hill now, and it seemed so high and yet so close they felt the Germans could reach down and touch them on the shoulder.

The men's boots barely left the ground, their bodies rocking from side to side like clockwork dolls, as if that were the only way they could move their feet forward; using their last ounce of energy to shift their legs. Yet, somehow, there was an enduring stolidity about them, as if they could march for ever.

Their faces, blurred by a fuzz of beard, were filthy and the eyes that stared from them appeared to gaze into space, seeing nothing. There was no singing or whistling and nobody spoke. Half of them had forgotten where they were going. They didn't care much, anyway, so long as they could sleep, get a hot bath and put on clean clothes before going into a town. It didn't matter which town, so long as there were pavements to walk on instead of mud; shops, even empty Italian shops; and cafés – even cafés that sold Italian vermouth and wine instead of good English beer. And women, of course. Above all, women; women they could joke with, torment, even just look at.

The Divisional General was waiting near the trucks with Yuell, the colonel of the North Yorkshires, to watch them march in. Because the mud was grey, the trucks were grey and the men were grey. Everything was grey. War, the general supposed, was a grey business.

Every vehicle in the world appeared to be rumbling up and down the road and every soldier in the world seemed to be waiting by its side. The line of vehicles was endless. Trucks packed with fuel, food and ammunition. Trucks packed with men in a dun mass, crammed close together with their equipment and weapons. There were clean soldiers moving north; and dirty soldiers, caked with mud, moving south. It went on continuously; the only difference between the British and the Americans was that the Americans drove faster.

It was a hybrid army. There were British from England, Scotland, Ireland and Wales, Americans from New York and the Deep South, New Zealanders, French, Poles, Sikhs, Gurkhas, all crammed together in a scene of vast confusion, their only common denominator their aim to destroy Nazi Germany in Italy. Small coloured signs dotted either side of the highway, telling you in pictures and numbers exactly where everybody was.

As the general waited, the weary soldiers passed him almost without seeing him, moving in a steady subconscious rhythm. As they reached the boarding point, an officer helped them drag their weary bodies into the backs of the trucks where they immediately lolled sideways into sleep. As the vehicles filled up and rumbled off, they jolted past the wayside graves and the tangles of telephone cables and the signs that warned of dangerous curves and the corners that came under shellfire.

They felt they had come through a furnace which had scarred them all, purging them of emotions, leaving nothing but the desire to rest.

t w o

The Germans watched them go. The artillery dropped a few shells on them as they went, but the gunners must have been in a good mood because they didn't appear to do any damage. Yet from San Eusebio, where Captain Werner Reis stood, you could see across the whole valley in front. From the monastery, Captain Reis sometimes felt, you could probably see all the way to Africa.

He studied the land about him, a lean hard soldier who, under the leathery skin and the strapped and belted authority, was surprisingly young. His face was thin, all high cheekbones and hard angles, as though the years of war had honed him down until there wasn't an ounce of flesh on him; and his body, already scarred with three wounds, was sinewy and strong. Despite the conditions, despite the rain, despite the cold, he was grateful to be in Italy, because he'd picked up his third wound near Stalingrad eighteen months before and had been evacuated by air just before it was too late.

Reis was a Rhineland Catholic from Andernach and he went to the church in San Eusebio every week. Despite the fact that most of the population had left, the priest, a doddering old man who couldn't bear to put his life's work behind him, still held Mass, and Reis never failed to attend. It didn't seem strange to him that he should believe so ardently yet still be serving the godless gang who ruled in Berlin. He was a good German and, though he didn't believe the propaganda that blamed the war on the enemy, he certainly believed in Germany and knew that after the First World War the Allied politicians had never given her a chance to get on her feet again. He was not unusual in his loyalties. The general who was running the show was not only a Catholic, he was also a former Rhodes Scholar and graduate of Oxford, an anglophile, an officer with known anti-Nazi feelings and, above all, a lay member of the Benedictine Order.

Reis lit a cigarette and looked over his personal stretch of front again. On his right was Highway Six, the road to Rome, running up the Liri Valley, and on his left, round the corner of the mountain, the ruined town of Cassino. Above and behind him was what was left of the monastery, and it gave him a comfortable feeling of security to know it was there. Just in front of it was the hill the British called Hangman's Hill. Behind that lay the ridge they called Snakeshead, and Monte Cairo. Behind the town was Castle Hill which he knew as well as everybody else was – after San Eusebio – the key to the monastery. With San Eusebio in their hands, the Allies could see what was taking place on Castle Hill, and Castle Hill dominated the other outlying spurs. One by one, they led to the top, to the monastery itself.

To the south of Cassino the land was flat until you reached the Arunci Mountains, the road heading across the plain for the town as straight as an arrow from south-east to north-west until it reached the iron bridge across the Rapido. On its south-western side was the railway, and both town and station were still securely held. Overlooked from the mountains behind, it had long been obvious to the Allies that an attempt to get at them would be spotted at once from the heights. The only way they could capture them was by crossing the river on the flank and moving along the bank on the German side, so that the strongpoints would wither on the stem. So far, after months of hammering, all they'd managed was a meagre foothold in the hills to the north.

In all his days of soldiering, and they were many now, Reis had never seen a stronger position. The whole art of defence was to choose a place where you could see the enemy without being seen yourself; and here, in front of Monte Cassino, everything fitted those requirements perfectly. San Eusebio looked like a watch-dog waiting in the entrance to its kennel. Behind the village and curling round its sides was a high escarpment of rocks, covered here and there with thin bushes and small trees. This was the position's only disadvantage because, unlike all the other German positions, it could not be covered by crossfire from the sides. With the village in British or American hands, the escarpment would protect the north end, where some of the buildings were actually built on to the cliff and where caves for wine cellars had been cut out of the rock. Leading from the river was a switchback road winding round its eastern slopes through a series of hairpin bends. In summer, trees softened the outlines but now, with the slopes bare and the gales sweeping the dark clouds across from the Abruzzi, the place seemed a stark symbol of defiance.

The last of the British lorries disappeared and a final flurry of shells dropped across the river among the smoke which had been put down to hide their departure. Because they were seen everywhere they moved, the Allies could not hold the river bank. The Germans could see everything, even a single lorry or a single man. They could slip patrols across the river after dark to lay minefields on the approaches to the river, and, if the Allies managed later during the night to clear them, could lay them again the next night. Indeed, German patrols could roam almost at will on the opposite bank, while no Allied patrol ever managed to survive long on this side.

'Wonder who's taken their place,' Reis said.

'Indians or Poles?' Lieutenant Maximilian Thiergartner peered through his binoculars alongside him, watching the land opposite. 'I hope it's not the Poles. The Poles have a special reason for being unpleasant.'

'You scared, Thiergartner?' Reis asked.

'Yes, Herr Hauptmann, I am.'

Reis glanced quickly at the younger officer. He was only twenty, blond, blue-eyed, innocent-looking, and Captain Reis often thought that after his years in the Hitler Youth he ought to have been a lot more dedicated. He had a violin which he played well and sometimes used to entertain them in the evenings. Once, further south, some humorist, opposite had heard it and yelled, 'How about Mother Machree, mate?' It had seemed to please Thiergartner.

'You damned well *shouldn't* be scared,' Reis growled.

Thiergartner remained unruffled. 'Aren't *you* scared, Herr Hauptmann?' he asked. 'When you think of what's in store for Germany? They'll accept nothing but unconditional surrender and they'll not even talk to anyone who's been a National Socialist.'

There was a lot of truth in what the boy said and Reis was thankful he'd resisted the temptation to join the Party in 1940 when it might have helped a career which seemed to have been marching a long time without getting anywhere.

'Shut up,' he said uncomfortably. 'We don't talk like that.'

The boy was probably a bit of a weak number, he felt. Though not a harsh man, Reis took his job seriously and didn't enjoy having someone in his unit who was likely to give at the first real shove. Which was why he'd posted Thiergartner on this knoll just to the east of San Eusebio. The position faced a stretch of rough ground where even a couple of good sergeants could hold back an enemy.

'Your people all right?' he asked.

'Most of them,' Thiergartner said.

'What's that supposed to mean?'

'Like the poor, Private Pulovski's always with us?'

Pulovski was a gentle soul, a country man from Thuringia, whose hands were all thumbs.

Thiergartner smiled. 'However, we also have some sound men, all under the good Obergefreiter Seidle.'

Reis grunted. 'Does Pulovski bother you?'

Thiergartner smiled. 'Not at all, Herr Hauptmann. I just feel sorry for him.'

'You're not here to feel sorry,' Reis growled. 'Can you handle him?'

'Oh, of course, Herr Hauptmann.' Thiergartner's smile widened. 'I make him laugh and then he eats out of my hand.'

'Who's down by the river?'

'Gefreiter Pramstrangl.'

Captain Reis grunted again. He didn't think much of Gefreiter Pramstrangl either. He was slow and cautious and an Austrian into the bargain, and Reis didn't trust him.

He put down his binoculars and glanced about him. The countryside was silent, and across the river the land seemed deserted again. It was the weirdest sensation, as though they were in an empty landscape. Yet he knew there were thousands of enemy troops just across the strip of grey metallic water, staring towards him, probably all thinking exactly as he was thinking.

'Well,' he said, 'they've gone. All we have to do now is sit back and let the war look after itself for a bit.'

As it happened, however, there was more to it than that. Because somebody had produced a plan.

And, as one of the New Zealanders had once said, there was nothing like having a plan – even if it was a poor one.

t h r e e

'*Object,*' the plan said: 'The crossing of the Liri and the occupying of the north bank near San Eusebio; to consolidate and expand the bridgehead, with the ultimate objective of by-passing the enemy position at Cassino.

'*Reasons:* The key to this sector is San Eusebio. With San Eusebio in our hands, all the land to right and left would be under observation. Within the past few days there have been increasing indications that, due to recent Allied pressure, enemy strength in this area is ebbing through casualties, exhaustion and low morale. From this it can be assumed that he has no fresh reserves, only a few tired ones, and it is considered that an attack on San Eusebio will cause him to withdraw.

'*Suggestions:* An assault crossing, the first flight to be silent and at night – launched from points on the near bank opposite San Eusebio to a mile upstream – to cross the highway and seize the far bank and escarpment east and north of the village. All to be undertaken with covering artillery fire, and preceded by an air strike by the RAF. A rapid follow-up in daylight, with tanks, under all available covering fire, to build up the bridgehead, then a rapid advance from the bridgehead to capture San Eusebio.

'*Details:* Initial attack, at brigade strength, should go in opposite San Bartolomeo Bucelli and Foiano di Miscano, and as soon as the bridgehead is established, a second brigade should pass through towards San Eusebio on D + 1. Rapid

16

consolidation is vital as enemy is bound to throw in counter-attacks from the direction of San Eusebio or further east. Steady pressure could be kept up elsewhere as a diversion.'

And so on and so on.

Two days before the idea hadn't existed.

It hadn't merely sprung into existence, however. It was something that had been growing for quite a while.

The political benefits of capturing Rome exercised a not inconsiderable influence on the people in London, just as its retention exercised an equal influence in Berlin. At first it had seemed that Fascism had been utterly discredited by the fall of Mussolini the previous year, but his rescue from captivity, coupled with the adherence to him of a few disreputable but well-known figures, had brought the Italians, who had thought they had seen the last of the war, back into the fight under the Duce's tattered banners. So the Italian campaign, which had been intended by the Allies to tie down German divisions, was now doing the opposite and tying down Allied divisions. At Alamein they had quoted *Henry V* on the emotions of St Crispin's Day, but that attitude had worn a little thin on the long struggle up the narrow peninsula from Sicily, and Cassino had finally stopped them dead.

It had been said as long ago as the Boer War – and doubtless even before that – that heights were the key to any military situation, and at Cassino most of them were in the hands of the Germans. Something had to be done to break the deadlock, and it was therefore inevitable that the plan would attract attention. It caught the eye of the army commander at once.

'Where's this come from?' he asked.

His chief of staff glanced at the folder over his shoulder. '19th (Indian) Division, sir. I gather it's actually the idea of the divisional commander, Royal Artillery – Brigadier Heathfield.'

The army commander was unimpressed. 'Seems to be assuming a lot about German weakness,' he observed. 'Outflanking Cassino with a crossing's already been tried by the Americans – with disastrous results – and, with the approaches as waterlogged as they are, I shouldn't imagine anybody's in favour of trying another until they've dried out.' He paused. 'But, you know, I think we *might* use the idea. If nothing else, it'll keep the Germans too busy to know what else we've got up our sleeve. Who've they got?'

'Tallemach's Seventh Brigade, sir. That's the North Yorkshires, the Yellowjackets and the Baluchis. And Rankin's 9th (Indian) Brigade, which is the Birminghams, the Rajputs and the Punjabis. 11th Indian's also in the mountains there. They're supposed to be earmarked already, but I suppose they could be used if they're needed.'

The army commander frowned. 'We can pull the Yorkshires and the Yellowjackets out and refit them,' he said. 'Then send them in again south of the town. Get hold of Corps.'

'You will make a strong thrust across the river towards San Eusebio. More than one crossing should be planned, and when the breach is created every effort will be made to link up rapidly.'

Not 'You will try to', Major General James Tonge noticed – as he always noticed, whether he were receiving the orders or writing them himself – but 'You will'. It was never a good idea to send a man into action with the suggestion of an option.

Tonge was a small man, round-faced and ruddy, with a clipped military moustache and a heavy limp, a relic of North Africa. Known to his troops as the Limping Limpet, he was a friendly man and, like most British divisional commanders in 1944, highly experienced. His faults were human rather than professional in that he was kind-hearted and too much inclined to let his subordinates have their heads. And, unfortunately, his 19th Indian Division was no longer as good as it had been.

The tendency since the desert to imagine that all future battles would be tank versus tank had been completely destroyed in Italy. Infantrymen were more important than ever and, with the rifle and the hand grenade once more the final arbiters of the battlefield, what was needed now was not vehicles, artillery or aircraft but men. A fresh brigade to throw in after a week's fighting would have made a great deal of difference; but Tonge's division had become depleted and weary, and the few replacements who had arrived had brought with them the established habits and practices of the army in England.

Italy was different. It was different from the desert and very different from England. They even had a different name for the Germans – not Jerries but Teds, from Tedeschi, the Italian word for them.

General Tonge was very much aware of his problems. He was a capable man, but suspected that since being wounded in Libya he had slowed down. And when he'd returned to duty it was to find himself saddled with a staff of whom he knew little and who, in many cases, were new to their jobs. Because he wasn't there to hang on to them, the experienced men he'd directed before his wound had all been whipped away to England to handle the problems of the Second Front, and he felt the new lot weren't as good and were never likely to be. This troubled him because when soldiers felt the staff were capable of making sure that everything worked, morale was high. Unhappily, General Tonge no longer felt he could guarantee this.

Despite his doubts, his headquarters reflected an atmosphere of brisk efficiency, rather like an important office in the City of London full of young executives keen on their jobs and well on top of it. It was situated off the main road in a villa set in its own grounds and marked with the tall dark flames of cypresses. Near the gateposts, military policemen stood on guard, and over the house the yellow divisional banner with its black dragon fluttered limply in the thin breeze. The house belonged to a wealthy Roman who was now on the other side of the front line, and that part of the building occupied by Tonge's headquarters looked a little like an English country club, with *The Tatler, The Field* and *Country Life* prominently displayed among the out-of-date copies of *The Times* and *The Daily Telegraph*.

Most of what had been done to make it comfortable was the work of Brigadier Wallace Heathfield. Heathfield was a thruster by nature, looked like a thruster and believed in being a thruster. He was a tall man inclined to plumpness, and his round face and smooth blond hair were instantly belied by his brisk manner. He had the energy of two men and, because he liked his comfort, enjoyed keeping an eye on the mess in addition to his own jobs as commander of the divisional artillery and the divisional commander's confidant and virtual deputy. A compulsive interferer, he felt he had found his niche on Tonge's staff, and his swift, ingratiating manner, heartily disliked by the men he dealt with, had seen him rapidly promoted. Heathfield got things done, whether it was the acquisition of clothing, ammunition or vehicles; the improvement of medical facilities; or merely the sorting out of the quarrels between the cook and the mess sergeant. He was also well-known in the army as a bridge player, though Tonge had noticed that he liked to win and that if he didn't he was inclined to sulk.

His handsome face puckered with concentration, he bent over the map spread across the general's desk, his plump white hands moving swiftly across its surface.

'I thought a straightforward head-on attack across the river by Brigadier Tallemach, sir,' he was saying, 'with Brigadier Rankin to leap-frog through him.'

Tonge rubbed his knee. Part of it was missing and when the weather was indifferent, as it was now, it ached.

'Not sure Tallemach's the man for the job,' he said slowly. 'He's not young any more.'

'He's only forty-five, sir.'

'With colonels of twenty-seven, it's still not young.'

'He has a good record, sir. And he uses his head. Rankin's noted for his doggedness. He'd be just the man to burst out of the bridgehead.'

Tonge glanced at his brigadier. Sometimes, he thought, Heathfield was inclined to let his enthusiasm run away with him. On the other hand, he appeared to be clever and he had ideas.

'Are you sure all your details are right, Wallace? This bit about German morale, for instance?'

Heathfield spoke stiffly. 'That's what Intelligence says, sir,' he said. 'It seems to be borne out by the facts.'

Tonge wasn't so sure. Heathfield was newly promoted and fresh out from England and Tonge wasn't confident he was yet properly attuned to Italy.

'Well,' he agreed. 'I have to admit 9th Indian Brigade's a bit rigid but, given a plan, Rankin's got the courage to pursue it to the limit. He's like a bulldog when he gets his teeth into something.' He nodded. 'Very well. Go ahead. Let me see what you propose. But if things don't look auspicious, we have to be prepared to call it off and try something else. And we might have to, because some of our armour's been taken away.'

'We've been given the South Notts Yeomanry, sir; Churchill tanks. We've also got 19th Div. artillery in addition to our own.'

'It should be enough.' Tonge looked at Heathfield. 'I have to see the army commander and then go down to Caserta to Army Group. It looks like being your baby for a day or two. Think you can manage?'

21

Heathfield smiled. He had no doubts whatsoever. 'I'm sure I can, sir.'

'Right. Remember 11th Indian's not ours and we can't call on them for the time being.'

'I have it, sir.'

Heathfield tapped his notepad, and Tonge nodded. 'How long were you intending for the planning?'

'A fortnight, sir.'

Tonge grunted. 'You've got four days,' he said.

And that was how it happened.

four

Lieutenant-Colonel Yuell's men awoke in empty houses, schools and war-battered villas, in tents and stables and barns, anywhere they could be packed in.

Known to the rest of the army as 'Dean's Dandies', because, in the days when a regiment was virtually the private property of its colonel, a certain Colonel Joshua Dean had lavished on their uniforms enough of his personal fortune to give them fashion parity with the cavalry, the North Yorkshires consisted of 22 officers and 642 other ranks. Or to be more exact, at that moment, 21 officers because Second-Lieutenant Marsden had overturned a jeep outside Caserta and been carted off to hospital with a broken leg; and 622 men because one man had died after an operation following a burst appendix in Naples, two men had fallen drunk out of the back of a lorry, and seventeen more had gone down with a recurrence of malaria contracted in Sicily and a variety of other illnesses. There were four rifle companies, the HQ company, and battalion headquarters, all ruled over by the awesome figure of the regimental sergeant-major who was appropriately named Mr Zeal.

'When James VI of Scotland became James I of England,' Company Sergeant-Major Farnsworth of A Company liked to tell his men, 'he and his court wore out their brogues on the journey south, so they sent a message back to Edinburgh asking for a thousand more. But by the time the message reached Scotland the word, "brogues", had become "rogues". And' – at this point CSM Farnsworth's voice always rose ' – their descendants all seem to be in this bloody battalion.'

They were sharp, suspicious and individual as Highlanders, which indeed many of them were because they came from the high country of the moors. Edward Yuell himself – a small, nervy, wiry man with jet-black hair and grey flinty eyes – came from a family which farmed two thousand acres of harsh Yorkshire Pennine land west of Ripon. The climate seemed to have bitten into his character so that he reacted to every crisis in the same way that his family had always reacted to crises of weather and livestock on their bleak uplands – in a Yorkshire way, quickly but with remarkably little fuss.

His men resembled him. Their speech was slow and strong and contained strange words nobody else understood. It was blunt and forthright, flat-vowelled but full of their own brand of humour.

They came from the hills, the dales and the riversides, and from the streets of ugly wool and steel cities. And although they had no real ill-feeling for the men of Lancashire, in one respect the Wars of the Roses were still being waged. The biannual counties cricket matches, which had always been played by the dictum of 'If you can't win, at least don't bloody well lose', had produced more boredom for the rest of the country than any other sporting spectacle. To the North Yorkshires, 'Ilkla Moor' was more of a national anthem than 'God Save The King'.

Because they were a regular battalion, many of them were in it for the sole reason that their fathers, or even their grandfathers, had been in it. Yuell's great-grandfather had been at Lucknow and the men of his family had served the regiment for over a hundred years. The father of Second-Lieutenant Taylor, who was newly arrived and as wet as a wet day, had been killed with the regiment on the Somme.

Mr Zeal, CSM Farnsworth and Corporal Wymark had all had fathers who had been NCOs in the regiment. At least two privates had actually been born into it, seeing life for the first time in the married quarters of the regimental depot at Ripon. Yuell's second-in-command, Major Peddy, round-faced, spectacled and looking like a schoolmaster, had not thought it possible, living in Harrogate, to join any other regiment. Mark Warley of A Company, though he had no regimental ancestry whatsoever, was as Yorkshire as Wensleydale.

Like all battalions, it included the good, the bad and the indifferent, individuals despite their uniformity of dress and equipment. In Major Warley's company alone they were as varied as circus performers.

First of all among them was Private White. White was an old soldier. After his first term of service in the 1914–18 war something had happened that they often debated but never established, and it had caused him to join up again for the rest of his life. He had a string of good conduct stripes halfway up his arm, three ribbons, two from the last war and one for the North-West Frontier, and he had resisted every attempt to promote him. Though they tormented him unmercifully, his comrades also regarded him with a certain amount of awe which showed in the fact that he was probably the only White in the British army who was not nicknamed Chalky'. Private White had been in so long he seemed to deserve more respect than that and he was always known – even to the officers – by his Christian name, Henry.

His tattooed sinewy body was still that of an athlete but he had the haggard face and sunken cheeks of an old man, and a set of wobbling false teeth which looked, according to Private Parkin, as if they'd been rifled off a corpse. He was sober, hard-working, frowned on bad language, tended to keep himself to himself, smoking and staring into space because he didn't read, and never received letters and never wrote any. Nobody knew where he came from because he never mentioned his home or his childhood, but he had an old soldier's knack for making himself comfortable and for finding women – what he called his 'parties' – like himself usually past their youth and usually with families, as if he gained something from being with them that he'd missed in his lifetime in uniform. In England they'd come across him occasionally sitting in a pub with one of them, both staring silently into space as if they'd been married for thirty years. Private Parkin liked to suggest that Henry had worn a red coat and carried a musket at Waterloo.

Mind you, Private Parkin – known like all Parkins as 'Pedlar' – himself was no slouch when it came to being odd. He had once done a season as a busker in Bradford, and knew every song that had ever been sung on the music halls and quite a few that hadn't. He had a mop of greasy black hair that hung permanently over his eyes, a mouth like a post-office slit and, like Henry White, a set of false teeth – ' 'Ad 'em all out when I was sixteen! Saved all that brushin'.'

Another butt for Parkin's humour was Dickie Duff, all five foot three of him, with tiny fists and tiny boots like the Gurkhas. In the desert Duff had seemed to be all shorts, but he was good-humoured enough not to mind the chaffing he suffered and, because he was always willing to do what the big men did, never considered himself small. Inevitably he was known as 'Lofty'. Matching him in equanimity, but for a very different reason, was Lance-Corporal Fletcher-Smith. Built like a small ox, Fletcher-Smith had once aspired to swim the Channel, and, considering himself a cut above the rest, liked to prove it with his knowledge of books. Known as 'Brains Trust' to the rest of the Company, he was a serious young man regarded with a measure of wonder by his less educated comrades, yet possessed of a curious naivety that made ridicule difficult and sometimes caused him to be a hell of a bind.

His complete opposite was Private Martindale – once a ploughman – who cared about nothing so much as his pipe. He smoked it awake and asleep, standing up and lying down. The front of his battledress was so scarred by the showers of sparks his pipe shed, it looked as if it had suffered from some sort of fiery scarlet fever. On one memorable occasion he had even appeared, all unaware, on parade with the pipe sticking from his face like the muzzle of a gun. The more ribald of his friends claimed he even smoked it when he went to bed with his wife.

There were two Bawdens, each identified by the last three figures of his number – 766 Bawden and 000 Bawden. 766 Bawden was known as 'Clickety-Click' Bawden and 000 Bawden as 'Bugger-All' Bawden. Though they came from the same town they were from opposite ends of the social scale but, perhaps because of having the same surname, they were the greatest of friends.

Known as 'Dracula', Private Rich had a voice that appeared to have been rubbed up with a file so that everything he said seemed full of menace. Similarly full of menace but also largely unintelligible were the utterings of Private McWatters, a Glasgow Irishman who had no time for any other breed. Most of what McWatters said – when he bothered to say anything at all – had to be guessed at, and there was an apocryphal story that the only time he'd got on the walkie-talkie, his 'Cam' awa' forrit, Wullie, ye greit gleekit gowk, an' gi'e 'un a wee bitty burrust wi' y' Bren' had been mistaken by Lieutenant Deacon for German.

The ladies' man of the company was Private Hunters, christened 'Poker' by the erudite Fletcher-Smith. Most of them thought it was a tribute to his virility, but in fact it was nothing of the sort and was a joke that probably only Fletcher-Smith and a few others appreciated.

'Poker Hunters,' he explained. 'Pocahontas. Get it?'

'No,' Private Hunters said.

Private Puddephatt was not only large, heavy-featured and ugly but also lazy, sloppy, indifferent, irresponsible and utterly untrustworthy. On the other hand Corporal Gask, who looked about sixteen and innocent as a shorn lamb, was one of the toughest men in the battalion. Tall as a telegraph pole and thin as a willow-wand, he had once marched fifty miles without water when he'd been cut off in the desert and had reported for duty the day after his return, apparently not much the worse for wear. Barry Lloyd Evans, who came from Aberystwyth but had somehow managed to be a milkman in Bradford, was known as 'Evans the Bomb' because he was a mortar expert. As Private Rich, not very happily married to a Welsh girl he'd met during training in Cardigan, liked to say, Evans was like all bloody Welshmen and could not only sing like an angel but also argue the hind leg off a donkey.

Finally there was Private Syzling from Cleckheaton. Syzling was supposed to be a Piat man, the operator of a Projector Infantry Anti-Tank, that spring-loaded 'Heath Robinson' device which gave no flash but had one or two disconcerting habits which Syzling never seemed able to master. When firing on a trajectory below horizontal, for instance, the bomb had an embarrassing habit of sliding out of the tube to fall at the firer's feet. This was something which Syzling never seemed able to grasp, and it regularly threw his platoon commander, Lieutenant Deacon, into a screeching fury. In the end, in fact, he had accepted that Syzling would never make a Piat man, given the weapon to someone else and banished Syzling to outer darkness with more menial tasks.

Known inevitably to his associates – not friends, because he didn't have any, and hardly comrades, because he spent all his time stealing from them what items of equipment he lost – as 'Frying Tonight', Private Syzling was one of the King's Hard Bargains, always in trouble, always scruffy, always minus half his kit, and always unreliable. Along with

Puddephatt – almost as bad but not quite, because nobody could ever be as bad as Syzling – he made life a permanent misery for Lieutenant Deacon.

Lieutenant Deacon, smooth-faced and fair-haired as a girl, was the product of a happy home and a good school; an only son who had everything he wanted, a doting mother, a sober father, two adoring sisters and a place in the family firm when he was free of the army. Private Syzling couldn't have been more different. His school had been a street-corner slum school, black and depressing, and before he had been swept up into the army he had been unemployed. When the army had finished with him, he would without doubt be unemployed again because he was virtually unemployable.

Deacon found Syzling's personality about as endearing as a bloated vulture's; to Syzling, Deacon was as exciting as a pile of sand. But together they were better crowd drawers than Ginger Rogers and Fred Astaire. When Deacon started on Syzling, everybody's head was cocked so as not to miss the gems that fell from his lips. Syzling on Deacon was never less than quotable.

'Hitler's secret weapon,' Deacon liked to call Syzling.

'That bloody Deacon,' Syzling would retaliate. 'He's as mean as cat shit and I wish he'd stick his head up his arse and get 'isself sold as a jug 'andle.'

'They're as good as Laurel and Hardy,' Fletcher-Smith observed.

In fact, that was very much what they were – Deacon, too clever by a mile, pompous and careful of his dignity; Syzling, dim as a Toc H Lamp, blank-faced, perpetually puzzled, but possessing an animal instinct for comfort that always managed to acquire for him those things like food, warmth, drink, girls, that all Deacon's cleverness never did.

As they came to life in the town of Trepiazze, they moved like drugged bees, scratching themselves, passing dirty hands over dirty faces as if they could wipe away the weariness. There was a thin rain falling, but the cooks had established a cookhouse in a battered warehouse, and the petrol cookers had settled down to a steady glow that could produce seven hundred breakfasts in just over an hour. There was a smell of bacon in the air and it brought them out, sniffing hungrily.

It also brought out the small Italian boys touting for their sisters. They had picked up the army slang as fast as the soldiers had picked up Italian.

'This bloody chow's no bloody buono,' grumbled Private Puddephatt. The corporal-cook responded with a bitter 'Fangola, you! Zozzone! Fuck off!' while the small boy to whom Puddephatt had 'dashed' it yelled delightedly, 'You no want it? Okay, bob's your ankle. Is bloody whizzo.' Which, to him it undoubtedly was.

'You don't know when you're well off, you lot,' Henry White observed gloomily. 'We didn't get food like this in the last lot. It used to come up in a sandbag and was usually covered with mud.'

'Ah, but they made up for it in peacetime, didn't they, Henry?' Parkin said. 'Queen Victoria was always red 'ot at lookin' after 'er soldiers.'

White gave him a dirty look. 'The peacetime army was all right,' he growled. 'The peacetime army kept England going until you lot decided to join up, didn't it? If it wasn't for the peacetime army where would North Africa be?'

'Right where it always was,' Parkin retorted cheerfully. 'Two thousand miles of shit-coloured fuck-all on the south side o' the Med.'

They ate like famished wolves, savouring the taste of the greasy bacon and hot sweet tea, while CSM Farnsworth prowled among them, concerned as an old aunt and on the lookout for anybody who, rather than leave his friends, was hiding an injury or some minor illness.

'You all right?' he asked Fletcher-Smith.

Fletcher-Smith, stuffing away his food in the shelter of a cottage wall, looked indignant, as Farnsworth knew he would. Despite his spectacles and owlish expression, Fletcher-Smith was as tough as Old Nick's nag nails, but Farnsworth had never much liked him since the day he had tried to give him a lecture on war; something Fletcher-Smith had learned from books and Farnsworth from being shot at while winning the Military Medal in the other bun-fight in 1914.

Mail arrived and billets were scrubbed – to the amazement of the Italians who couldn't understand why they threw down buckets full of water inside while the rain came down in bucketfuls outside. When they'd finished, they were fallen in and marched to the mobile bathhouses which had been set up, and their filthy clothes were replaced by clean ones. Nobody chivvied them and the sergeants spoke to them with an unexpected gentleness. In the afternoon they were allowed into town. Trepiazze was like all small Italian towns. It might have looked better in sunshine, with foliage on the trees, but the trees were bare and the rain fell on the painted houses, turning the yellow stone of the older buildings to a depressing grey.

It was a shabby little place, and the first joy of liberation had long gone. The names of protesters shot by the Germans that had been painted on the walls were growing fainter, and the fascist posters and the communist hammers and sickles scrawled over them were becoming more tattered in the rain with every day that passed. In the Piazza Garibaldi, the main square, there was a large notice – TO FORWARD AREA, 10 MILES – to which Private Parkin promptly added the nostalgic comment, 'TO BRADFORD, 1500 MILES'. Not far away the ditches were still cluttered with the rubbish of war – cartridge cases, articles of clothing, tins, cartons, broken weapons and German helmets by the dozen. One bar owner had lined the front of his veranda with them, cementing them in a metallic frieze to the top of the wall.

'I just hope the bastards don't come back,' Private Rich said. 'He'd have a champion job explaining.'

But you could get beer and wine; and above all there were women. Even to those men who weren't interested merely in satisfying their craving for female flesh, that was a point in favour of Trepiazze because in the male world where they'd lived – that harsh, uncomfortable, cold, cheerless, noisy world of the front line – to be able to look at a woman – merely to *look* at her, knowing she was warm and soft and quiet and comfortable – was enough.

five

The dead had been buried in the hills before they'd left. The plaintive note of the Last Post had died away and as they were forgotten, Major Warley brought out A Company office, which consisted of a tin trunk newly arrived from B Echelon, and set about listing the casualties and informing the adjutant. With the personal belongings of the dead packed, he then sat down, faintly depressed, to write to the relatives. He tried to do it as always without hypocrisy because he felt the dead men would have preferred it that way, and after so long with the battalion he felt he knew them.

He had been through all the fighting up and down the desert, for the battalion had originally been with the Eighth Army and had only been switched to the Fifth since landing in Italy. He'd slogged through Egypt, Libya and Tunisia, across Sicily, and now up the length of Italy, progressing from lieutenant to major as others fell by the wayside. He hadn't particularly enjoyed it, yet his temperament was such that it hadn't made his life miserable either. He was an adaptable man, quick to adjust to good or bad conditions, able to ignore the war and the dullness of sustained repetition as an interruption of the life he had planned for himself. He intended eventually to leave journalism for the law, and if the war took ten years, very well then, so be it; that was when he would start becoming a lawyer. It was as simple as that.

As he finished the letters, and without considering it at all odd, he began immediately to fill the vacancies among the junior NCOs and reorganise his sections and platoons to absorb the newcomers and make use of the old hands. The company quartermaster-sergeant appeared, to be told the revised ration strength and bring replacement kit, sitting opposite Warley to await instructions, bolt upright, on parade, as if he were attending a funeral and owed the dead man some money.

Needs weren't just confined to ammunition and food. They required a great many fresh battledresses, socks and boots, as well as those deficiencies which always existed after a period in the line but which Q Branch could never understand. The CQMS studied the list cautiously, holding it at arm's length as if it might spit in his eye.

'It's a long one, sir,' he mourned.

'We were a long time up the line,' Warley said.

Pay was dealt with and the minor worries at home were referred to the padre. They played football against anybody who would oppose them, and a lot of them gave away their rations to the hungry, stick-legged Italian children, offering them first their biscuits, then their tea, and finally their entire meal – 'Here, for Christ's sake, take the lot!' A few of them, out of sheer high spirits, argued with the Italian police, small men with rifles and bomb-burst badges, who preferred to disappear if possible whenever there was trouble and leave it to the Provost Department. The uproar they created didn't worry Colonel Yuell too much. His men needed the gentleness of women, he knew, and hid their need chiefly in loud voices and sexual aggressiveness, which as often as not came to nothing.

Their impressions of Trepiazze were crude, blunt and to the point.

'I don't think she had a stitch on underneath,' Private Hunters said.

'The beer,' Private Rich announced in his graveyard voice, 'wun't get a possum pissed.'

'Vermouth's too sweet. I always did say so.'

'When I said "What about a kiss?" ' Private Puddephatt was saying earnestly, 'she said "Proibito". What's "proibito" mean?'

'Same as in English, you bloody great twit!'

'Well, she said I was "simpatico". Does that mean the same, too? Because I wasn't trying to be sympathetic. I was tryin' to get 'er up against a wall.'

The shops appeared to be full, a small indifferent cinema was functioning, and there was opera further south at Caserta where Fifth Army HQ was now situated. Anyone could visit it provided they could get a place on a lorry, but, being newcomers of course, they couldn't. Khaki appeared everywhere in the streets, some soldiers on rest, some merely lines of communications troops engaged in bringing the town back to life. When they'd first passed through Trepiazze going north, there'd been only infantry, tanks and guns. Now all sorts of people were crawling out from under the stones and Corporal Wymark was stopped by a fat little lieutenant emerging from a restaurant, whom he'd omitted to salute.

'Hey! You there!'

Wymark stopped. He was forty-five if he was a day, built like a dray-horse and quiffed in the manner of the other war, and he had long since forgotten more about the army than it was most people's privilege ever to learn. He was quite undismayed by the officer's pink-faced rage because he knew that if a report landed on Warley's desk, all he'd do would be sigh and toss it into the cardboard carton he used for waste paper. He'd seen him do it before.

'What's your unit?' the officer was demanding.

'Yuell's Yorkshires, sir. A Company, sir.' Wymark was full of exaggerated respect for rank. 'What's yours, sir? Mersey Docks and Harbour Board? That's a nice outfit, sir. And now, if you'll excuse me, I'd better be off, sir. I've just left the war for a day or two to get me breath back and I'm due to return before long. It's been lovely seeing you, sir.'

The Via Garibaldi was packed with people, all jostling each other off the pavement, and there were two restaurants filled chiefly with officers. There was a false gaiety about the place that came from the rapid turnover of money. But it was an atmosphere of well-being, too, that was a change from the starkness of their lives up near Cassino. Though the prices were astronomical, they were largely the fault of the soldiers who were determined to buy something – even if it were only rubbish – and the black market was flourishing.

CSM Farnsworth found himself in the Bar Roma, being accosted by a smooth-looking individual in a clean shirt and suit. The Italian was very different from the rest of the town. Most of the Italian males seemed to have been killed or taken prisoner in the desert; this man was the sort that always came out of the woodwork; and he claimed to be anti-Fascist, pro-British and a personal friend of King George.

'You will perhaps take a glass of vino with me,' he suggested to Farnsworth.

Since the local wine – what Fletcher-Smith called 'Proprio brutto vino', proper rotten wine – left you with a feeling that someone had worked over your mouth with a rasp, Farnsworth wasn't very impressed with the offer. 'No, thanks, mate,' he said.

'I am a businessman,' the Italian persisted. 'I belong to the *mondo degli affari*. You would like silk stockings, perhaps? A girl?'

Farnsworth looked round. There were a lot of men in the bar and the noise was like the Charge of the Light Brigade.

'You speak good English,' he observed.

The smooth-looking man smiled and spread his hands. '*Ma, naturalmente*. I have learned. In the course of business.'

'Then – ' Farnsworth's face was expressionless ' – you'll know what I mean when I say, "Bugger off before I clock you one", won't you?'

A few of them found girls, some even ended up in bed with them. A few got drunk, some so drunk they couldn't walk. But it was freedom after being in prison. Christmas wasn't too long past and for most of them the festive season had been as wet and miserable as every other period, with nothing but a bottle of beer, a toffee and an egg to mark the occasion.

Inevitably, Henry White was seen sitting in a bar with a line of beer bottles in front of him and a 'party' alongside, pasta-plump, sallow-skinned and dark-eyed.

'Why don't you pick 'em younger, 'Enry?' Rich asked.

'Because I'm a bloody old man, that's why!' Henry snorted. 'I used to 'ave 'em young when I was your age.' He produced a photograph and showed it round. 'That was the bint I 'ad in India.'

'Who's that 'andsome young feller standing beside her?' Parkin asked innocently.

'Me.'

'It's never!' Parkin gasped, elaborately disbelieving. 'What's that thing you've got on your 'ead then?'

'It's a topee.'

'I thought that's what Red Indians lived in.'

Quite by accident, Fletcher-Smith met a girl who turned out to be a librarian. He crashed into her as she came out of a shop and sent her parcels flying. Like him she wore glasses, of which one lens had been cracked in an air raid and never replaced. Fletcher-Smith bent down to help retrieve her purchases and, feeling somehow that because they both wore glasses they must have something in common, insisted on helping her carry them home.

When he learned that she worked with books, he tried in his halting Italian to discuss literature. But despite his erudition, he knew very little about the Renaissance and nothing at all about Dante or D'Annunzio, while the girl was totally unaware of Rupert Brooke, Housman, Eliot or the other poets Fletcher-Smith considered essential to an ordered life. In the end, as it grew dark, they decided to forego literature and simply clutched each other in dark corners. She was plump and soft and smelled clean, and it was a long time since Private Fletcher-Smith had clutched a girl. Because Fletcher-Smith was inclined to be romantic and the girl was an ardent Catholic, it led to nothing more than a visit to Mass and sighs and groans and the swearing of an eternal oath by Fletcher-Smith to return for her after the war.

'Get invited 'ome then?' Parkin asked when he returned to his billet.

'Yes.'

'Nothing like getting invited 'ome,' Parkin agreed. 'Sooner or later the old folk go to bed and there you are on the settee and 'er afraid of kicking up a fuss when you start stripping 'er in'ibitions down to 'er ankles, in case they wake up.'

To someone of Fletcher-Smith's temperament it was an insult, and he gave Parkin a hot, indignant stare. Parkin, happily, was fireproof.

Captain Jago, who looked like a dissolute Ney, found himself a buxom, black-haired piece almost as tall as he was – which was tall for an Italian and went in for a much more earthy companionship. He didn't have to try hard. As he'd once said himself, he wasn't really a ladies' man; the crumpet just rushed at him.

Private Hunters wore himself to a frazzle trying to prove himself, but the Italian woman he picked up was giving nothing away without a good evening out first. When he finally got back to her flat his brains were slopping about as if they were liquid, and as he sat on the bed to untie his bootlaces the room spun round and he fell forward on to his head. She had to call his friends to carry him away.

The most dramatic success of all was that of Private Syzling. The only real asset Syzling possessed was a gift for getting on with people whose language he couldn't speak. Since he could barely speak his own and was so scruffy he couldn't get on even with his comrades, this was remarkable. Yet in Egypt, Libya, Tunisia and Sicily, despite standing orders to the contrary – which he never read anyway – he somehow managed to communicate with the locals, to buy beer from them when no one else could find any, and to dig from them the name of a willing woman while everybody else was still sniffing warily round the bars. There had been one in Ismailia, one in Benghazi, one in Sousse, one in Syracuse and more all the way up Italy. Now, in Trepiazze, within a day, he had found an Italian widow – thick-legged, with hips like two house-bricks and smelling strongly of garlic – who had lost her husband in the desert. She possessed a name he couldn't pronounce but she could cook like a dream, was eager for a man, and was quite indifferent to the whispers of her neighbours. Warm and comfortable in her bed, Private Syzling considered himself blessed among men.

With everybody sorted out within an inch of their lives, it was only right that their company commander, who had ordained most of their comfort, should also have a degree of contentment himself and, happily enough, that was how it worked out.

Major Warley, who could never have been called a ladies' man, found himself billeted with Captain Jago, Lieutenant Deacon who was twenty, and Second-Lieutenant Taylor who was nineteen, some distance from the rest of the battalion with a family called Vanvitelli on the edge of the town. Vanvitelli was a prosperous lawyer with an office in Naples. As one of the few wealthy men in the area who hadn't made his fortune from Fascism he had been swept up by Allied Military Government, Occupied Territory, to assist them, and was never home for long.

Vanvitelli's house was backed up by fields, allotments and smallholdings so that there was no lack of food. A widower, he had two daughters, one fifteen years old called Francesca and one roughly Warley's age called Graziella. Somewhere in between there was a son but no one knew where he was. He'd gone as a soldier to North Africa and had simply disappeared: it was not known whether he was dead, a prisoner of war, or back in Italy and hiding in the hills to avoid being forced to fight for the Germans.

There was an orchard of fig and peach trees, a grapevine over the door, a small vegetable garden, and a big kitchen where the company runners could wait and the duty sergeant could sip a glass of wine. Warley had a bed in a room with white walls, faded green curtains, a carpet, a large walnut writing table he used for company business, a silver candelabra for when the electricity went off, as it often did, and a painting of the martyrdom of St Sebastian which he'd seen ad nauseam all over Southern Italy.

He was lucky in his billeting companions. Captain Jago was always able to look after himself and was already, as they said in Yorkshire, 'set up', while Deacon and Taylor clearly considered Graziella Vanvitelli far too old for them and spent all their time chasing her younger sister. By the second day Warley had become aware of the glances he kept receiving. Again and again he saw the older sister's eyes flicker away from him as he looked at her, and he knew she was watching him. For a long time they didn't speak to each other, and then she shyly offered him a glass of wine which he accepted just as shyly. After that they managed to conduct a conversation in Italian mixed up with a precise sort of English, which she'd taught in Naples before her mother had died and she'd returned to help run the family home, and sometimes with German. It seemed odd that they had to keep falling back on the language of their mutual enemy but, whenever they couldn't make themselves understood, they slipped easily into it because Warley had learned it at school and Graziella Vanvitelli had had Germans in the town for nearly two years.

'What is your name?' she asked him timidly.

'Warley,' he said. 'Mark Warley.'

'Marco Uoli.' She made it sound like the plural of an Italian noun. 'That is a nice name. I think you do not look so much tired now.'

'No,' Warley agreed. 'Much better.'

'It is good to feel not so much tired.'

'Yes.' When his ability to recover ran out, Warley thought, he was finished as a soldier. 'What's *your* name?'

'I am Graziella.'

'That's a nice name too.'

'No. *E brutto.*'

'I don't think so.'

'You don't?'

'No, of course not. It's pretty. Like you.'

Her eyes lit up mischievously. 'I am growing too old to be pretty. My face cracks all over these days – like an old vase.'

'Rubbish. How old are you?'

'Twenty-three. That is old for an Italian girl. How old are you, Uoli?'

'Twenty-five.'

Unlike her father or her sister, she was blonde and blue-eyed, and had a type of face he'd seen a dozen times in medieval paintings.

'My mother came from Florence,' she explained. 'Many northern Italians are fair. I have my mother's looks.'

'You're very unusual,' Warley said. 'Blonde and pretty.'

'What should I be?' she asked. 'Dark, squint-eyed and long-nosed?'

Like everybody else, like Deacon and Taylor, Warley had taken army rations – chocolate, tea and tinned meat – back to his billet to help out. She was grateful but wary, too, because soldiers liked to use army rations to bargain hungry Italian girls into bed. But Warley made no attempt to suggest anything of the sort; and the first evening, he remained distant but obviously delighted with the house, his room and, as she very quickly suspected, with her.

Intrigued, she wondered what sort of man he was and began to probe gently, starting, so to speak, on the outer perimeter of his character.

'What do you do when you are not a soldier?' she asked.

'I'm a journalist,' Warley said. *'Giornalista.* But after the war I'm going to be a lawyer, like your father.'

She clapped her hands delightedly, then looked at him gravely. 'You will be a good *avvocato,* I think,' she said. 'And what do you think of Fascism?'

'Not much,' Warley said bluntly.

'Ma, naturalmente. What *are* your politics?'

'Why?'

She shrugged. 'Because the war will end eventually and everybody must believe in something.'

'I believe in staying alive,' Warley said simply. 'As for politics, well, I suppose I'm a sort of liberal. What about you?'

She shrugged. 'I am a sort of a liberal too. But not a real one because in Italy we are never really anything, always just *almost* something. Perhaps we haven't the courage to be anything proper. We weren't even really very good Fascists, because we haven't the ruthlessness, and Mussolini, for all his bombast, could never make us behave like them.'

Because she enjoyed music and Warley had once been keen on it himself, they began to talk about it, and in the end she opened the piano and pulled up two stools.

The found themselves hammering out duets – Chopin and Schumann – collapsing in a gale of merriment when Warley's fingers, clumsy through lack of practice, played wrong notes which he promptly changed into one of the jingling army tunes she'd heard the soldiers whistling as they passed through the town in their lorries. Lieutenant Taylor's request that they try 'Roll Out The Barrel' and 'Lili Marlene' was tacitly ignored, and in the end he and Deacon gave up in disgust and went off to the officers' mess. It was an indication of Warley's interest in her and hers in him that they never noticed them leave.

'Do you know many soldiers?' Warley asked.

'What do you mean by that?' she asked, on the defensive at once.

'Nothing. But there are a lot of soldiers here. And a lot of girls like soldiers.'

'That is fortunate for the soldiers,' she said coolly. 'Because they behave badly sometimes. Sometimes many policemans have to come.'

'It's a long time since they spoke to girls,' Warley explained. 'They've missed them.'

'Yet you sneer at the Italian girls who go with them. You destroy our cities and lay waste our fields, but you consider that a hungry girl who goes to bed with one of your men is someone who disgraces herself.'

There was a lot of truth in what she said and it was Warley who was thrown on the defensive this time.

'I respect Italian girls,' he said.

'*Si*,' she smiled. 'Like all soldiers. *Nella camera da letto.*'

'What's that?'

'In the bedroom.'

Warley pulled a face, then he grinned an impulsive boyish grin. 'Well,' he said, 'it's as good a place to respect them as any, isn't it?'

His grin touched her heart and his comment made her laugh. She tried to explain how the Italians felt.

'We don't live as we would like to,' she said, 'but as we must. Italian men no longer have any money, and their backbones have gone because they've suffered one defeat after another. They complain about the girls going with the English and the Americans, but it is often the girls who bring them the money they use for cigarettes and the wine they drink.'

Warley studied her. 'Do *you* go with soldiers?' he asked.

'No.'

'Why not?'

'I'm too busy here.'

'Nobody's *that* busy,' Warley said.

She didn't say that the real reason was because she felt it was safer; sometimes strange things happened to girls who went with soldiers. She passed to the attack. 'Do *you* go with girls?' she asked.

'I have done,' Warley admitted.

'In Naples?'

'Yes.'

'And doubtless in Caserta too?'

Warley didn't argue. He felt too happy to argue. For once the army had done him an enormous kindness. It had granted him a clean billet and a room where he could be alone. And there was nothing to describe the joy he felt that it had also given him a pretty, intelligent and friendly girl to talk to. It was a tremendous gift and it filled him with such a quality of thankfulness that he went to bed in a blank-eyed wonder of delight, and for the first time in months fell asleep looking forward to the next morning.

s i x

For a few days it was like being in Heaven, a heaven that was disturbed only once by any interference from the enemy. For a brief hour or two on the second morning the sky cleared and the sun came out and almost at once two German fighters flew over the town. They were very high, like small silver minnows moving across the heavens in an indecisive sort of way. Anti-aircraft fire pursued them and eventually they dropped half a dozen small-calibre bombs.

They barely disturbed the routine and the sun seemed much more important, but the Italians ran for the shelters, clutching holy pictures and shrieking that they were about to be killed. There seemed little danger but Warley found himself with Graziella Vanvitelli in the deep cool cellars of the house where he was billeted.

It was strange to be alone, and to both of them faintly disturbing. They had known each other only for a little over twenty-four hours but already they were aware that the brittle shell of their chatter covered unexpected emotional currents.

Warley was still faintly dazed by his good luck and was inclined simply to enjoy it; Graziella, less inclined to take things for granted, wished to know more about him.

'Where do you come from?' she asked.

'Yorkshire.'

'I do not know of Yorkshire?' She pronounced 'Yorkshire' as if it were spelt 'Giorccia'. 'What like is Yorkshire?'

'It's in the north,' Warley said. 'It has a lot of high ground.'
'Like Italy?'
'Yes. But it's different.'
'I think I would be cold in Yorkshire.'
Warley looked at her happily. 'No,' he said. 'You'd be warm anywhere.'

She was suspicious of his meaning, and he tried to explain. 'I meant that you make me feel warm. There's something about you that makes me feel warm.'

She blushed with pleasure. She was silent for a long time and they could hear quite clearly the sound of aeroplane engines and the cries of people in the town.

'What are you thinking about?' Warley asked.

She was thinking that there was something about Warley that appealed enormously to her, but since she could hardly say so, she fenced a little.

'What *does* an Italian think about?' she asked. 'I know what you British think we think about: pasta and opera. Spaghetti and *La Sonnambula*. Lasagna and *Lucia di Lammermoor*.'

Her beauty troubled Warley and he went on quickly. 'We used to have a neighbour who thought all the time about opera,' he said. 'She was very fat, so she probably thought a lot about spaghetti too.' He smiled in a way that pleased her because it was a warm, intimate, sharing sort of smile. 'Whenever my mother and father gave a party, she liked to sit at the piano and sing. But she forgot her voice had been trained to reach the back row of the gallery, and it used to shake the windows. The dog crawled under a chair and the cat bolted upstairs at the first shout. It wasn't just the neighbours who complained. They used to complain from the other side of the town.'

She laughed, as much at his expression as at the story. Then she saw him studying her and her face became grave again.

'*Do* you think of pasta and opera?' he asked.

'No. We think of many subjects.'

'What?'

She refused to tell him, because she was thinking now of all sorts of unexpected things. What was he like, for instance, when he was away from the army? Whether he was really as kind as he seemed? And unexpectedly, what life was like in Yorkshire? Instead she asked him what *he* thought about.

He found it hard to tell her, because most of the time he'd thought only about whether he was cold or hungry or whether his men were cold or hungry and what a rotten war it was. Sometimes he'd thought of the girls he'd known in England, and – only very occasionally these days, however – of a girl in Manchester he'd become engaged to. He knew, and he knew that the girl in Manchester knew, that nothing would ever come of it. Sometimes he wondered what had happened to all the other girls he'd once known, and where they were now. Once he'd enjoyed their youth and the way their dresses caught the breeze and the way their hair moved as they turned their heads. That seemed to have gone now, and often – though not at this moment – he thought instead how nice it would be to be in bed with one of them. It sprang less from sexual desire than the need for security. He decided he was growing old.

'What do we think of in England?' he said. 'Roast beef, beer and Shakespeare. That's what Englishmen are supposed to think of.'

'I think perhaps that you don't think always of that.'

'No,' he admitted. 'Not all the time.'

'Sometimes, I think, you think of your men.'

'Yes.' He looked at her in surprise. 'I do, often, because they're good men on the whole. How did you know?'

'Because I have watched you with them. You are that sort of man.'

'I try to look after them. As I'm looking after you now, with the German planes overhead.'

She smiled. 'The Church protects *us*,' she said. 'We have to be grateful to it for something.'

'That's cynical.'

'What is cynical?'

He explained what he meant, and she shrugged again. 'Sometimes I think the Church is like Il Duce. Neither has much improved the lot of the Italian people.'

He was staring at her, entranced, indifferent to what she said. 'I think you're beautiful, Graziella,' he said.

She stared back at him. Warley wasn't handsome in the sense that his features were perfect, but they were strong and there was a transparent honesty about him.

'You are also beautiful,' she said.

'You should see me with my hair combed.'

'Please?'

He smiled at her puzzlement.

'I'd like to kiss you, Graziella,' he said. It came out unexpectedly and certainly without forethought. In a wonder of shy excitement, he spoke tenderly and quickly.

She looked at him calmly. Her large clear eyes carried no secrets and no dishonesties.

'Do you try to woo me?' she asked.

He was tickled by the phrase and he raised a hand to touch the soft fair hair falling against her cheek. 'No,' he said.

'But you are not in love with me?'

'No.' Though I'm already well on the way, he admitted to himself. 'But just being here, being allowed to talk to you, to look at you – it means a lot when all you've looked at for a long time is men and ugliness.'

She frowned, a little worried because things seemed to be getting beyond her control. 'Do not be cross with me,' she said quietly. 'I try to understand. But Italian girls are different from other girls.'

'I've noticed that.'

'You must be careful with Italian girls. Nevertheless – ' she smiled ' – I think you had better kiss me and get it over, because the all clear is sounding and soon the others will return.'

The few days in Trepiazze were like no other days they'd spent for months. They all knew that before long they'd be back chasing the Tedeschi and that it would be cold again and uncomfortable and bloody dangerous, because the Teds knew their stuff too well. But for the time being they made the most of what they had.

They drank sweet vermouth and pale beer like soapy water, and fought off the old men who begged for cigarettes – *'Sigaretta, Signor Soldato. Ancora una sigaretta!'*

They thought blissfully about home and beer and football, and discussed their minor triumphs.

'This officer,' Parkin was saying. ' 'E 'ad a face like a dog's be'ind, and 'e was always complaining about the food. So the cook-corporal got this goat shit, see, mixed it with mashed potatoes and a bit of bully beef stew and served it to 'im as rissoles. 'E asked for more.'

'Remember that time at El Adem?' Duff said. 'When Puddephatt chased them Arab women and nearly got shot.'

'And when Rommel started us on the Gazala Gallop,' Martindale grinned. 'We was swimming in Benghazi when the panic started. Next day we were up to the neck in desert, running like hell for Cairo.'

One of the men who had not joined the battalion until Sicily, started to sing 'Sand In My Shoes'. It stopped the reminiscences dead.

In the opposite corner of the bar an argument was going on about girls.

'She will,' Hunters insisted.

'She wouldn't for me,' Evans the Bomb said.

'You don't know the rules, man.'

'They don't make rules for love.'

'What do you lot know about love?' Fletcher-Smith was armoured by memories of the previous evening with his Italian girl, which had taken the form of an adult discussion on literature interspersed with clumsy embraces. 'To you lot it's just an itch in a ditch.'

'Don't worry, kid,' Hunters said cheerfully. 'She's got it where it counts – under the left bloody Bristol.'

Rich pulled a face. 'Tha wants to stop swearing,' he said sternly. 'The Archbishop of Canterbury says it's because we swear so fuckin' much that we're losin' t' war an' worryin' our families.'

'What 'appened to *your* family, 'Enry?' Evans the Bomb asked White.

' 'E didn't 'ave a family,' Parkin said. ' 'E came in a box of soldiers.'

A few of them remained totally indifferent to the town. McWatters, in his soured, surly way, disliked Italians. In fact, he disliked everybody except Glaswegians – and he didn't like them very much – and remained most of the time in his billet; like Corporal Gask who spent all his spare time with a frown of concentration on his blank youthful face, cleaning his kit, writing home to his widowed mother and trying to think like the sergeant he intended to become.

Two men who beat up a military policeman and started a fight in a bar were brought up before Warley. Another man got knocked down by a lorry when he was drunk and both his legs were broken. To Warley, it seemed God ought to leave infantrymen alone when they came out of the line. The most vulnerable of mortals in wartime, they were surely entitled to a bit of safety when they weren't being shot at.

A special cinema show was put on for them in a marquee. The film was about Jack the Ripper, and hardly fun, while the marquee wasn't dark enough and the seats consisted of ration boxes. Even the unaccustomed smell of perfume that wafted down from a group of nursing sisters from the nearby hospital at Calimero, seated at the back, didn't adequately compensate for the numb behinds.

'I think the Navy would do it better,' Captain Jago observed. 'My brother's in the Navy and they always make sure that any girls who appear at their functions are properly paired off. I wouldn't mind the one with the fair hair, as a matter of fact.'

Major Warley said nothing, because he'd already found one with fair hair. He was itching to return to his billet and had already cried off from a visit to the mess on the excuse that he had letters to write.

Colonel Yuell hated deceiving them, hated allowing them to believe they were resting instead of merely having a brief respite in which to recover their spirits before being called on once more to pit their unwilling flesh against the steel of the German guns.

Orders had arrived. Like the good, the bad followed the same route downwards – from division to brigade, from brigade to regiment. The divisional general's conference was held in the mayor's office in Trepiazze, with only lieutenant-colonels and above in attendance. Many of them were still in their twenties and early thirties, young men with old eyes and the whole weight of the war on their shoulders. The soldiers watched the jeeps arrive with sardonic expressions on their faces. Conferences meant battle and battle meant death; and it was usually the troops, not the generals and the brigadiers, who were involved in that part of it.

The plan would normally have been discussed in outline by General Tonge with his staff – and perhaps even amended – at a meeting with the infantry brigade commanders and the commanders of the engineers, artillery, signals, supply and medical services. But, with things brewing up further east and Tonge constantly in Caserta, much of the plan had been drafted by Heathfield, and it was now all set up for the lower echelons to inspect.

Heathfield was doing most of the talking, and Brigadier Tallemach and Brigadier Rankin were listening hard, their brigade majors and DAQMGs in the background scribbling like mad with chinagraph pencils on the talc covers of their map cases. Brigadier George Rankin was a bull of a man – heavy-featured, heavy-shouldered, moustached and red-faced. Insensitive and not considered over-bright, he had, however, a good reputation as a fighting soldier. Brigadier Thomas Tallemach was thin and sensitive and looked more like an artist. In fact, a lot of his spare time was taken up with painting. He was good at it and it calmed him, because his was a nervous spirit and he was able to do a lot of thinking as he applied colour.

His orders were simple – '7th Brigade will attack northward from the area San Bartolomeo-Capodozzi-Foiano', followed by instructions about routes, timings, advance parties, administration, preliminary arrangements for the positioning of supplies and transport, and the movement of artillery ammunition.

He had studied them carefully. It was always important to impart clearly the mass of information, the method, the signals and the location of units on the flank; and these orders seemed curiously hurried and at the same time surprisingly rigid. Tallemach suspected that the uncertain methods which had produced them had begun to extend in the 19th Indian Division to other departments such as Intelligence. To Tallemach, who had made a point of exploring the forward area, Heathfield's assumption that the Germans were ready to throw in their hand was the height of wishful thinking.

When the idea of a river crossing had first been put to him, in fact he had been sceptical enough to make a joke of it.

'Is this just a casual enquiry?' he had asked. 'Or an order? Because I have very few men trained in walking on water.'

Heathfield now set up the position for them. 'This will not be an easy operation,' he said. 'But we expect it to be made easier by the Liberators and Fortresses drenching the area with anti-personnel bombs. The aim is to knock the enemy back from the river bank so we can dominate it by patrols and fire, and the attack will go in after a heavy bombardment.'

He went on to explain that the advance up Italy was in danger of coming to a stop and that it was necessary to keep up the momentum. Colonel Yuell listened thoughtfully, knowing only too well how right he was. There was no difficulty with a single rush, but wherever the line had paused to be regrouped it had always lost its forward movement.

'There'll be an artillery bombardment,' Heathfield was saying, 'and then the infantry will advance with close support fire from tanks.'

Provided, Yuell thought, that the Germans hadn't held their fire to conceal their positions, so that when they opened up the infantry would have to entrench or withdraw; and then, with the attack halted, the artillery would have to start up again and repeat the rhythm, as it had been repeated all through the dark foggy weeks of winter.

'7th Infantry Brigade will make the crossing,' Heathfield said. 'Your people, Yuell, going in by Route A along the main road in front of San Eusebio; and the Yellowjackets further east by Route B in front of Castelgrande where the footbridge used to be. As soon as you've established your bridgeheads and the tanks have crossed, the Baluchis will push across to join you, giving the greatest support at whichever bridgehead appears to be most successful. It's expected that the crossing will take roughly three minutes; the infantry will be behind the barrage and there will be a safety period for the artillery to plaster the opposite bank. However – ' Heathfield paused – 'some of our guns are so worn they can't guarantee there won't be an odd round up to six hundred yards short. That means we shall have to form up three hundred yards short of the bank on our own side, and the artillery will have to lift six minutes before the start.'

'Which,' Tallemach pointed out quietly, 'will give the Germans six minutes to emerge from their shelters.'

After the divisional commander's conference with the brigadiers asking the questions, it was the brigade commander's turn with Heathfield sitting alongside, holding a watching brief, and the battalion commanders doing the worrying.

Brigadier Tallemach gestured at the blackboard behind him where a simplified plan of the countryside in front of and around San Eusebio had been chalked up.

When he had been forward to look over the territory they were to attack, what he had seen hadn't encouraged him. Heathfield and his staff had worked with feverish activity to prepare the detailed plans but they seemed to have overlooked the fact that the river, the main line of resistance, was unfordable, twelve feet deep and fifty feet wide, with steep banks, a swift current, only one bridge – with its centre span smashed – and a rumoured 24,000 mines sown on both sides.

Behind the river, beyond the railway line that ran to Rome, San Eusebio was built on a bluff. Once there, they could expect to be protected by the surrounding escarpment from the German guns above and on the flanks. But since the Germans would be just as much aware of this as they were, it was clear they'd have taken every possible precaution to prevent the capture of San Eusebio taking place and Tallemach's battalions would be in full view of the heights until the minute they'd finally captured the village.

He had tried to point this out to Heathfield, but Heathfield had seemed to be wearing blinkers. Despite all protests, he determinedly held to the view that the piecemeal methods used during the winter would again cause the Germans to withdraw.

However, it wasn't Tallemach's role to question orders, and now he tried to make some sense of them for the men under him.

'The idea's to establish a bridgehead to the east of the village,' he said. 'We know that it's built on a bluff a hundred-odd feet above the river, but to the east the ground's broken and rolling and should provide plenty of cover for us.'

For the Germans too, Colonel Yuell thought.

Tallemach cleared his throat and went on briskly.

'The Yellowjackets will be crossing well to the east of the town,' he said, his voice crisp but unusually low, 'so between them and the North Yorkshires we ought to be able to keep the enemy busy. When we've linked up, and the 3rd Baluchis are across in support, 9th Indian Brigade will go through us for San Eusebio.'

'It's difficult country down to the river on this side, sir.' The words came softly and Tallemach studied Yuell over his spectacles.

'The river's inundated the land, sir,' Yuell continued, 'and the country's flat and open to observation from San Eusebio. And we all know the Germans have established posts and strongpoints right to the river's edge and there isn't a scrap of shelter to hide a gun or a tank.'

There was a long silence. 'Go on,' Tallemach said.

'There are minefields on both sides of the river and, on the other side, gun emplacements built into the river bank itself and near the railway. Farm buildings have been fortified with pill-boxes and tanks dug into the ground. Every one of these strongpoints will have to be reduced individually.'

'Don't you think you're making rather a lot of it?' Heath-field interrupted from his chair alongside Tallemach's desk.

'My men are going to have to face them,' Yuell retorted stubbornly.

'We're trying to get at Cassino from the side,' Heathfield explained patiently. 'Going at it from the front's produced surprisingly little mileage so far. Both the Americans and the New Zealanders have been thrown back. And you won't be under fire from all those posts you mention because you'll be crossing in darkness.'

The regimental officers exchanged glances. The one thing nobody liked was a river crossing by night. There was another long silence before Heathfield asked:

'Would you be satisfied if the heights on your flanks were under attack, although not actually in our possession?'

'So long,' Yuell said, 'as the attacks are powerful enough to force the Germans to use every gun they've got to oppose them. Just two or three concealed 88s would be sufficient to destroy our bridges.'

'I think we can guarantee we shall be able to prevent that. Division will be giving everything they've got and we also have Corps backing. Guns are being transferred even now.'

Heathfield didn't say how many, but nobody quibbled and the conference came to a halt. As he returned to his room, Tallemach took out a cigarette. He felt tired and knew he was inclined to be crochety and over-critical. The war seemed to have been going on such a long time, and now that it was showing signs of approaching its final phase every day seemed to drag. Reaching across his desk he picked up a lighter, and as he did so his eyes fell on a photograph of his wife and the two sons she had borne him. Only the previous month he had learned that he now had only one son; his younger boy, barely out of school, had died from wounds received in a grenade accident while rehearsing in England for what they all knew was to be the Second Front.

Tallemach drew a deep breath. Keep the other one safe, God, he begged under his breath, knowing all too well that Bomber Command was hardly a secure haven from which to fight a war.

Lighting up the cigarette quickly to stop himself from thinking, he moved to the window and peered through the rain-swept glass. If they were to keep their preparations out of sight of the Germans on Monte Cassino, he thought, there was going to be remarkably little elbow room to manoeuvre. Bridges couldn't be established easily; there was no concealment for the Engineers in the open plain, and even smokescreens wouldn't work because it would be no problem for the Germans to estimate where the bridges were and plaster the whole area with fire. When the Americans had tried it, at the beginning of the year, the result had been considered by them the worst disaster to their forces since Pearl Harbour.

He thought again of Heathfield's plan. He'd even protested that it wasn't wide enough in scope. There weren't enough crossings, and too much pressure could be brought to bear on the ones that had been proposed. Heathfield had been smoothly ingratiating.

'No enterprise in war ever turns out quite so well or so badly as the first reports lead you to believe,' he'd said cheerfully. 'I've no doubt we shall be worried at first, but I think it'll work.'

Tallemach drew on the cigarette and stared out of the window. The sky was a violet grey and the rain was lashing into the puddles.

'Let's just hope the weather gives us a chance,' he observed to his brigade major, 'because all that sunshine Italy's supposed to have is nothing but a fallacy. I often think the photographers who take those picture postcards you see with all that blue sky in 'em sit waiting in the cafés for the clouds to clear; then, when it stops raining, rush out, take their pictures, and bolt back to the bar before the next cloudburst. One of the things the travel brochures have always been reticent about is that Italy's mostly mountains and that where there are mountains there's usually rain.'

In Trepiazze, Yuell studied the map with Major Peddy.

'It would make a lot of difference,' Peddy said, 'if *we* were on the hills instead of the Germans.'

Yuell nodded. 'It's notorious that enemy strength and morale always appear weaker to headquarters than they do to the chaps in more active contact.'

He turned to the battalion Intelligence officer. 'What do *you* think of the appreciation of the German capabilities, Harry?' he asked.

Lieutenant Harry Marder considered. He was an Oxford graduate with the university man's habit of dissecting everything minutely – so minutely, in fact, you couldn't sometimes see the pieces – and a superficially fluent command of French, German and Italian that would have been more valuable to the army if it had extended to a fuller understanding of some of the finer nuances of those languages. He liked to be amusing about the Intelligence branch, claiming it consisted of out-of-work journalists, Latin scholars, booksellers, unwanted clergymen and fugitives from university common rooms; but he was proud of his job nonetheless and regarded himself as making a considerable contribution to the war effort.

'I understand, sir,' he said, 'that in the other war, General Marshall-Cornwall used to crawl out into No Man's Land to listen to the Germans talking. He was able to judge whether they were from Bavaria or Saxony by their accents.'

Yuell frowned, wishing that Marder would sometimes give him a direct answer.

'That's no help,' he said testily.

'No, sir,' Marder agreed. 'But until we have some prisoners to question, I can't see how we can ever give a proper appreciation. The Duke of Wellington used to say that all the business of war, indeed all the business of life, was to endeavour to find out what you don't know by what you do – what he called guessing what was at the other side of the hill. But that's a bit difficult with a river between us. Whose was the appreciation, sir?'

'Brigadier Heathfield's.'

'They say he intends to go in for politics after the war,' Peddy observed.

'It's a measure of how safe he feels that he can plan for after the war,' Yuell growled. 'I wish I could. All the same, it's not entirely a bad plan, though it'd be better if there were more crossings. It's the first principle of forcing a river position that there should be plenty of points of attack, so that the enemy can't deal with any of them in strength. On top of that, we're too close together. The Germans can deal with both crossings with the same defence.'

He lit a pipe and sucked at it for a while, before going on. 'However, I gather we've been promised everything we want – boats, artillery, tanks, the lot, and all the back-up services we need. What's more, if things begin to look dicey, it's to be called off and something else tried.'

'When's it to be, sir?'

'The thirteenth.'

'Three days,' Peddy mused. 'That's not long. Will there be a rehearsal?'

'No time.' Yuell frowned again, feeling this too was a mistake. 'They decided, after all the rivers we've already crossed, that we ought to know something about it.'

A Company officers received their first briefing the following day in Warley's room. Graziella had swept and polished and dusted it as if he were the Pope about to give an audience.

'It's only a bunch of soldiers,' he said.

'Nevertheless, they must not feel you are neglected.'

It had delighted him but, faced by his officers, he was in a thoughtful mood. 'We're for it,' he said. 'We're to be part of a push across the river. In front of San Eusebio.'

He explained the plan as he'd received it from Yuell, and Jago sniffed.

'Bit optimistic, isn't it?' he said in a flat voice. 'All this business of the Yellowjackets going across at Castelgrande half a mile away and then hacking along the river bank to San Eusebio.'

'That's the way I've got it, Tony.'

'It's too bloody obscure,' Jago grumbled.

'Well, it doesn't exactly run out and bite you in the leg,' Warley admitted with a grin. 'But I suppose they know more about it than we do.'

Jago grinned back at him. 'It's always been my impression that the staff know a bloody sight less than the chaps who're going to do the job,' he said. 'Come to that, how *are* we going to do it? The bloody place bristles with guns and that's God's plain unvarnished and unbuckled truth, and you can't get away from it.'

Warley shrugged. 'Brigade seems to think we can manage it; but then, of course, so do Division, Corps and Army. All the way back to Naples and London and Number 10, Downing Street, I expect. Let's have Farnsworth in.'

In front of the officers, CSM Farnsworth was so stiff he seemed all bone. Warley offered him a cigarette and pushed a chair forward.

His first meeting with Farnsworth had been on the Egypt-Libya border. Standing upright by a heap of sandbags, staring across the empty desert with his binoculars, Warley had asked, 'Where's the front line?' Farnsworth, crouching well down, had hesitated for a second before answering, 'At the moment, sir, I suspect you're standing on it.'

Warley had ducked out of sight and they had grinned at each other, Warley faintly sheepish, Farnsworth with no sign of superiority, and it had been the beginning of a long and easy relationship that made the passing on of orders a very simple business.

'We're moving up, Fred,' Warley announced briskly. 'In two days' time.'

Farnsworth smiled. It was like a crack appearing in concrete. 'This river crossing, sir?'

Warley's head jerked round. 'How did you hear about that?'

'It seems to have been around since yesterday, sir.'

'Does it, by God? Where did it come from?'

'HQ Company runner was at Brigade, sir, you'll remember. He brought it back. He didn't like the sound of it. Come to that, sir, neither do I.'

Warley frowned; then he shrugged. 'I expect,' he said, 'that, as usual, the ordinary common or garden soldier will salvage everybody's reputation.'

Perhaps he would, but he wasn't very keen all the same. Unlike the people, sitting at home in clubs complaining about the slow movement of the army up Italy, unlike the Prime Minister who felt they were being wasted and should be allowed to get on with the job; unlike everybody except themselves and their friends, in fact, they had no particular wish to be part of the battle. People got hurt in battles.

It was all right planning battles, seeing them in great sweeps on the map. It was a bit different when you were up at the sharp end. The descriptive phrases used by newspaper correspondents and war commentators about 'flinging in armour', 'pouring in reserves' and 'launching pincer movements' gave a fairly reasonable impression to those at home with a map in front of them; but most of the men involved would have found it difficult to recognise just what part they'd really played, even if they'd had it pointed out to them.

It had come as a surprise to them to read in such newspapers as found their way out from home that the time when they'd spent three days cowering in the mud behind a wrecked farmhouse, they were reserves being 'poured in', and that the shambles at Sant' Agata di Militello was part of a 'pincer movement'. They hadn't been aware that these occasions even were battles. They'd merely thought they were just continuing the painful advance up Italy through mud, mountain and river, which seemed to have been going on ever since the dawn of time and, as far as they could see, would continue until the Last Trump sounded.

The more intelligent of them, of course, knew that the war was on the home straight at last and that if they could only get going again in Italy, the Second Front could be launched across the Channel while the attention of the Germans was occupied in trying to hold on to Rome.

'After all – ' Fletcher-Smith spoke with the authority of scholarship and the romantic view of a man heavily involved with an Italian girl – 'they're bound to try. Italy's the land of the Romans.'

'You know what they can do with Italy?' 766 Bawden said. 'They can fold it three ways and stick it where the monkey sticks its nuts.'

'If they up-ended the mountains and slotted 'em into the valleys,' 000 Bawden chimed in, 'they'd be able to roll it reasonably flat.'

'Tha ought to suggest that to t' staff,' Rich said enthusiastically. 'It'd make transport a 'ell of a lot easier.'

For just a little longer Heaven continued to lie about them, but soon it began to dawn that with all the new equipment and new weapons that were flying about, something was in the wind.

A river crossing, they were told, and they were even less happy when they heard that. River crossings were the worst possible means of getting from one place to another. Without the Navy around to help, the launching of small boats by rank amateurs, weighed down by heavy equipment, was bad enough even in daylight. At night time, while being shot at, it was about as horrifying as anything that wartime could produce. And added to that they were all too well aware that the boats, flat-bottomed and not possessed of much in the nature of bows or stern, wouldn't lend themselves to anything much more demanding than a duckpond on a calm day; especially when their occupants were being shelled, mortared and raked by machine-gun fire.

'River crossin's are bloody 'ard work,' Duff said, his small face full of alarm.

'An' 'e knows all about work, don't you, Lofty?' Parkin said. 'All that flannel about "Hi-ho, hi-ho, it's off to work we go" comes natural. 'E's one of the Seven Dwarfs.'

Martindale gestured with his pipe. 'Yon river's fifty feet wide an' twelve feet deep,' he pointed out aggrievedly in his slow, plodding, ploughman's manner. 'And when you can't swim like me, that's enough to drown in.'

As he spoke, showers of sparks threatened to set light to the straw on which they were lying and Private Rich, having beaten out the threat of fire in his immediate vicinity, moved away a little to avoid being blinded. 'They'll 'ave to clear t' near bank,' he grated in his Dracula voice. 'They'll 'ave to ave a 'olding force to stop t' Teds puttin' us off as we go forward.'

'There's a fat lot of good a holding force will be,' Evans the Bomb said. 'With the whole bloody area open to observers on the hills.'

'Under the circumstances –' Hunters looked up from where he was scraping mud off his greatcoat – 'I'm going out tonight to find myself a dame.'

'They say there's a concert,' 766 Bawden said. 'An ENSA job.'

'They never 'ad concerts when I joined up,' Henry White observed.

'Gi'e o'er, 'Enry,' Parkin said. 'Look what fun it was when they turned the lions loose on the Christians.'

'Did you know' – this time the voice was Fletcher-Smith's – 'that a squad of Yellowjackets got down to the river a week ago to lift the mines the Teds laid? The next night they went again and lost five men from mines.'

'Obviously didn't do a very good job of it,' 000 Bawden said.

'That's just the point,' Fletcher-Smith insisted. 'They did. They were *new* mines. The Teds had crossed the river again and laid some more.'

Private Syzling summed up the prevailing feeling better than anybody. He could see ahead of him days of cold, wet misery with the Germans shooting at him and probably even killing him. At the very least going without food and having that stupid nit, Deacon, nagging at him to stand up straight or keep his head down, to clean his rifle and find his kit, and above all to behave like a man with some pride in himself and his company. All in all the future outlook – and Syzling's future outlook rarely went beyond the next week – was sheer unadulterated gloom.

'A battle!' he said indignantly as he pinched out his fagend and stuck it in his pocket. 'You'd think they was tryin' to get us killed.'

seven

Curiously enough, the thoughts that Syzling was thinking were much the same as those running through Captain Reis' mind on the other side of the river.

To Reis it stuck out a mile that Germany had already lost the war, but the lunatics in Berlin seemed to want to see the German army – the whole German nation – go down in some sort of fiery Götterdämmerung. No wonder Wagner, with his love of gods and gloom and Valhalla, appealed to the feverish and twisted intellects that were running the country.

Reis had lost a dozen good friends since he'd become a soldier and he couldn't help thinking uneasily, and not for the first time, that there must be something wrong with the popular conception of the Almighty, with His mercy and His justice, when He could allow such things to happen while the monsters in Berlin continued to wax and grow fat. Though Nemesis was clearly approaching, *they* were still alive and still enjoying the fleshpots while far finer men had long since gone to their graves – German and enemy alike. The idea that it was sweet and fitting to die for one's country seemed to have become just a tired old platitude. As a good Catholic and a good German, it worried Reis.

Standing by the sandbagged window of the cellar of the farmhouse in San Eusebio which he had made his headquarters, his elbows resting on the sill, his eyes glued to his binoculars, he tried to push the bitter thoughts from his mind and concentrate on the job in hand. But it wasn't easy.

He had a wife he hadn't seen for over a year and a child he had never seen at all and, though the Rhineland where he lived was safer than Hamburg, Berlin or the Ruhr, these days nowhere in Germany could be called secure. Enemy bombers ranged over the country twenty-four hours a day.

They had been promised airy sunlit homes: Well, thanks to the enemy bombers they'd got them. Anybody who *hadn't* got an airy sunlit home these days – a home with the roof still on and the windows still in – could be called lucky. Even along the rural areas of Rhine there had been raids and attempts to mine the stream. Yet still the gang in Berlin seemed quite happy to go on as they always had, as if they were untouchable. *Alles klapt* was the saying. Everything's ticking over. *Hitler ist der Sieg.* Hitler is Victory. But with men of sixty-five being called into the Volkssturm and the cracks in the national façade appearing faster than the Nazi propagandists could paper them over, such sayings took on a hollow ring. And in the meantime, men continued to die.

Reis sighed, aware that he was not without guilt himself for what had happened to his country. He too had once cheered, in the days when he'd believed National Socialism could overcome the evils wished on his country after the last war. Even in 1940 and 1941 – when foreign capitals fell to the Wehrmacht like skittles in a skittle alley – he had still been able to think that despite the disturbing things he kept hearing, perhaps the Nazi leaders were right. It had long since changed for him, of course, as it had for the rest of Germany; but the change had come far too late, and the wild talk he sometimes heard of a plot to remove the regime remained merely wild talk because no one dared move with the Nazi grip on the country's throat.

He was just wondering how it would all end, and if he would be alive to see it end, when his attention was caught by movement on the road that ran from below him, straight as an arrow into the hills where the roofs of San Bartolomeo were just visible. Directly beneath him, he could see the bridge that brought the road to his own side of the river, with its centre span neatly removed by German engineers as they had retreated.

Bending low, jamming his eyes into the rubber cups on the glasses and concentrating fiercely, he thought he could see tanks outside San Bartolomeo. The haze that hung over the valley after all the weeks of rain was confusing, however, and after a second or two the vision faded and he began to wonder if he were imagining things. But it seemed safe to assume that things *were* moving across there, if only because patrol activity had increased in the last few days and observation posts had reported that the British were lifting the minefields on their own side of the river as fast as they could. If they intended staying where they were until the end of the winter, they wouldn't have bothered.

He reached for a message pad and began to jot down what he had seen in the last twenty-four hours. There had been guns, a column of vehicles moving in and out of the hills, what looked like a dump growing among the trees just out of artillery range, and now possibly tanks. It all pointed to *something* being in the wind. Lifting the telephone, he cranked the handle. Thiergartner's voice answered.

'What's it like down there?' Reis asked.

'Quiet, Herr Hauptmann. As a graveyard.'

'Nothing happening?'

'Nothing of moment, Herr Hauptmann. Only Pulovski kicking the stove over just as the coffee was coming to the boil. That's the worst of our ills just now. Why? Do you see something from up there?'

'No.' Reis forced his voice to sound calm. 'It's nothing. I'm just worried a little.'

'Aren't we all, Herr Hauptmann?' Thiergartner's voice came back full of humour and slightly mocking, and for a moment Reis thought that he might well be worth talking to for his views on the political situation at home. At least he'd be amusing. He rejected the idea sadly. Once that sort of thing started, it could only lead to demoralisation. He had to believe – they all had to believe – in what they were fighting for, or there would be no point in fighting. Even Reis, who was fighting chiefly for his wife and child, realised that he could not honourably give up the struggle. The things he'd seen in Russia gave him sleepless nights at times, and Germany's borders had to be kept inviolate.

'Have you seen anything across the river lately?' he asked abruptly before his feelings could burst out of him.

'Movement, Herr Hauptmann,' Thiergartner said. 'Lots of movement.'

'I thought I saw tanks just now.'

Thiergartner laughed. 'Doubtless from the monastery, on a clear day and with a good pair of glasses, they can read the arrows on the Tommies' maps in Caserta. It isn't worth worrying about.'

Reis thought it was, but Thiergartner's voice came again. 'We all know we're the sacrifice, Herr Hauptmann. That fact is clear. The bait, you might even say. *Morituri te salutamus.* We who are about to die salute thee. Pity there's no one at the top *worth* saluting.'

'Shut up, Thiergartner,' Reis snapped, realising he had allowed the younger man to go too far.

Thiergartner was quick to apologise. 'I'm sorry, Herr Hauptmann,' he said. 'That slipped out before I realised. But I think I'm right, all the same. It *is* no use worrying. They'll come. When they've made their plan, they'll come.'

In fact, the plan had already been finalised. Colonel Yuell knew as well as anyone that the date wasn't far enough ahead. It never was, of course, but the few days they'd been granted wouldn't even be sufficient to bring the battalion back to its former skill and quality.

A whole new bunch of men had joined – curiously pale and innocent-looking to the old hands. They'd come up from Naples, newly out from home to make up the numbers. But they'd been in England for most of the war and didn't know that 'Ted' wasn't your girl friend's brother but a Tedesco and a German, the same article they'd been facing across the Channel for three years without ever coming to grips. There were also a few old hands who were rejoining after being wounded, but these weren't many and they were wary because there was nothing like a wound to make a man realise he wasn't immortal.

Colonel Yuell was no happier than the rest of them. With Warley, he was squatting in a ruined farmhouse in the hills overlooking the river. They had driven up that morning to make sure they knew the country ahead. In front of them the land flattened out, dropping gently towards the river which meandered slowly past on its way to the sea. From where they crouched, they could see the whole width of the valley with the slow-winding steely thread of the river, the railway line to Rome, and Highway Six in the shadow of the mountains. At that moment it all seemed empty, but occasionally on their own side they saw a vehicle move, spotting it at once and realising that the moment they came into the open, they too would be spotted.

The colonel of the Sikh regiment holding the sector was with them, and he gestured towards where San Eusebio sat on its bluff above the river. 'We put a patrol across there two nights ago,' he said. 'Not a man returned.'

Warley pointed. 'Sir, how're they going to get a holding force down there near the river? The Germans'll see every move that's made, and their observation posts'll be able to shell 'em to Kingdom Come'. He studied the land below them again. 'It's also a hell of a long walk under fire, sir,' he went on. 'And if we're going to be down at the river bank at the right time, we're going to be starting *while it's still daylight.*'

It was something that bothered Yuell, and he determined to have it out at Brigade HQ.

It so happened that his arrival at Brigade HQ coincided with a visit from Brigadier Heathfield, and the three of them – Yuell, Heathfield and Tallemach – got down to it together.

'I'm concerned less with the business of getting across,' Yuell admitted, 'than with getting into position.'

Heathfield looked up. His features were plump, pink and smooth with self-satisfaction. He had produced his plan and he could see no reason why it shouldn't work. Dammit, Yuell thought, no wonder he wants to be a politician after the war. He looks like one. He even has a politician's self-righteous belief in what he has created.

'It's a straight enough road,' Heathfield said.

'That's just what bothers me,' Yuell pointed out.

'You'll have it all to yourselves. The Yellowjackets go down by a different route.'

Yuell's eyes flashed. 'Have *you* marched down to the river bank from cover, sir?' he demanded.

Heathfield paused then came back to the attack. 'No,' he said. 'And I don't suppose you have either.'

'No,' Yuell admitted. 'I haven't. And neither has anyone else. That's the whole problem. Nobody knows how long it's going to take. There's only one real road down to the jumping-off spot and that's the road from San Bartolomeo to San Eusebio. You can bet the Germans have it pin-pointed down the whole length. It's so straight they've only got to have a battery opposite the end and drop a few shells on it for markers, and they can cover the whole length of it simply by raising or lowering their sights.'

Heathfield seemed unable to see the difficulties. 'I think you're making rather a lot of it,' he said. 'And we're making great efforts to clear the minefields on our side.'

'Are we clearing them quicker than the Germans are slipping back to re-lay them?' Yuell asked.

Heathfield ignored the question because he wasn't sure of the answer, and went on, sweeping the map with his hand, always pleasant and smooth, never angry. 'We shall try to put a holding force by the river to deter them.'

Yuell didn't ask who they were, merely where they were to be positioned.

Heathfield's finger jabbed at the map. 'There.' His hand moved. 'And along this ground here.'

'That bank slopes *towards* the Germans,' Yuell pointed out. 'Not away. There's nowhere there they can dig in with safety. They'll be under observation the whole time.'

'I think we can leave that to the holding force,' Heathfield said confidently. 'We expect to use the Baluchis, then they'll be in a good position to join you across the bridge as soon as the Engineers have repaired it. Don't worry about this side. Worry about the other side. Because only when the ground there's in our hands will the bridgehead stand any chance of success.'

The new conference at Divisional HQ didn't go quite as easily. General Tonge had left it to Brigadier Heathfield because he was due to confer with the army commander. He'd already come to the conclusion that perhaps Heathfield had been a little too precipitate and that it would be a good idea to call the whole thing off before they became too involved to do so. In the meantime, since he had this feeling nothing might come of it and since it was Heathfield's plan and Heathfield had made all the arrangements, he had considered Heathfield quite capable of handling the details.

Perhaps because Tonge wasn't there, everybody was more pernickety, and it was Colonel Baron of the Yellowjackets who first voiced his doubts. 'What's the river like there, sir?' he asked. 'We ought to know.'

Heathfield was blandly reassuring. 'No high banks,' he said. 'Not like further along. It's low and there are beaches of mud with patches of shingle. It should be easy to launch the boats.'

Baron still wasn't satisfied.

'What are the grounds, sir,' he asked, 'for imagining that German morale's sagging? I've seen no sign of it.'

Heathfield lifted a bunch of papers. 'We've been picking up letters from German bodies,' he said. 'I have five here, all taken from the same man – one unposted from the dead man himself, quite obviously hating being here in Italy; one from his father in Russia to him, saying they're enduring hell; one from a cousin on the Adriatic front; one from a brother in France; one from his mother in Germany. They all follow the same theme – how much they're suffering from allied attacks and from the bombing.'

'With respect,' Baron persisted, 'only one of them refers to this sector – the one that wasn't posted. Aren't we reading too much into them?'

Heathfield paused, aware that the divisional Intelligence officer's enthusiasm – and his own too, for that matter – had failed to take this point into account. 'There are plenty of others,' he said.

As Baron sat down, the colonel of the 717th Field Company, Royal Engineers, raised his objections. 'That bridge at the end of the San Bartolomeo road,' he pointed out. 'It's no good for tanks.'

'I know that,' Heathfield said. 'We all know it. There's a span down. It'll be your job to repair it.'

'I didn't mean that. I mean it's not strong enough. I put in a report myself.'

Heathfield frowned. 'Are you sure?'

'I've had a look at it, sir. It was dark and they were shooting at us, so it was a bit perfunctory, but I'd stake my career on it. If you want to get tanks across, you're going to have to push up a Class 40 Bailey bridge.'

Heathfield frowned because the Engineer's report seemed to have gone astray somewhere, then he nodded. 'You'd better attend to it,' he said.

It was the bridge that brought Colonel Vivian, the officer in command of the armour, into the picture. Vivian had fought all the way along the north coast of Africa and through Sicily before arriving in front of Cassino. He was a tall man with a limp yellow moustache, but he wore the ribbon of the DSO on his breast. He was said to be enormously wealthy and to have given a tremendous amount of time and money to keeping his Yeomanry up to scratch before the war, and he clearly had no intention of being pushed into something that might destroy it unnecessarily.

'If we're to get across the bridge,' he said, 'we'll need to be grouped well forward so we can get across it at first light the minute it's finished and before it's knocked out.'

'You go as soon as a good bridgehead's been established,' Heathfield agreed. 'Until then, your tanks will remain concealed.'

'What about the approach?'

'What about it?'

'How do we get into position?'

'Why can't you be in position already?'

'Because in front of San Eusebio, where we'll be, there's only one surfaced road down to the jumping-off spot, and that's going to be jammed with infantry, artillery and lorries carrying assault boats. To say nothing of the Engineers with all their bridging equipment who'll have to be ready to start throwing the bridge across the minute the infantry reach the other side.'

Heathfield lifted his head. 'A timetable's been prepared,' he said shortly. 'When you want to use the road, it'll be clear. The guns will also be in position when they're needed. It's been worked out carefully from timetables in other successful attacks. There's no reason why it shouldn't work here; especially as you're going to be backed up with every bit of artillery we've got.'

'The river's only fifty feet wide,' Vivian pointed out. 'The artillery won't be able to give all *that* much support for fear of hitting the infantry. And, just in case you haven't been down there, sir, I might point out that I have. In the summer of 1939.'

'Before the war,' Heathfield said.

'The countryside hasn't changed. Along the riverside there's a lot of tangled undergrowth. I remember it well because I was rather hopeful of taking a girl I'd met for a swim. We didn't make it. And, from what I remember, there's nothing down there to provide cover. For anybody. Don't you think, sir, we ought to lay an extra track alongside the road so that when the time comes, my tanks can get down there like bats out of hell?'

The Engineer colonel frowned. 'My men will already be working at full stretch,' he snapped.

'I wasn't aware, anyway,' Heathfield said, 'that tanks were dependent on the roads.'

'They're not.' Vivian had no intention of backing down. 'But it's hardly stopped raining for weeks. With the inundations the Germans caused by diverting the river, the fields are nothing but artificial marshes far too soft for tanks.'

'It's only a straightforward river crossing.' Heathfield was beginning to sound exasperated.

Vivian shook his head. 'I'd submit, sir,' he said briskly, 'that there's no such thing especially by night. It certainly wasn't simple for the Americans in January.'

'Perhaps they hadn't our experience,' Heathfield retorted.

'My men haven't had our experience either,' the colonel of the Rajputs in Rankin's brigade said bluntly. 'I've never come across an Indian regiment that was ever any good in boats, in fact. Like artillery and armour, it's something they don't seem to master.'

They moved on to supplies, the Engineer officer drawing attention to the lack of basic engineering necessities. 'There are no standard footbridges,' he said. 'And all other items have become scarce since they started preparing for the Second Front in England. We have to produce around sixty wooden assault boats, forty pneumatic boats and four improvised footbridges. I'm hoping to pick up about a hundred additional craft of each type, and we've found fifty sections of cat-walk which will make a footbridge for the follow-up. We can provide vehicle-bearing bridges for support troops.'

'There's – only – one – road,' Vivian said, dragging their attention back to his problems. 'And it'll have all this engineering equipment on it. An attack without suitable approach routes and blocked by organised defences behind an unfordable river could create an impossible situation.'

Heathfield frowned, realising that, with his inexperience of this theatre, his estimates and plans were running into difficulties. 'I'll see what I can do,' he agreed.

'What about the air?' Colonel Baron of the Yellowjackets asked. 'Are we certain of support? Because we shall need it.'

Heathfield felt more at ease. He'd already tackled that problem and received promises of assistance. 'There'll be a strike on the enemy positions at last light before you go in.'

'Let's hope it *is* on the enemy positions,' Baron said dryly. 'There've been too many instances lately of them landing on *our* positions.'

'I'll get in touch with the RAF and ask what they suggest. The infantry can carry iridescent panels to show where they are. At least, we can assume they'll quieten the Germans enough for the Engineers to get on with their job.'

'There's one other thing, sir,' Yuell said. 'We still haven't put a patrol across the river and we don't know a damn thing about what's waiting for us on the other side.'

At roughly the moment when the conference was drawing to a close, General Tonge's car was braking to a halt outside Corps HQ.

The general in command of corps was a tall, hook-nosed man with so many medal ribbons it was difficult to separate t'other from which. He had a sense of the dramatic and a flair for publicity that went with it. He was also intelligent and knew a lot about war. He listened to Tonge with sympathy and, when he'd finished, offered him a cigarette before sitting back and studying the map on the wall.

'Unhappily, James,' he said slowly, 'I'm afraid it *can't* be called off. Fresh orders have just come down from Army Group. They've set up an attack of their own. The New Zealanders are having another go. Unfortunately, the weather's been against it and they've been sitting on it over a week already.'

'I've heard nothing of it,' Tonge said.

'They've kept it pretty dark.'

Tonge glanced at the envelope the general had pushed across the desk. It contained his orders.

'You have the doubtful honour of opening the bowling,' the corps commander went on. 'They reckon the Germans will be so damn busy holding you off, they'll not notice what's going on elsewhere.'

Brigadier Heathfield was inclined to be indignant at the thought that Tonge had tried to put aside his plan.

'I got the impression we had a straightforward go-ahead, sir,' he said stiffly.

'We did indeed, Wallace,' Tonge explained patiently. 'But I decided that it was a whole lot harder than we'd imagined. As it happens, it makes no difference, anyway, because orders now are that it *will* go ahead.'

Heathfield made no comment and Tonge went on. 'Unfortunately,' he said, 'the imponderables of war are beginning to appear. What was merely an idea which could be called off if it wasn't likely to work now has to go on willy-nilly. However, we might make it a bit easier all round. I'm not sure I like the idea of using just two roads – the Foiano-Castelgrande road for the Yellowjackets – what you've called Route B – and the San Bartolomeo-San-Eusebio road – Route A – over the bridge for Yuell's men.' He jerked a map forward and jabbed a blunt finger at it. 'This cluster of houses here – Capodozzi – between Foiano and San Bartolomeo. There's a cart track runs down from there through these orchards to the river where there used to be a ferry for getting the fruit across to the railway. It's gone now because they built the bridge and tarmacadamed the road from San Bartolomeo, but I think we ought to use the track. We'll call it Route C.'

Heathfield gave a little sniff at the suggestion that he hadn't thought of everything. Tonge heard it and looked up.

'We could use it for Yuell's men,' he said, 'and prevent congestion on the San Bartolomeo road. So let's have it recce'd. I want a strong patrol put across the river to the east of San Eusebio and I want this cart track from Capodozzi to the river examined. The San Bartolomeo road's going to be crammed with vehicles because it's the only hard-surface road that's wide enough. Therefore, we've got to make sure it's not cluttered up with infantry. There's a good path along the river bank on the other side so I think we should send the North Yorkshires down from Capodozzi and have them join the road to San Eusebio where it leaves the river by the bridge.'

'Very well, sir.' Heathfield's indignation was still marked but he was recovering quickly. 'I understand. I'll see to that.'

'Right away, Wallace.'

'Of course, sir.'

The officer Heathfield chose was a middle-aged man of no great drive or skill on the staff of the GSO1. But, with everybody else occupied with the plans for the crossing, he was the only one left.

And it so happened that, just as he was preparing to leave, the malaria he'd contracted in Sicily struck him again. The last thing he needed that evening was a drive down to the river bank. He put on every article of clothing he could manage and, shivering alongside the driver of the jeep, roared off from headquarters.

Heathfield's briefing had been quick and casual.

'We want to push infantry down to the river from Capodozzi,' he explained. 'Just do a recce on the road there, will you, and see if it's suitable.'

Aware of his state of health, the officer was glad it wasn't more. The job would consist merely of driving to the river and making sure the road was wide enough for the infantry to get down there safely with their Bedford lorries, Bren gun carriers and jeeps. Heathfield hadn't explained why they were going down there, and he imagined they were going to occupy the river bank as part of the holding force for the river crossing.

As it happened also, his driver was new to the area and, with the officer half dozing with a high temperature beside him, he missed his turn so that instead of arriving in Capodozzi as darkness fell, they found themselves in a totally different village several miles further on. Weakly, the officer cursed the driver, knowing perfectly well it wasn't his fault. Signs got blown down by shellfire, or nudged over by lorries.

Sometimes some Italian – or even some swaddy – stole them and used the wood to make a fire.

They retraced their route, the officer reading the map with a shaded torch and urging on the driver who narrowly averted collisions with ill-lit vehicles that groped their way past. By now, the officer was feeling worse with every mile they covered, and he knew perfectly well that by the time they reached Capodozzi it was going to be far too late to drive down the road to the river. It would mean waiting a whole day. They could find someone to feed them and it might even be possible to find a bed, but he didn't relish the thought.

It fell to the Yellowjackets – the Lincolnshire regiment that had been so called because of the yellow facings they'd worn on their red tunics during the first century of their existence – to throw the patrol General Tonge had asked for across the river, and they arranged to do it from near the ferry at the end of the cart track Heathfield's officer was about to take.

The officer in command of the patrol had been in the war since the beginning and felt as if he were a hundred years old. He couldn't even remember what his wife looked like, it was so long since he'd seen her, and her letters lately had grown so few and far between he suspected she'd dropped him for someone else. In his heart of hearts, he felt he could hardly blame her.

He was tired because he felt he'd been fighting the war ever since he was a youth – which, indeed, he had – and the idea of crossing the river to see what was on the other side angered him. Doubtless, some little shit at headquarters had looked at an air photo he couldn't understand and found some unimportant squiggle that needed explaining. For this, he and six men were going to risk their lives. If only, he thought wearily, the bloody rain would stop! It seemed to have been raining for ever. They'd almost forgotten what sunshine looked like, and the mud made everything so tiring.

The men with him were all volunteers. He had found their willingness to risk their necks for him surprisingly moving, because they'd certainly get no medals for it.

They climbed into the boat – one officer, one sergeant and five men – all with blackened faces and wearing cap comforters instead of steel helmets. A sergeant of Engineers and two of his men were standing by the boat ready to push it off. They'd muffled the oars and the rowlocks with rags so they wouldn't clatter or squeak.

'Right, sir?'

'Yes, fine.'

'Best of luck then, sir. Be sure you're back before daylight.'

'Don't worry. We'll be back.'

But they weren't. During the night, the Engineer sergeant crouching among the brambles on the river bank, sucking at a cigarette and wondering how much longer the war would go on, heard shouts from across the river. Then, startlingly sudden, shattering the silence, three short bursts of machine-gun fire. Then silence again.

He waited until it was almost daylight when he knew they couldn't wait any longer. He and his men climbed into their lorry, three this time instead of the ten who'd driven down, and set off up the long narrow track. It was muddy after all the rain, and the driver had to handle the vehicle carefully in and out of the potholes. For most of its length the road was raised above the surrounding fields, which were flooded after the steady downpour of the past days.

As daylight came, they were spotted by a German observation post across the river. The forward observation officer picked up the telephone and spoke to the battery on the slopes behind him. The battery commander listened carefully and then picked up his binoculars. Staring through them for a while, he turned to his men who were preparing for the new day and were directing their guns towards the road beyond San Bartolomeo.

'Fresh target,' he instructed.

The men in the lorry heard the whirring sound growing louder until it became a shriek and the shell dropped just ahead of them thirty yards from the track, sending up a shower of water, mud and wet gobbets of earth.

'Get that bloody foot down!' the sergeant snapped.

The lorry leapt forward, the springs groaning in protest as they slammed in and out of the potholes. Two more shells dropped before they reached the shelter of the trees and slipped between two small hills, the second shell spattering them with more mud, water and stones.

An officer stopped them as they retreated thankfully into the mountains. 'Where's the patrol?' he demanded.

'No sign of 'em, sir,' the sergeant said. 'We waited until it was almost daylight. We heard firing so I think they must have been nabbed.'

As the officer vanished, another appeared, climbing from a mudstained jeep. He was an older man, his face grey and drawn, and the sergeant realised he was ill and was shaking with fever.

'That road, Sergeant,' he asked. 'What's it like?'

'Muddy, sir,' the sergeant said.

'That all?'

The sergeant stared back the way he'd come from the river, wondering just exactly what the officer wanted to know. 'Well, there are plenty of potholes, sir.'

Heathfield's officer grimaced. It was meant to be a smile but by this time he was feeling as if he were at death's door.

'I meant the width, Sergeant?'

The sergeant glanced at his own vehicle. It's wide enough for two lorries to pass,' he said. 'Just.'

'Fields on either side? Plenty of room at the end to turn round?'

The sergeant considered. If this bloke was going to do a quick belt down to the river bank in daylight for a recce, he thought, he was barmy. However, it wasn't his job to argue and he tried to answer the question. 'Yes, sir,' he said. 'There's room to turn round.' They'd had to do a bit of backing and filling in the dark to get the lorry facing the other way, but it ought to be a damn sight quicker in a jeep.

The officer nodded. 'Thanks, Sergeant.'

'You all right, sir?'

'No, Sergeant.' The officer was clearly struggling to stay on his feet. 'I'm not. I think it's a recurrence of malaria.'

'You'd be best in bed, sir.'

'That's just where I'm going, Sergeant.' The ghastly smile came again. 'If I live that long.'

Watched by the sergeant, the officer turned away and climbed back into the jeep; then, huddling into his coat, fell almost at once into a fitful doze. By the time they reached Divisional Headquarters, they had to help him from the seat because he was shaking with fever and could barely see for the blinding headache that had attacked him. The doctor they brought to him made his decision at once. 'You're for hospital,' he said.

The sick man struggled to make his brain function. 'Just one thing to do,' he said. 'Have to make a report.'

'I doubt if you'll last that long. Is it important?'

The sluggish brain stirred. It didn't seem to be. The road appeared to be wide enough, though muddy, and, with fields on either side, there should surely be no difficulty about lorries passing.

'Not really,' he said. 'But I'd be grateful if you'd tell Brigadier Heathfield that the road he sent me to look at's okay. It's muddy but it'll take lorries. There's room for two vehicles to pass and a place to turn by the river. Can you telephone him and let him know?'

eight

The message reached Brigadier Heathfield at the same time as the report from the Yellowjackets about their lost patrol landed on his desk.

Heathfield's expression became increasingly grim. He had also just received a report from the brigadier of the 19th Division Artillery, complaining that the mud was hampering him from getting his guns into position and that when one of his lorries, reconnoitring the road to the river from San Bartolomeo for the move forward into the bridgehead, had had to leave the track it had immediately hit a mine.

'Weren't those mines cleared three nights ago?' Heathfield asked the AAQMG hovering anxiously beside him.

'Yes, sir, they were. But it seems Jerry keeps slipping back across the river and replacing them.'

Heathfield stared at the Yellowjackets' report on the loss of their patrol. 'How is it,' he demanded fretfully, 'that they can put patrols across to our side without being interfered with, yet we don't seem to be able to put patrols across to their side?'

'Because we can't see what they're up to, I suppose. *They* can see everything that goes on.'

'The patrol didn't cross until after dark.'

'They probably saw the boat being carried down, sir.'

'It was kept in San Bartolomeo until dark.'

'They can see beyond San Bartolomeo from Monte Cassino, sir. Well beyond.'

'Well, tell them to have another go. And inform the Sappers that those mines will have to be cleared.'

'At the moment they're trying to lay tank routes to the river, sir. They've got hold of wire matting from the American air force. They use it for temporary landing strips, I believe.'

Heathfield's frown deepened still further. He could foresee this damned road from San Bartolomeo causing trouble. He was well aware that in his determination to force his plan forward, he had cheated a little when he'd said a timetable had been worked out based on other similar movements. So it had, but it had been worked out on hard winter roads whereas the verges from San Bartolomeo were soft with rain.

All the same, he felt, he was right to push the thing. It had to go on. They'd been told it had to go on. And nobody got promotion by refusing responsibility. Perhaps it was as well orders had come down from the high altar, because already there were too many people raising objections, too many people finding difficulties which ought not to exist. In his warm and comfortable office, Brigadier Heathfield believed firmly that a little more spirit was needed, a little more determination, a little more enterprise such as the Engineers were showing with the air force strips they were building for Vivian's tanks.

'Who put 'em up to these wire mat things?' he asked.

'The Yeomanry, sir. Colonel Vivian, to be exact. He says he has to have some means of getting past all the bridging material.'

'What's happening about assault boats?'

'I'm still trying, sir. But Corps seem to have grabbed them all for their effort further north.'

'Try the Americans. They'll probably let us have some.'

'Very good, sir.'

'How about DUKWs? Aren't there any of those? They had 'em at Anzio and Salerno.'

'I gather they're being rounded up and sent home, sir. For the Second Front.'

'Well, we can't cross rivers without boats. Why wasn't the matter put in hand before Corps grabbed them all?'

'Sir – ' the other officer stiffened at the suggestion of inefficiency – 'I was only informed two days ago that boats would be needed.'

'How the devil did you expect to cross a river?'

'Sir, I gather the plan was made five days ago, but I've never been told what form it was to take. We could have been using parachutists.'

'Don't be bloody impertinent!'

'I'm sorry, sir, but I had no idea.'

Heathfield waved the other man away irritably. 'Anyway, get on with it! There must be boats somewhere. Corps can't have grabbed them all. Try to round up a few from the local Italians.'

'I gather the Germans thought of that, sir,' the AAQMG said bleakly. 'What they couldn't move, they sank.'

In Trepiazze, Yuell's men were coming to the end of their rest period. They all knew it.

Food increased, new uniforms were issued, and there was a rash of kit inspections. Inevitably, Syzling was short of several things. Not only had he lost them but, knowing his reputation, everybody else in A Company had kept a sharp eye on their own belongings and he hadn't been able to lift anything.

Lieutenant Deacon, his smooth round face pink with rage, stormed at him.

'You're the most useless bloody object I've ever had to deal with, Syzling,' he said, his voice rising until it was almost a screech.

Syzling stared at him dully, trying to look defiant without looking defiant enough to be put on a charge. He was put on a charge, anyway.

Watching him shuffle off with Corporal Wymark towards the barn that did duty as a stores, Deacon felt exhausted. Syzling always made him feel exhausted. In Deacon's ordered world, there was no such thing as an individual like Syzling. When he'd been a sergeant in his school OTC, he'd had boys under him who were as keen as he was to get into a proper uniform and nobody had been difficult. A few had considered him an opinionated, self-important ass and had told him so, but, because they came from his own class, he could understand them. He'd never had to deal with anybody of the sullen stupidity of Syzling.

If only Deacon had possessed a sense of humour, he might have struck a spark from Syzling who somehow always managed to behave himself with people who could make him laugh, like Wymark or even CSM Farnsworth whose ramrod exterior concealed a whole inheritance of old army jokes that might have been invented as a means of getting through to the Syzlings of this world. Humour, however, was one quality that Deacon conspicuously lacked.

Seeking to distract their minds from what lay ahead, Major Peddy organised a concert party in the cold and comfortless marquee that had been used for the cinema show and an ENSA troupe was summoned from Naples. It contained no famous names because the marquee wasn't big enough to hold the crowd famous names would have attracted, and in any case there just wasn't time enough for the famous names to fit in so relatively unimportant a place as Trepiazze with all their other commitments.

'They should shove Deacon on the stage with Frying Tonight,' CSM Farnsworth remarked. 'Set to music, and with a troupe of belly dancers in support, they'd have 'em rolling in the aisles.'

The ENSA troupe were late arriving, and there was a lot of slow clapping and 'Why are we waiting?' until they began to sing their own particular song, the song of the army of Italy:

'We are the D-Day dodgers, out in Italy,
Always drinking vino and always on the spree.
The desert shirkers and the Yanks,
We live in peace and dodge the tanks.
We are the D-Day dodgers,
The boys D-Day will dodge.'

They sang it to the tune of 'Lili Marlene', which they'd pinched from the Germans in North Africa, and the lilting melody gave the words a curious poignancy. And when they appeared to have finished, somebody at the back began to sing an extra verse on his own. He had a good voice, and the men around him pushed him to his feet so that he could be heard still more clearly:

'Look around the mountains, in the mud and rain,
You'll find the scattered crosses, some which bear
no name.
Heartbreak and toil and suffering gone,
The lads beneath them slumber on.
They are the D-Day dodgers,
Who'll stay in Italy.'

The soloist was young, with a face like a choirboy's, and the truth in the words he sang brought a dead silence to the marquee that lasted for several moments after the last note died away. It was uncomfortable and uneasy and spoiled the mood; but it expressed the bitterness they all felt at having a thankless task, unappreciated at home where nobody could think of anything but the forthcoming invasion of Western

Europe. It was a bitterness they shared with the Fourteenth Army in Burma.

When the ENSA show finally got going, it consisted of a tenor whose voice was so embarrassingly high it provoked wolf whistles from the back; an ageing soubrette with arms like thighs and breasts like buttocks, who worked through her numbers wearing a death's head grin to show she was enjoying it; and a pianist who also played a fiddle, a piano accordion, cymbals, a penny whistle and a set of motor horns, eventually placing them in a frame and playing them all at once. 'Why not shove one up your arse, mate,' Private Parkin yelled, 'and fart "God Save The King"?' Finally, there was a pub comic who seemed to be suffering from a hangover because he obviously couldn't have cared less whether they enjoyed his efforts or not.

It wasn't a very inspired affair and, deciding they could do better than the falsetto tenor, they pushed up Evans the Bomb who gave them 'Rose Marie', 'The Desert Song' and 'The Song of the Vagabonds', and they enjoyed it so much they wouldn't let him go until he'd sung everything else he knew and finally retired breathless. Encouraged by his success, Private Parkin gave them a tap dance, a few jokes that fell like lead balloons, and a few dubious ballads. Then, to Lieutenant Deacon's shame, Private Syzling – of all people! – appeared blinking and dazzled in front of the footlights that had been rigged up by Vivian's Yeomanry.

Seeing him, they all settled back for some fun. Syzling had already found his way into the bell tent that had been erected as a dressing-room for the concert party and lifted the bottle of whisky Colonel Yuell had provided. Climbing on to the stage, half-shot and stinking of booze, he proceeded to go through his repertoire. It was the only original thing he'd ever done in his life, and even then it wasn't all that original because he'd seen it done first by a South African medical orderly in a Cape Town bar when his troopship had docked there on its way to the Middle East. It wasn't very extensive either and consisted of only two items.

First of all he stood with his back to the audience with his arms wrapped round himself so that his hands appeared to belong to someone out of sight beyond him. Then, waggling his behind, he put on his act of a sailor in a shop doorway with a girl.

Everybody hooted with delight and waited with baited breath for his pièce de résistance, even though most of them had seen it before. It was known as 'The One-Armed Fiddler', and Syzling never missed an opportunity of presenting it whether he was asked to or not. The routine began with his donning his battledress blouse with the right sleeve empty and his right arm and hand out of sight and tucked into his trousers. Usually all the props he had were two sticks, one for a bow and one for a fiddle, but tonight realism was added by the loan of the pianist's violin. Holding the instrument in place with his chin, Syzling used his left hand to pass the bow lightly over the strings, imitating the high-pitched sound of the violin with the side of his mouth until, suddenly, he stopped short with a raucously discordant squawk of a note. Keeping the violin clamped firmly under his chin, and still grasping the bow with his free hand, he then began to pluck at the strings to the accompaniment of suitably pizzicato noises until he found the one that was supposed to be out of tune. Syzling was no comedian and it was all done with a straight face – not the straight face of the professional actor but the dogged stare of a stupid man who'd learned one party piece by heart and was struggling not to forget it. It was perfect.

The grand finale consisted of tuning up the fiddle. Since he had only the one arm and hand free, Syzling needed this to turn the pegs that held the strings and had to dispose of the bow while he worked. Gazing blankly around him, he first seemed to be about to put it on the floor, then on the piano.

Finally, with a shrug of despair, he held it in front of his trousers where through the flies appeared a fat white finger to hold the bow against his groin.

There was a shriek like an engine whistle from the nursing sister Jago had brought along from the hospital at Calimero and she hid her face in Jago's sleeve, weeping with laughter, while the tank men and the newcomers who'd never seen it before clutched each other and howled. It was so blatantly vulgar, it wasn't even offensive, and the pub comedian had nothing in his repertoire half as good.

Colonel Yuell had been too busy to attend the show. He was trying to make sure everything was prepared, because Division appeared to be having difficulty producing the boats they needed. It was going to be difficult in any event but they'd get nowhere at all unless someone produced some soon. There was one thing he could do, however, and that was make sure that there was a proper supply of mortar bombs and hand grenades. When they'd attacked at Sant' Agata, they'd found themselves obliged to suffer the German mortar bombardment without being able to retaliate and when they'd gone in, they'd had to use bayonets.

'There's a whole lorry-load of them,' Tallemach insisted when he telephoned. 'Mortar ammunition, too. It was a point I raised myself and Brigadier Heathfield said he'd handle it. And so that you won't be short when the build-up begins, he's promised to send a second lorry-load down with it. They'll be leaving Ordnance today and they'll be in San Bartolomeo ready to move up with your people.'

'There'll be no mistakes, sir? We lost a lot of men at Sant' Agata because we were short.'

'You won't be short this time,' Tallemach said. 'Two lorry-loads ought to be enough to bomb your way to Rome!'

If they could have left the next day, everything would have been all right. But they didn't. They waited another twenty-four hours, and during those twenty-four hours it seemed as if the last of the Italian winter did its damnedest to destroy every ounce of good spirit the concert had engendered. The rain lashed down with incredible ferocity so that it was impossible even to queue up for food without being soaked. It was impossible to go into the town, impossible to keep warm. During the afternoon the *tramontane*, the winter wind from the mountains, found all the cracks and holes in the billets and made them wretched.

'In case of inclement weather,' Fletcher-Smith said, 'the battle will be held indoors.'

Tempers grew frayed. CSM Farnsworth put Puddephatt on a charge which he knew he'd never press. McWatters shoved at Lofty Duff for getting in his way, and in return received a kick on the backside which was as much as the tiny Duff could manage. It was Wymark who got between them as McWatters, his vicious temper boiling over, reached for his bayonet. Martindale was sitting brooding in corners, sucking at an empty pipe as if it were a baby's dummy. The two Bawdens, who had happily done their fighting, drinking and fornicating together for nearly three years, ended up in a punch-up for no other reason than that 766 Bawden had called 000 Bawden a snob and 000 Bawden had retorted that 766 Bawden was so bloody dim he'd never be in a position to be a snob. It was Gask who separated them, his pale face expressionless as usual, as if he regarded everybody who didn't polish his buttons and go through a war in the same detached way he did as something considerably less than worthwhile. His large white bony hands flung them aside so that they sat glowering at each other until finally 000 Bawden sheepishly offered a cigarette and 766 Bawden came across with a light.

Since it was their last day, Graziella Vanvitelli decided to give Warley, Jago, Deacon and Taylor a lunch party with a very special meal. Jago, Deacon and Taylor had a lot less to do with it than they realised and it was really put on for no one but Warley. She had ironed his shirts the night before, because she'd wished to, and when he'd thanked her she had suggested he might like to go to Mass with her.

'I'm not a Catholic,' he explained.

'The Catholic Church will not mind,' she said softly. 'And I would like it. I shall pray for you.'

Warley studied her. There was pride and possessiveness in her attitude, and a little more too.

'Very well,' he said. 'I'll come with you.'

She sighed. *'Che brutta guerra. Quando finirà.'*

They said nothing as they walked to the church, but on the way back, surrounded by women in black wearing shawls on their heads, they saw one of Warley's men with a girl in a doorway. Graziella sighed.

'Wars are all the same,' she said. 'The men become animals and the girls become more willing.'

'It's worse in Naples,' Warley pointed out gently.

She gave him a sad smile. 'Everything's worse in Naples.' She shrugged and became silent. 'Do you have a girl, Uoli?'

'Yes.'

'A *fidanzata*? A fiancée?'

'Yes.'

'Do you love her?'

Warley considered. His fiancée was the daughter of a wealthy Manchester clothing manufacturer. She had a perfect figure and was always exquisitely turned out, but if he'd seen her at that moment her clothes could just as well have been draped round a garden roller.

'I don't know,' he said honestly. 'I doubt it. I haven't seen her for three years. I've almost forgotten what she looks like.'

When they reached the house Graziella busied herself with pots and pans in the kitchen while her sister Francesca laid the table, and Jago – ridiculous in a frilled apron – used his enormous hands to cut up the pasta into long strips like tapeworms.

With as much whispering and nodding as if the whole Provost Corps of Trepiazze were after them, Deacon produced two tins of bully and Taylor two tins of milk. Avvocato Vanvitelli, released unexpectedly from his duties with AMGOT to share the celebration with his daughters, contributed a bottle of Orvieto and a large flagon of rough wine. He was a plump, handsome smiling man who seemed quite happy to leave his elder daughter in the hands of Warley, though he appeared more doubtful of the fate of Francesca at the hands of Second-Lieutenant Taylor. He brought with him an elderly woman, whom he introduced as *La Nonna* and two well-scrubbed and cherubic small boys in suits of snow-white linen.

'My cousins, Leonardo and Giovanni,' Graziella said. Since Jago had provided chocolate, the two small boys regarded him as Christ come to earth again.

As they gathered round the table, grace was said and the home-made tomato sauce was poured over the pasta.

'*Ancora, ancora,*' Avvocato Vanvitelli insisted as they finished their platefuls. 'In Italy is always much pasta. *Oggi, festa – mangiamo molto.*'

Chicken appeared, cooked with tomato and pepperoni, followed by fried salami and slices of pork with peas.

'Where did you get it all?' Warley asked Graziella.

She gave him a shy, happy smile. 'My father is a lawyer,' she said. As you will be one day. He has always something to offer in exchange. A lawsuit for a piece of pork. A will for a case of wine.'

The Orvieto, what was called 'the real wine', appeared with the main dish and by the end of it Taylor was trying to sing 'Lili Marlene' in Italian to Francesca, watched by the sharp eyes of *La Nonna,* while Avvocato Vanvitelli kept up a running commentary on the lot of Italy.

'*E sempre la miseria! Siamo poveri, tutti poveri! Quando finirà la guerra?*'

So full they could hardly move, Avvocato Vanvitelli called for music. *La Nonna* sang a shaky '*0 Sole Mio*', and then they started to dance to the gramophone. Stupefied by the wine, Taylor had fallen asleep but Deacon danced with Francesca, Avvocato Vanvitelli with *La Nonna,* Jago with one of the adoring little boys, and Warley with Graziella. It was an Italian dance and gravely, wearing her calm smile, Graziella advanced and retreated before him, hands on hips, bobbing and circling with a strange cool dignity, her face as calm as if she were at Mass.

'I am so happy, Uoli,' she said.

Beyond the cypresses at the end of the garden, the greyness of the day was everywhere, stretching away to the horizon, hill upon hill. Graziella stared at it as they stopped dancing, faintly pink in the face, her breath coming quickly. She looked at Warley, then looked away again, quickly, as if she were embarrassed.

'*Quando finirà la guerra,*' she whispered. '*Quando finirà?*'

The last night seemed the worst of all the nights. Few ventured out, not even for the ritual evening stroll that always took place in Italian streets. Syzling braved the rain and spent most of the time in the bed of his widow, with his clothes steaming in front of a fire she built up. Well-fed and satiated, he left her just as the rain stopped for the first time, wearing clothes that were dry again.

Captain Jago borrowed a half-tonner and went to see his nursing sister in Calimero. What he intended was obvious from the fact that he'd tossed his bedding roll and a ground-sheet in the back, but it proved unnecessary because the nursing sister had a room in a small house near the hospital and the other sister who shared it with her was on duty, so they didn't argue and slipped into bed there and then.

Private Fletcher-Smith, his teeth chattering with cold and damp, clutched his girl between the stacked winter logs and a pile of straw in the barn of the little farm where she lived with her mother. Her warmth made him forget all about literature and they took off their glasses, which were becoming steamed up anyway, and considering life too short for intellectual exercises decided to use the pile of straw instead. His love-making was hurried and clumsy because they were both virgins; but afterwards, while the girl returned to the house shivering and fearful of what she'd permitted, a proud and overjoyed Fletcher-Smith almost danced back to his billet, feeling that he didn't care now if it rained for ever.

Warley's parting from Graziella was quiet and subdued. Although she was the older sister and ran the household, she was still young, her slim body moving freely inside her loose dress. Her smooth fair hair, piled on her shoulders, framed a face that was oval in shape with a pointed chin. The impression she had given Warley was one of shyness and purity, but he'd seen her glance at him occasionally with eyes that were as old as woman herself. He wasn't a man of great experience with girls, but he suspected she wasn't the type to play at love and he was intelligent enough to realise that one couldn't make hard and fast rules for the reactions of a member of one sex on a member of the other. Graziella had been educated in Rome and she displayed an instinctive womanly wisdom that was curiously secretive and independent.

With Avvocato Vanvitelli heading back to Naples with *La Nonna* and the two small boys, and Deacon and Taylor at the cinema with Francesca, they were alone and spent the evening playing the piano. It seemed a ridiculous thing to do under the circumstances, and Warley knew that Jago would have laughed like a drain at the time he was wasting.

But he was supremely, bewilderingly at peace. He had brought a bottle of brandy and had insisted she have a drink with him. He finally forced two on her, which was a lot more than she normally drank, but it made her happy. Warley was a little tipsy, but he was well-behaved and clearly content just to be with her.

'Have another?' he asked.

She shook her head. 'I think it would be better if *you* did not have another, also,' she said. 'It is not very good brandy.'

'I paid eight hundred lire for it.'

'It is not the brandy we used to have.'

He smiled sadly. 'Your lire aren't the lire you used to have either,' he said.

It wasn't meant to hurt, though it did a little with its reminder that the Italian nation was on its knees; but she managed to overlook it, and they sat alongside each other, playing and drinking, until their fingers touched. Warley's playing faltered and she half-expected him to use the opportunity to take her hand.

But he didn't. He simply let his hands fall to his knees and sat silently. Graziella played a few more notes; then she stopped too, and sat looking at him. Without a word, Warley leaned forward and kissed her on the mouth. For a second she stared back at him, her eyes huge and starry with long lashes. Then, impulsively, she reached out for him and kissed him back.

She kept her arms round him for some time in a frightened, gentle way. Then Warley turned to the piano again. He didn't play but just sat staring at it.

'What are you doing?' she asked.

'I'm communing with God.'

'Why?'

'Today is a crisis.'

'In Italy every day is a crisis.'

'It's not that. I'll be leaving tomorrow and things have reached a climax and I felt I needed to think about God.'

'Why?'

'I've a lot to thank Him for.'

'What?'

'You.'

'We've only known each other four days.'

'It's long enough.' Warley shrugged. 'And I'm grateful for being able to get to know you in a quiet atmosphere. If I'd met you at a party you might have seemed different, and so might I. But because we've been blessed with the chance to talk – not party talk, but ordinary talk about ordinary things – and not about the war, I feel as if I've known you all my life.'

Graziella studied him carefully. It wasn't the first time a man had told her he was in love with her. There had been an Italian in 1940, and in 1941 and 1942 Germans who seemed to be attracted by her fair hair and Aryan appearance. Some were sincere, kind men – the British and the Americans didn't have a monopoly of kindness – and there had even been one from Heidelberg who had played duets with her, exactly as Warley had.

With Warley, however, it was different. There was a quality of restraint about him that told her he was sincere. It was possible that being in Trepiazze and in safety had swept him off his feet, but somehow she didn't think so. She had a feeling she knew every movement of his body, every twitch of every muscle, every beat of his heart. She had dug down into her deepest mind for someone she'd ever felt this about before and had discovered she couldn't find one.

She had even started to think thoughts she felt she had no right to think, intimate thoughts that should never have passed through the mind of unengaged girl, and guiltily, the night before, as she had prepared for bed, she had paused in front of the picture of the Virgin in her room. 'You'll understand,' she had murmured. 'You are a woman and I know you will forgive.'

Warley was still sitting with his hands on his knees, and suddenly he looked desperately serious and a little lost. She was shelter, warmth, knowledge and common-sense and he felt he needed the embrace of her limbs, the smoothness of her skin, and the fire with which he knew she would envelop him.

'I can think of nothing more beautiful,' he said, 'than to be allowed to make love to you. Properly, I mean. As men and women in love should.'

With a sharp sense of disappointment she felt she'd been mistaken in him after all, and that he was going to spoil everything by proposing that while the house was empty they should go upstairs together. He had carefully avoided physical contact with her and he hadn't declared his love for her as so many others had with far less reason. Nevertheless she'd believed that something unexpected and unusual existed between them, and his words troubled her.

But he didn't fail her. It was ridiculous, he knew, to imagine their relationship could ever mean anything after only four days of knowing each other, yet he stubbornly felt it would.

'But making love to you now,' he went on slowly, 'would be wrong. And what I was thinking of wasn't *that* sort of thing, anyway. I was thinking of the sort of love-making that a man does with his wife, with the woman he loves. I don't know, but I think *that* must be different.'

The indignation had gone from her eyes, and she was shocked to realise she could as easily have offered herself to him as not.

'I'm jealous of anyone who looks at you,' Warley went on gravely. 'Even poor little Taylor, who's still wet behind the ears.'

She said nothing because she didn't know what to say. If he never returned to Trepiazze, if he went on to Rome and the north, if he went home to England, even if – and she caught her breath as the thought crossed her mind – even if he were killed, she felt she would still like to remember and cherish the moment.

She turned a lost face to him. 'We must not jump to conclusions,' she said cautiously.

He sat up. 'Why not?' The words were full of indignation and surprise.

She tried to tread carefully. 'There is a war on and things are different in war.'

'My father met my mother in the last war,' he said briskly. 'They seemed happy enough. I was the result.'

'That war was different.'

'Men died, didn't they? I can't see the difference.'

'The difference,' she pointed out gently, 'is that in that war we were on *your* side.'

'Not all the time.' He felt he'd caught her out. 'In the first days we thought you'd come in on the German side. But, in fact, you came in on ours.'

She smiled. 'This time, you also thought we'd come in on the German side – I remember your merchant ships going through the Mediterranean in 1939 at full speed in case our warships sank them – and this time we *did* come in on the German side.'

'It makes no difference, Graziella.'

'It must do.'

He paused then went on seriously. 'What do you want more than anything else?' he asked.

She was about to say that she wanted the war to end, but she realised it wasn't just that she needed.

'To feel that when you come back,' she said slowly, 'it will be possible for me to be here. To know that you *will* come back.'

'There you are,' he said. 'The one thing *I* want is to *come* back, and to know *you'll* be here.'

'It might not happen that way,' she warned. 'You might go on to Rome. You might be sent to the Adriatic. You might be sent back to England to fight in this Second Front they say is so imminent.'

'Not me,' he said. 'I'm here for good. We all are. Nobody wants us. We're stuck with Italy, and you're stuck with me.'

nine

There weren't many as lucky as Warley. But there were a few like Jago and Fletcher-Smith and Syzling who went to their blankets that night feeling better than they had earlier in the evening.

For most of them, however, it was a wretched night and they tossed and turned trying to stay warm. They were used to sleeping rough and, because they lived in the open air so much, they usually slept like animals, indifferent to the weather. But the few days in Trepiazze had spoiled them; they were just beginning to expect the spring and a little sunshine, and the weather had betrayed them.

The following morning, the barns, sheds, schoolrooms and houses rang with the stamping of heavy boots, the thump of falling packs. The clatter of weapons and the impatient voices of men.

When the sergeants arrived, they clattered out into the square. You could hardly say that their blood was quickened by new impulses of vigour and enthusiasm, because it was hard to feel enthusiastic or blood-quickened after a cold night in damp blankets and wearing clothes that were already heavy with rain and smelling of wet wool. Further towards the coast there had been flooding and families were having to be rescued. It had been going on for days – as long, it seemed, as they could remember.

The solid block of khaki filled the piazza under the statue of Garibaldi, the lines of helmets swathed in nets or sacking like so many rows of brown beetles.

Henry White stared at the sky hanging over them, violet-grey and threatening.

'I don't like all this bloody rain,' he said.

'Well, you can't always be fightin' Zulus in the sunshine, can you?' Parkin pointed out.

Rich didn't like the look of it much either. 'But they say t' Black Watch are coming up wi' us to 'elp,' he said hopefully. 'Or one of t' 'Ighland regiments.'

'The Black Watch's no' a regiment, ye reid-heided gowk,' McWatters growled. ' 'Tis a bluidy reeligion.'

As they squatted in their ranks, eating their breakfasts from their mess tins, the last really good meal they could expect for some time, there was an unexpected hint of sunshine. The town was awake to see them off, standing in the streets to watch them leave – whole families, from wrinkled grandparents to babies in arms, all busy chattering and commenting. A few girls, bolder than the rest, penetrated the ranks to talk to the men they'd been seeing for the past two or three days. A few drew apart: Henry White with his 'party'; Private Syzling and his woman; Warley with Graziella Vanvitelli; the two fresh-faced lieutenants with her fifteen-year-old sister. Occasionally, a whole household crowded round a single soldier whom they'd taken in and who was now having to leave them behind. Some of the soldiers had the prune-eyed Italian children in their arms, stuffing army stew into them as hard as they could go.

'I've never known anything quite like the British soldier,' Yuell said to Peddy. 'They know they'll probably not get another hot meal for days, and here they are giving it all away.'

In the end, however, it was Yuell who gave the orders that what was left was to be handed to the Italians, and as the information was passed round there was a yell of delight and the crowd dispersed to fetch bowls, cups and plates. Bottles of wine and vermouth appeared, and breakfast turned into a communal feast.

As the dubious sun disappeared again and a misty rain started once more, the ranks were cleared.

'Company – !' Heads lifted, and as the orders came they turned and began to move off, the tramp of their boots echoing between the houses. For a moment the town, which had known them for only four days and had seen dozens of other units pass through, watched them dully. Then the children moved forward, followed by the girls, the women and the old men, until there was a whole crowd of them running alongside.

Fletcher-Smith felt a little bit taller as he saw the wretched expression on the face of his girl friend and her worried eyes behind her cracked spectacles. He thought it was because she was going to miss him, but in fact it was because she was worried in case he'd given her a baby. Lieutenant Deacon and Second-Lieutenant Taylor waved at Francesca Vanvitelli. Warley gave Graziella a somewhat staid salute, but it meant more to her than the smiles the others had to offer. It went with Warley – serious, sober, a gesture of respect as much as anything else – and he saw her lift her handkerchief, balled in her fingers, to her mouth as she stifled a sob. It had been his intention when he'd arrived in Trepiazze to do a lot of drinking and sleeping, but he hadn't done much of either – only talking late into the night and playing the piano. As they'd parted, their kiss for the first time had been one of painful intensity and she had cried, hard sobs through clenched teeth and taut lips. Now she looked small and lost as she smiled damply and waved, whispering as she watched him go.

'Holy Mary, Mother of God, pray for us sinners, now and forever – '

Warley sighed. He hadn't come to Trepiazze to see anguish on a girl's face as she watched him leave.

As the last of the civilians dropped behind, the soldiers turned, lifting their thumbs in acknowledgement, to assure them that it was all going to be okay. The British thumb, Warley thought. When the Last Trump sounded, the British would disappear into outer darkness still sticking up the good old British thumb, but it didn't really alter the lonely lost feeling that now came over them as they marched.

The lorries were waiting outside the town, drawn up in rows, and as they began to cram into them, they moved off in ones and twos, making a long column like a string of broken beads, heading north. It was over. Promises would be forgotten for the most part; letters would be answered for a week or two, then dropped. The comfortable memories would slowly vanish as they found themselves back on the bleak mountainsides. What they had considered home for a short time had vanished. Home from now on was in the front line. They were on the move again.

PART TWO

The Hilt

'Often cold and soaked to the skin, and
with little or no sleep or hot food...
the will of these men, for the most part children
of the Great Depression of the Thirties...to
close with the enemy never faltered. Morally,
in comparison with them, the military bureaucrats
in the vast Headquarters, warmly housed and
regularly fed, looked small indeed.'

Major-General Hubert Essame

one

Things began to go wrong even before they arrived in San Bartolomeo.

It wasn't the most inspiring of routes and the mist made the landscape soft – full of grey forbidding mountains, some even peaked with snow – with a strange lack of definition. The smudgy white walls of houses and farm buildings were sprayed with brown liquid mud from the wheels of speeding lorries, and the rust-red roofs took on a bluish tinge in the haze that rose stealthily from the valleys.

All along the road, as they moved forward in three-tonners of the Indian Army Service Corps, there were smashed hamlets and small towns. Drenched by the downpours of the past weeks, they were sometimes garishly lit by odd streaks of sunshine that broke through the heavy clouds to make distant groups of white houses momentarily blaze like jewels set in sharp relief against the prevailing dark blues, greys and violets of the mountains.

Italy was trying to stay alive, trying to claw itself back to a normal existence among the waste of destroyed buildings and devastated fields and vineyards. Heavy two-wheeled carts, dragged by lean oxen, held up the convoy, so that not infrequently they found themselves waiting alongside groups of peasants or even monks working by some ruined building. The roads were packed full of refugees – men, women and children pushing into the rain, umbrellas down against the wind, struggling along with all they possessed on their backs or piled on to a hand-cart, sodden bedding, mattresses and clothes all exposed to the rain as they plodded forward over the wet surfaces.

Of all the countries they'd seen since the beginning of the war, Italy seemed the worst hit. In the desert the fighting had gone on with no harm to anyone but the combatants. Here, the desolation was everywhere. It had become part of their lives, with each house a hazard course of mines and booby traps, the Germans using flame throwers that consumed everything in their path, the Allies using tanks that were supposed only to demolish machine-gun nests but invariably wrecked the houses as well.

Occasionally, in half-darkened rooms, they had found whole families crouched round a single table, muttering imprecations against Mussolini. Once, as they'd searched for rations, 000 Bawden had found an old dead woman sitting in a chair in a farmhouse, with four dead children lying on the floor, their hands on their breasts, their eyes closed, their limbs decently composed, the victims of blast.

The contrast between the British and American columns was marked. The British moved at a steady speed, each vehicle the regulation distance from the one in front, very orderly, correct and sedate – and very, very slow. The American columns – convoy after convoy of powerful six-wheeled trucks – swept past, the vehicles usually driven by black men with cigars in their mouths, so casual it wasn't true. In North Africa they had liked to dangle one leg out of the cab window while the other operated the accelerator. There was no concern with spacing. They just went flat out for their destination and usually got themselves there in the end.

There was a big traffic block outside San Ambrosio. The convergence of two columns brought staff and military police into the growing confusion to pluck machines and vehicles from its centre and head them on to their separate routes. As the North Yorkshires waited, they tried to snatch a few winks of sleep; then suddenly the core of the jam came loose and they were on the move again.

As the vehicles disentangled, drivers and commanders watched for the traffic signs and guides. Because tanks blocked the road to troop carriers and guns, Tallemach's ammunition dumping programme had begun to fall into arrears, and nobody dismounted at the halts because there were still 'Beware of mines' notices along the verges.

A painted board came up – 'Go Slow. Bridge Ahead. Await Signal By Military Policeman'. But the bridge was down, and a military policeman directed them on to an already crowded diversion. One of the lorries, trying to edge past a parked Scammell, swiped the lower shutters from a house, bringing the owner into the street wailing with dismay, because shutters meant shadow in the heat of the summer and a freedom from draughts in winter. The railway station was only a mass of twisted wreckage, torn-up track and lopsided engines. Beyond it the road was flooded, the water lapping round the poplars as far as you could see. In Ferni, they halted for food in the piazza among lorries parked beneath the army signs – 'Chaos Corner', 'This is a Star Route. Keep it open'. Then on they went again, the officers clutching bundles of new maps they'd picked up, the drivers hooting furiously at the creaking carrozzas hauled by skeletal horses.

In the hills they passed Indians working on the bends to scrape the mud off the surface, and pioneers filling in ruts, potholes and old latrines. There were mules everywhere now, caked with mud, their ears drooping wearily as they stood bent-kneed in front of shattered buildings. They jolted past to shouts of 'You lucky people' from troops billeted in houses with shattered roofs and holed walls. They passed burnt-out tanks, the debris of earlier battles, ditched lorries, once an aircraft bogged down and lopsided in a flooded airfield near the road.

It was a long way from Trepiazze. They were all tired, and a lot of them were wet because the misty rain had changed to a downpour. A few of the newly-joined wondered what they were in for. Then, as they descended the mountains towards San Bartolomeo, they were held up for a long time by an accident. A lorry had skidded on a hairpin bend and slithered into the vehicle in front. They were lying on their sides now below the road among the sparse trees beyond a broken stone wall, and the Red Cross people were hoisting a stretcher up.

'Some poor bastard's copped it,' Rich said.

'Ordnance Corps,' Hunters observed. 'Nothing to do with us.'

But, as it happened, it was.

They were approaching the front line now and the traffic had thinned out. It always thinned out as you drew nearer to the battle area. Wrecked vehicles, rusted, blackened and ugly, lay by the roadside. Telephone cables crossed and recrossed the ditches and hedgerows like an old woman's knitting. Signs indicated mines or the possibility of shellfire, and one said 'Stop here or – !' followed by a macabre little figure of a man being separated from head and limbs.

The wayside graves indicated just what the signs meant, and all the time the ambulances with the wreckage moved back – converted Bren carriers, scout cars and jeeps, all painted white and marked with a red cross.

At last Yuell's men reached San Bartolomeo. Because the northern end of the town was still just within range of the German guns across the river, the lorries set them down on the southern outskirts. Here they were hidden from view by the buildings, though they all knew that the German telescopes high up on Monte Cassino must have spotted the column as it came over the hill.

San Bartolomeo had all the appearance of a town that had only recently passed out of the front line. Houses were wrecked and their beams carried away, like the trees, for firewood. The ground had been churned by tanks and lorries into a morass of mud. Ahead there were shell-pitted fields, the grass torn or trampled but always lush in the spots where it covered minefields. A few shattered buildings were marked with the red cross or the insignia of headquarters.

Outside the Mayor's office the statue of Garibaldi had lost its arm and head, and the plinth was pitted by shell fragments. Telephone lines trailed, and an ugly stench arose from the bodies of dead soldiers, dead mules and dead civilians in the bombed houses. It was cold and squalid in the extreme.

There was no hot food, though Yuell had sent Major Peddy, his second-in-command, ahead with the advance party to arrange it.

'A shell got the kitchen, sir,' Peddy explained. 'It knocked out three of the cooks and wounded four other men. I'm sorry, but we'll have to manage with bully beef until we can get organised.'

By late afternoon they learned that the replacement food Peddy had hoped to send up in hot boxes had also been lost; this time because the farm where a fresh set of field cookers had been set up was flooded to a depth of four feet when a small dam burst in the hills behind the town. They would now have to wait for their hot meal until after dark.

There was nowhere to brief the battalion as a whole, something Yuell liked to do. In the desert he'd always been able to get them sitting round in the sunshine in the Montgomery manner and tell them exactly what their job was; but no one wanted to sit down in the mud and rain, and it was far too dangerous, anyway, because the Germans on the heights opposite knew exactly where they were.

As darkness fell, he scattered his men in groups while the officers were assembled in a dimly lit barn to see a mock-up of the battlefield, complete with the Liri, the high slope of San Eusebio and a stick to indicate the height of Monte Cassino. Yuell outlined to them what they were to do.

'Intention,' he said, 'to seize and hold San Eusebio. That's all. No more. But no less either, so never lose sight of it. Method: this has changed a little – I hope for the better. To relieve the congestion on the San Bartolomeo road by Route A, we shall now be crossing by a new route – Route C – a dirt road from Capodozzi to the river and make our way along the river bank on the other side towards the end of the San Bartolomeo-San Eusebio road. This will place our crossing nearer to the Yellowjackets who'll be going over by Route B at the end of the Foiano road, towards Castelgrande. It will make linking up easier. Fire support will be pretty extensive and fighter-bombers will take on the enemy mortar and machine-gun positions.'

'If the weather improves,' Jago murmured.

Yuell heard him. 'Exactly,' he admitted. 'A, B and C Companies will form the first wave. A will lead, and will leave Capodozzi half an hour before the rest to enable them to get into position. B and C will start exactly on the hour, by which time A should be in position. It'll be their job to link up with A and move with them to the end of the San Bartolomeo road where the ground's more uneven and will provide more shelter. Mark Warley will be running the show.'

There was a little muttering. Yuell allowed them time for coughing, lighting cigarettes, and comments; then he continued: 'D Company will be in San Bartolomeo ready to reinforce as soon as the Engineers have a bridge across. This shouldn't take long because I understand they're proposing to use the broken span as the basis for a footbridge. They'll also throw across a new Class 40 Bailey for the tanks alongside, where the stonework will give them some protection from the guns on the left.'

He glanced at his notes and went on quickly. 'Boats: lorries will move them down to within three hundred yards of the river. Once on the other side, the plan of what we have to do is relatively simple. We have to get into San Eusebio. That's *all* we have to do. We have to get in and dig in at once because they're bound to counter-attack. The Yellowjackets should join up within an hour or so. If we get San Eusebio quickly, it'll give the Engineers a few hours freedom from observation. Once they get their bridge across, we can be supported by tanks.'

It sounded simple but Yuell knew as well as any of them it wasn't likely to be.

Warley certainly didn't think so, and said so.

'I didn't say it would be simple in execution,' Yuell pointed out quietly. 'Only that the plan was simple.'

'Planning and performing are two different things, sir.'

'I'm as well aware of that as you are, Mark. Until you're established, I shall remain on this side doing everything in my power to see you get every scrap of support you need. As soon as you're established, I shall join you with the vehicles and, I hope, the Baluchis.' Yuell paused to glance at his notes again. 'Greatcoats will not be carried because everybody will already have enough to lug along, and this thing will depend on speed and therefore on lightness of equipment. If it's raining, gas capes will be worn. Identification panels will be carried to show to the Air Force when they come in. Under no circumstances are these to be abandoned. We want no accidents, and if we have to call on the RAF again when we're across we want them to know exactly where we are. Pigeons will also be taken in case anything happens to the radios or field telephones.'

After the officers were dismissed, Major Peddy reappeared. His face was grave.

'What the devil's wrong with you?' Yuell asked. 'You look as if you've lost a shilling and found sixpence.'

'Well, we *have* lost our mortar bombs and grenades,' Peddy said.

Yuell stared. 'What do you mean? The brigadier promised us two lorry-loads.'

'Those were the two lorries that ran off the road through the mountains.'

Yuell's heart sank. 'Aren't they salvaging them, for God's sake?'

Peddy pointed through the open barn doors to where the night was full of the hiss and rattle of water.

'That doesn't help,' he said. 'I gather they're trying, but there's a mist up there now and you can't see your hand before your face. A few have been stuck on other lorries, but nobody has that much room and they're arriving only in dribs and drabs. Unfortunately also, some of them have gone to Capodozzi and I don't suppose in the darkness anybody will know where the hell they are.'

Yuell did not reply but stalked off through the rain to the headquarters he'd set up in a small farmhouse.

'Get me Division – Brigadier Heathfield,' he snapped to the man waiting by the rear link telephone.

Heathfield was already a little worried because of an earlier telephone call from a friend at Army HQ who he suspected had been deliberately chosen to make it just because they knew each other well.

'How's it going up there?' he'd asked.

'We're very confident,' Heathfield had said. 'I think there'll be little opposition.'

'That's just as well,' the man at HQ had continued. 'Because we want to know if you can let us have the 19th Division Artillery down here as soon as you're across.'

Heathfield had hesitated and the other man was quick to take advantage of him.

'I thought you were confident,' he said.

'We are.'

'Then, how about it?'

Heathfield had reluctantly agreed and the request had been followed at once by another.

'We've found your boats, by the way, but we'd like the lorries down here as soon as they've delivered them to your jumping-off point. We need everything we can raise. Good-bye, Wallace.' The line went dead.

Now Heathfield listened to Yuell angrily. He had a feeling that he'd been outmanoeuvred over the artillery and it roused in him the same feeling as when he was out-thought at bridge. He wasn't worried about the lorries because he'd told Tonge about them, but he'd omitted for the time being to mention the artillery because he wasn't sure that Tonge would approve.

Hearing about the mortar bombs and grenades, he was quick to defend himself because he *had* heard about them.

'I'm organising mules,' he said. 'But it's not easy because every available bloody mule on this front seems to have gone north. However, I'm rounding a few up here and there and we'll get your bombs and grenades to you in time. It'll be only *just* in time, I'm afraid, but I'm watching it personally.'

Yuell hesitated before he answered. He was as aware of the difficulties as anybody. An army that could call on 600 tanks, 800 guns, 500 aircraft and 60,000 vehicles of one sort or another had become terribly dependent on that obstreperous object, the mule.

'There can be no success without them,' he said. 'The Royal Sussex found in February that grenades more than anything else are needed for close fighting in this kind of terrain.'

'I know that,' Heathfield said sharply. 'But I've promised them and they'll come.'

Yuell seemed to be satisfied but, as Heathfield was about to put down the telephone and pick up the cup of coffee standing by his elbow, Yuell spoke again. 'What about the air strike?' he asked. 'When does that go in?'

'Late tomorrow afternoon.'

'In this weather?'

Heathfield sounded irritated. 'The RAF said they'd laid it on. They usually keep their word. Don't you feel up to this thing, or something? Because if you don't, we'd better find someone else.'

Yuell held on to his temper. It was always easy for the men at headquarters to talk about determination when they were rarely expected to show any.

'I'm up to it,' he said quietly. 'We shan't let you down, but I'm interested to know what the result of the patrol was.'

'Which patrol?' Heathfield was anxious to get at his coffee.

'Sir – ' Yuell's temper gave at last 'you were putting a patrol across to find out what it's like at the other side. Nobody's passed anything down to battalion level.'

'Yes, well – ' Heathfield shifted uneasily in his chair – 'the Yellowjackets put a strong patrol across. But nothing came of it.'

'What do you mean, sir? – nothing came of it.'

'No one came back.'

There was a long silence. Then Yuell's voice came again, slow and icy. 'I see.'

There was a click as Yuell replaced the receiver and Heathfield stared at the silent instrument angrily. Banging it down, he picked up the coffee, took a sip, and shouted for the corporal clerk.

'Sir!'

Heathfield jerked a hand at his cup. 'This coffee's cold! Bring me some more! And this time make sure it's hot!'

t w o

It just wasn't good enough. They needed to know more.

'I'll go,' Jago offered. 'All it needs is two determined men.'

Yuell looked at him as he leaned with one hand on the side of Yuell's jeep, smiling and self-assured, like a big red, rangy fox. Jago was an invaluable officer. Immensely strong, daring, and indifferent to danger, in everything they'd done he'd always been well to the fore. Yuell had no wish to lose him, and he suspected he'd been pushing himself too hard for a long time. Nevertheless, he was also probably the only man who *might* take a patrol across to the other side and come back.

'What have you in mind?' he said.

'Go across in a two-man dinghy, sir, knock the first chap we see on the head, chuck him aboard and bolt. Then turn him loose for the Intelligence wallahs to go at. If they can't knock the truth out of him, let 'em turn him over to me. I bet I can.'

Yuell suspected that Jago was a man who could be brutal, and it must have shown in his face because Jago frowned.

'Sir, there's no such thing as clean fighting,' he protested. 'Only dirty fighting and dirtier fighting. We're not playing kiss-in-the-ring, and the Gestapo wouldn't hesitate if the boot were on the other foot.'

Yuell nodded because what he said was right. Jago had no head for plans but in small affairs like this he seemed to have a flair for doing the right thing.

'Who would you take?'

Jago grinned. 'McWatters,' he said. 'He's a murderous sod, sir. I think he belonged to a Glasgow razor gang before the war. Just the sort for a thing like this.'

Yuell stared at him for a moment longer, then he nodded.

'Let's see if we can get you a dinghy from the Engineers,' he said.

Faces blackened, cap comforters on their heads, Jago and McWatters climbed into the dinghy just after midnight. They were armed only with revolvers and clubs, which McWatters had made by winding barbed wire round the end of a stave. Anybody who received a blow from one of them would suffer a very nasty wound.

With the rain coming down now in thin wavering lines of drizzle, more mist than rain, the night was pitch-dark. Yuell had driven them down the road from San Bartolomeo in his jeep.

'One prisoner,' he said. 'That's all. Someone who'll tell us a few things. I've told our Intelligence boy wonder, Harry Marder, to stand by for when you get back. How long do you expect to be?'

'Hour, sir. Two hours. If we're not back by then, I reckon we shan't be coming back.'

The two men faded into the darkness, blurred figures with black faces. Patrolling was an art and the job for a specialist, and, though the best ones were often ghillies, poachers and gamekeepers, there were also the other kind who'd lived in city streets all their lives and had an instinctive sense of direction and an ability to make a quick decision.

Jago had rarely moved from his native Leeds before the war, but he was aware of possessing a special kind of skill and cunning when it came to affairs like this. He also didn't like the Germans. He'd seen the fly-encrusted bodies of peasants shot by them, the tiny bits of flesh and clothing after the SS had tied dynamite to partisans and blown them up, the scarred wall of a village church where the men had been dragged from Mass and shot. So he'd never hesitated when a fighting patrol was asked for, and in the line had gone out nightly because there was always the need for information or a party to repair the gaps in the wire. Going out on patrol was always a cold-blooded business, and a lot depended on the experience of the leader; but as an unexpected finger of panic clawed at his stomach, he asked himself if he hadn't volunteered once too often.

'No fight if we can help it,' he said to McWatters.

'Nae fecht, sorr?' McWatters turned.

'No fight, I said.'

McWatters shrugged, thinking that Jago was changing. He'd been on many patrols with him and had never known him back away from a fight before.

'Wha' aboot mines, sorr? They say yon place is thick wi' 'em.'

'It's my guess they'll be behind the path along the bank,' Jago said. 'In any case, it's a chance we'll have to take. If we get a prisoner and anything happens to me, it's up to you to get him back on your own. Okay?'

'Aye. Okay, sorr. Where are we gaein', sorr?'

'There's an observation post forty yards downstream from the bridge. That's where we'll head for. It's my bet somebody'll be there or will come there before long. They must have some idea there's something in the wind and they'll be watching.'

'Aye. Richt, sorr.'

'No arsing about,' Jago warned. 'We're not playing ring-a-roses. We want a prisoner, but don't be afraid to hit the bastard.'

As they whispered together the current was carrying them further downstream than they expected, and as the rubber dinghy grated softly on the bank at the far side Jago decided they couldn't be more than twenty yards or so from the observation post. Climbing from the dinghy, they made fast to a willow growing from the water's edge, and Jago tied a clean white handkerchief to the branches.

'We might have to move fast when we come back,' he said. 'But we ought to spot that even in the dark. Remind me to pick it up.'

They made their way gingerly up the muddy bank to the path. They could just make out scrubby bushes on their right and the dimly looming slopes rising towards San Eusebio. They were just about to move ahead when McWatters laid a hand on Jago's arm.

Petrified into silence, they saw the flash of a torch coming from the direction of the slopes, going on and off as though whoever held it was using it only over the more difficult stretches.

Jago touched McWatters' shoulder and pulled him gently to the side of the path.

'They'll spot yon handkerchief, sorr,' McWatters breathed.

'That's what I'm hoping. If they do, they'll stop. That's when we go for 'em.'

The approaching party consisted of Gefreiter Pramstrangl and three men. They were on their way to relieve the men in the observation post, and two of them were armed with rifles and two with 32-shot Schmeisser machine-pistols.

Pramstrangl was a small wiry man but wore spectacles, which didn't help in the dark; especially now when they were blurred by the drizzle. As they reached the path, the leading man stopped dead so that Pramstrangl and the others crashed into him.

'Gottverdammte – !'

In the dark Pramstrangl saw Jago's clean white handkerchief on the tree, hanging limply as it grew heavy with the damp, and they all crowded round, wondering what it meant and puzzled how it got there. Then it dawned on Pramstrangl that it was a sign or something similar and, peering into the darkness, he spotted the rubber dinghy on the mud below.

He was just about to shout a warning when Jago shouted for him. 'Now!' he yelled, and he and McWatters leapt through the darkness swinging their clubs. The man who had spotted the handkerchief went down first, his skull fractured, his scalp laid open to the bone. McWatters' big shoulders sent another man flying into a ditch, but the collision put him off his stroke and the swinging club caught Pramstrangl on the upper arm, paralysing it and sending him spinning down the bank towards the water. The third man was still struggling to get his rifle off his shoulder and screeching 'Englanders!' when McWatters shot him in the chest.

'Englander be buggered,' he yelled. 'Ah'm a Scot, ye German hoor!'

'We've got one!' Jago said as the noise died down. 'He went down the bank! Grab him, McWatters, and untie the dinghy! What happened to the other bastard? There were four of them.'

But the man who had disappeared into the ditch was wise enough not to attempt to climb out in a hurry. Instead he got quietly to his hands and knees, pawing the ground for the machine-pistol he'd dropped as he fell.

By this time McWatters was already waiting at the water's edge, one hand twisting the dazed Pramstrangl's collar until he was half-throttled, and the other unhitching the rope of the rubber dinghy. More to show off than anything else, Jago was unknotting the handkerchief.

'Right,' he said after what seemed to McWatters to be a delay of several weeks. 'Let's go.'

As McWatters released Pramstrangl to push the dinghy into the water before scrambling aboard, Jago picked up the

German, flung him into it with a bone-cracking heave, and then flopped in after them.

'Christ,' he said, 'that was quick! Can't be more than a quarter of an hour since we left.'

They were out into the stream now and paddling hard. They could hear shouts on the bank and running feet, and guessed that the men at the observation post had realised that something had happened to their relief and were on their way to find out what.

'Turn the wick up a bit,' Jago panted, digging at the water. 'A bit further and the bastards won't even know where we are.'

As they paddled still harder, the man in the ditch struggled to his feet, holding his machine-pistol. He couldn't see the dinghy now but he could still see the white handkerchief, which Jago had stuffed carelessly into his blouse pocket, and it seemed to glow through the darkness. As he raised his weapon to fire, however, the dinghy slid to his left on the current, and the willows got in the way. He cursed and, moving a little to the left, stepped on to the mud to get a better shot.

The explosion lifted heads on the far bank.

'We got a patrol across there, Sarge?' somebody asked. 'Yes, keep your eyes open for 'em. They'll probably be on their way back.'

The first speaker was silent for a while. 'Not them, Sarge. That was a mine. They just walked into it. You ask me, they're napoo. Kaput. Finis.'

From across the water, German weapons had opened up, blindly spraying the bank. It sounded like all hell let loose.

The soldiers peered into the darkness. They could hear voices at the far side. They seemed almost opposite them.

'Give 'em a go with the Bren,' the sergeant said. 'At least it'll make the sods keep their heads down.'

As the Bren ripped out a short burst, a voice came from among the bushes just below them. It sounded angry.

'For Christ's sake, stop that firing! You almost blew our bloody heads off.'

Jago appeared, pausing just long enough to tie the dinghy to a tree. Between them, he and McWatters dragged Gefreiter Pramstrangl up the muddy slope to the footpath and there let him sprawl among the puddles.

'He don't look so good, sir,' the sergeant said.

'You should see the other bastards,' Jago said. 'Where's the nearest transport?'

'End of the San Bartolomeo road, sir. About two hundred yards in that direction.'

Aided by one of the sergeant's men, McWatters hauled Pramstrangl to his feet and they set off after Jago who was already striding out in search of a vehicle. Though they didn't know it, and Jago had no intention of letting them know it, his whole body was shaking. There had been more than a touch of bravado in his volunteering yet again, and he could only feel that God's hand had been in it somewhere. By sheer chance, they'd put their dinghy ashore at one of the gaps in the German defences and someone endeavouring to reach them as they'd left had clearly stepped on one of his own mines.

'There he is, Herr Hauptmann.'

Lieutenant Thiergartner turned and looked up at Captain Reis.

The injured man was lying in a heap on the mud, his life's blood draining away into the river. He had trodden on a Schu mine, one of the Germans' more delicately contrived inventions which flung up a charge to explode chest-high in front of its victim. Even if his chest hadn't been punctured, he would still have been of little use to anybody because an eye was hanging out on one cheek and the other cheek was ripped open to show his teeth.

Alongside him, two grenadiers, one of them the farmhand Pulovski, were waiting.

'Get him up here,' Reis said.

Pulovski began to move to where the dying soldier's head lay on the mud and Reis barked at him. 'For God's sake be careful where you tread, you damn fool,' he snapped.

'Jawohl, Herr Hauptmann.' Pulovski looked up, his simple face that of a sixteen-year-old boy, bright and helpful in the light of Thiergartner's torch. In his life at home on the Thuringian farm, the most difficult thing Pulovski had ever had to handle up to joining the army was harnessing a horse. He had no mechanical bent and no idea of danger – though he was an expert shot and an excellent provider of extra rations, always knowing just where to look for eggs or rabbits or pheasants.

'All right, pick him up,' Reis said.

Smiling and full of willingness, Pulovski began to lift the wounded man, forgetting once more where he put his feet. Reis saw the other men moving back. Nobody wanted to be too near if Pulovski set off a mine, and Reis himself edged away. Showing an unexpected confidence in the slow-witted countryman, Thiergartner didn't move and Reis had to admire his courage.

As they got the man on to the path, Reis bent over him. There was little they could do for him.

'What about the others?' he asked.

'One badly hurt, Herr Hauptmann,' Thiergartner said. 'God knows what they hit him with. A mechanical saw, by the look of his head. The other's in the bushes. He's already dead. There's no sign of Pramstrangl.'

'All right.' Reis nodded. 'See that they're brought back, and inform the burial squad. You might also get in touch with headquarters and tell them to send a new relief party down. The Tommies wouldn't have sent a patrol across if there weren't something in the wind, and if there is we must be on the look-out for it.'

three

Jago's prisoner was the first thing that had gone right. Yuell had spent the whole evening worrying about the missing bombs and grenades and he was immensely grateful to Jago for his success.

'I'll see you get something for this, Tony,' he said.

Jago shrugged. He knew he didn't deserve a medal but it would be nice, he thought, to have a ribbon up like Warley. 'McWatters, too, sir,' he suggested. 'If they don't give McWatters something, you can send mine back.'

McWatters, who was a communist and was fighting less for the British Empire than to bring down the Fascist beasts who were standing in the way of world socialism, hadn't much time for such baubles as medals and told Jago so.

'Ah dinnae wan' no medal,' he growled.

He was going to be put down for one all the same, Jago thought, and even if he still refused it Jago had no intention of sending back anything of his own. What he'd said had sounded good, however, especially with Mr Zeal listening, because it would get back to the men and that sort of thing never did any harm. There was a lot that was false about Jago, but at least his courage wasn't part of it.

Despite having gone through the desert and up the length of Italy doing the preliminary interviews of German and Italian deserters and prisoners, Lieutenant Marder still remained a bit of a hothouse intellectual. He was also too much inclined to look on the bright side, to jump to conclusions, and to believe what he wanted to believe. What was more, because he'd learned a few tricks, he'd begun to think he was clever.

It was one of the ill chances of the day that Gefreiter Pramstrangl *was* clever. He wasn't sophisticated like Lieutenant Marder because he'd never been to university, hardly even to school, but he'd lived most of his life in the mountains and had the sharp wiliness of a mountain fox. During the winters before the war he had run a ski-shop at Igls and during the summers driven the tourist bus from Innsbruck. He took an immediate dislike to Marder because he looked so much like the haughty British tourists who'd so often treated him like dirt.

Marder had already got Pramstrangl's name, rank and number. There was no need to ask for his unit because it was shown on his collar, and Marder knew all the collar insignia. He also firmly believed in what Caesar had said in Shaw's play: When a man knew something, the chief difficulty was to prevent him communicating it to all and sundry. According to the Duke of Marlborough, no war could be conducted without early and good intelligence, and a good Intelligence officer, to quote another of Marder's idols, had to be courageous, adroit, patient, imperturbable, discreet and trustworthy. Lieutenant Marder considered he was all the lot.

Now he studied Pramstrangl knowingly. Prisoners, he believed, were much more inclined to be communicative immediately after capture, if treated with kindness. The knowledge that he'd survived a violent meeting with an enemy filled with murderous intent always loosened a man's tongue, and it was important to create a climate of confidence between the questioner and the questioned. He pushed a cigarette across to Pramstrangl who frowned warily.

'I'm not a Nazi,' he said.

'You people never are, I notice.' Marder smiled smugly, making Pramstrangl dislike him even more.

The interrogation was taking place in the Intelligence truck, which was like a newspaper office just before edition time. There was always someone arriving or a telephone ringing and men were working to get maps of the intelligence summary up to date. Marder glanced at the big 1/15,000 map where oblongs and squares denoted enemy minefields and blue marks indicated machine-gun posts, headquarters, supply dumps and trench systems. Then he opened Pramstrangl's pay book. 'Medal for the Einmarsch in Czechoslovakia. Medal for Poland. Iron Cross, Second Class, in France. Iron Cross First Class, in the Crimea.' This wasn't a new boy. He jabbed a hand at the map.

'You were taken just here,' he said. 'What were you doing there?'

'I was going to the observation post about thirty yards further along the bank.'

'What were you observing?'

'You people, of course.'

'Don't be impertinent!'

'Well, what else would I be observing? The moon?'

Marder frowned. He jabbed at the map again. 'This point here,' he said. 'Is it fortified?'

Pramstrangl studied the map. Since it ought to be obvious even to an idiot that the point would be fortified, he didn't see any reason why he shouldn't admit it. 'Yes,' he said. 'Of course.'

'And this?'

'Yes.'

'Minefields? Where are they? Here and here along the bank?'

'Yes.' All this was obvious too, and Pramstrangl saw no point in backing away from it.

'What about the approaches to San Eusebio from this direction?'

Pramstrangl hesitated before answering. He didn't like the Nazis. He was a good Austrian and had loathed them since the day they'd walked into his country in 1938 for no other reason than that they believed it needed their special brand of efficiency. But his wife and two teenage daughters lived in Steinach, which was just north of the Brenner Pass on the route from Rome into Austria, and having seen what the war had done to Italy he had no wish for it to do the same to Steinach. The longer, therefore, that the fighting remained outside Austria the better. Much wiser to let the Germans be knocked out in the north by the Russians or the RAF, or by the Second Front which they all knew was bound to come before long, and hold the enemy back in the south.

He pointed to the rough ground to the east of San Eusebio. It was full of machine-gun nests because the Germans believed that the Allies would never try a frontal attack but would approach from the side.

'Not much there,' he said. 'They've got Russians there. Conscripted men. They've just arrived. There are some Czechs there, too.'

Marder's heart leapt. Nobody had heard of defecting Czechs and Russians on this front before. It seemed to indicate a shortage of troops.

'Here?' he asked and Pramstrangl nodded.

'What about the river bank?'

Pramstrangl shrugged, chiefly to give himself time to think again.

'Not much,' he said eventually. 'They haven't the weapons because they're withdrawing them. They're building a new line near Valmontone.'

'Why?'

'Well, it's clear you'll break this one eventually – '

'Where does the line go?'

'Along the mountains towards the Adriatic.'

'You sure of that?'

'I was up there with a lorry last week. They'll pull back when the pressure here gets too much. They're saving the troops for when you get to Germany.'

Pramstrangl decided this was a stroke of genius because it was just the sort of thing the Nazis would do.

Marder pushed the map across. 'Machine-gun nests,' he said. 'Where are they?'

Pramstrangl almost smiled. This one was a pushover, he thought.

Lieutenant Marder was elated when he reported to Yuell. He had watched Pramstrangl being marched off to where a lorry was waiting to transport him to Division, then turned to find the colonel waiting for him. He spread a map across the blanket-covered table and opened his notebook.

'Machine-gun nests, sir,' he said. 'Here, here and here. This route from the end of the San Bartolomeo road should be easy. There are only Russians and Czechs there.'

'I didn't know there were Russians and Czechs on this front,' Yuell said.

'They've just come,' Marder pointed out. 'We'd better inform Division, because it surely means our job's going to be easier than we thought. In fact, he said that with a bit of pressure the Germans would pull back. They're already constructing a new line along the mountains.'

After lunch and a long talk with Heathfield, Yuell decided to get his company commanders and the artillery, armour and engineers together again, to go over the final details.

He explained what Marder had told him. 'Personally,' he ended, 'I'm inclined to think he's a bit too optimistic and I'd warn you about rushing your fences. However, you all know how to go about things by now, so I'd suggest you do exactly that and move with care. Don't imagine that just because you've been told there's nothing in front of you, there won't be.' He looked at Jago who, as the only man who'd actually crossed the river, was also there. 'What about you, Tony? Can you add anything to what we know?'

'Only that the stream runs surprisingly fast, sir. There's quite a lot of drift.'

Yuell nodded. The plan was clear in his mind, clarified by pad jottings and lines, arrows and symbols drawn in chinagraph on the talc of his map. 'Let me say straight away,' he went on, 'that I think this is a pretty hasty operation we've been handed. I suspect the other side of the river – this side, too, for that matter – is more covered by mortars than we've been told, and I think we can expect the usual reception in the forming-up areas. Finally, the place is stiff with mines and we have no guarantee that they'll be lifted before we go in.'

As he sat down, the colonel of the 215th Field Artillery, representing the 19th Division Artillery commander, stood up, clutching a formidable-looking table of fire support tasks. He was followed by the mortar platoon commander, and as they all thrashed out what they were to do, their anxieties came to the surface.

'What disturbs me, sir,' Warley said, 'is the mine business. I'm wondering if the Sappers'll be able to clear enough space for us to work.'

It was worrying but, as timings, communication arrangements and administrative details were announced, order seemed to emerge from the chaos. During the afternoon, however, Yuell began to worry again about the air strike, and eventually he contacted Tallemach who immediately got on to Heathfield.

'They're having trouble,' Heathfield admitted. 'The floods have spread to their airfield and it's waterlogged. They can't fly because they can't take off.'

Tallemach frowned. What was the point, he wondered, in having a superiority in aircraft and tanks, if the planes spent most of their time grounded by the weather or the tanks sank to their bellies if they moved?

'What's happened to the strike then?' he asked.

'Don't worry,' Heathfield reassured him. 'We're watching it. We've appealed to squadrons further south for help and they've promised it.'

'They'll never fly all that way in this weather, with the mountains in the way,' Tallemach replied tersely. 'They wouldn't dare risk fighter-bombers like that. There aren't so damn many in Italy, anyway, since they started the build-up for the Second Front.'

'We're doing what we can. Tell Yuell to stop worrying.'

But Yuell went on worrying. Italy was a bastard of a country. They'd all thought when they'd landed in Sicily and the Fascist government had collapsed, that they were going to walk straight up its length to the flat plains of the north, ready for the assault on the southern flank of Germany. The loss of their North African empire had demoralised the Italian army, and with Mussolini deposed it had all seemed so simple. But the Germans had reacted quickly, and what with the sea to guard its flanks, rivers running across it every few miles, and endless mountains with only a narrow coastal plain on either side, Italy had proved a hell of a place to win ground.

Yuell sighed. There were a thousand and one things to hold his attention. The MO was badgering him to know if there were any buildings on the route they'd chosen to San Eusebio where he might set up an aid post, and just where Division was proposing to put the forward dressing station; the signallers were concerned that their 'Eighteen' sets had always presented problems when working with tanks; the artillery were concerned that they might not see the red smoke with which it was proposed to mark targets; and the padre was insistent that morale demanded that he should cross with the first wave.

'The Yellowjackets' C of E chap's decided that it isn't *his* job,' Peddy pointed out. 'The Church of England doesn't seem to encourage the view that chaplains should get mixed up with the fighting.'

The Yellowjackets' chaplain was young, and not long out of theological college. Whey-faced, smoothed-cheeked and limp, he winced when the latrine squad were making their feelings clear and, probably because of his cloistered existence, seemed not to have the faintest idea how to minister to the needs of several hundred hard-boiled difficult soldiers.

'He prays well,' Peddy had once said in his defence and Yuell had often felt that was *all* he did.

'The chaps would have admired him if he'd gone all the same,' he observed. Though public opinion demanded that troops should have a padre handy to look after their souls, many of them were not only out of touch, they'd never even been in touch. As they struggled to promote the Kingdom of Heaven and tried to be funny in their sermons without mentioning sex, most of the men regarded them with frozen-faced contempt or, if they were well to the back, read books or played cards. In any case, Yuell reflected, if you wanted to see Christianity and brotherhood in action, you didn't have to go to church, only towards the front line. Ten to one, you'd see soldiers there who not long before had been engaged in trying to kill other soldiers, sharing their cigarettes and rations with the captured enemy.

Fortunately O'Mara, the Liverpool Irishman who looked after the spiritual welfare of the North Yorkshires, for no other reason than that he had to be attached somewhere and there were eighty-odd Catholics among them, was one of the good padres. He and the MO were not only working partners but also good friends who were known to the battalion as 'Body and Soul'. Their co-operation contributed more than a little to confidence, and they had jointly decided to cross the river early. O'Mara even seemed to be contemplating the prospect with enjoyment.

'It's my job,' he pointed out to Yuell, 'to be wherever the fighting's heaviest. The troops need more than sermons to inspire them.'

Yuell smiled. 'I sometimes think,' he reflected, 'that the Anglican church lost something when it broke from the Catholic stem.'

O'Mara returned the smile. 'That's just the strength of the Irish, Colonel, sir,' he observed. 'The Irish and the Italians are nearest to God's heart – as you can see at once by looking at the number of them in the calendar of saints.'

Yuell smiled. He liked O'Mara. He was a small red-faced man who looked like a jockey and – perhaps because he'd come from a Liverpool slum parish – never turned a hair at the troops' drinking. He did a little himself, in fact, and possessed a marked sense of humour that allowed him to regard his profession with a levity that never interfered with his faith – 'We celebrated Mass today,' he liked to report. 'There were no casualties' – while his attitude to bad language was easy-going. When one of the sergeants was at it hammer and tongs at some maladroit swaddy, he merely remarked that you could hardly expect a harassed NCO to be touched with celestial fire.

'It must have been a whole lot easier, Padre,' Yuell said, 'When you thought you were fighting a holy war.'

O'Mara smiled again. 'Are we not fightin' a holy war now, Colonel, sir?' he asked gently. 'Would you not consider Hitler and his minions part of the powers of darkness? Sure, I would. I'm a practical man and I believe in practical things – even in the practice of religion – and if these evil forces are to be destroyed, then it's up to us – and that means me – to destroy 'em. A crusade's better than making it seem as if we're asking men to risk their lives for one of the Water Board's by-laws, and, in any case, I always thought those people on the *Titanic* who stood around singing 'Nearer My God To Thee' were just wasting their time when they could have been building rafts.'

f o u r

It had rained all afternoon, slashing and crackling down so that their ears were constantly filled with the sound of rushing water. The barns where they sheltered were leaking, puddles covered the floor, and the hay was teeming with animal life.

'A louse born in t' morning,' Rich pointed out indignantly, 'is a mummy by midday and a grandma by evenin'.'

Spurred on by Peddy, and with a superhuman effort, the cooks had finally got their pressure cookers roaring alongside a reeking cowshed and had produced a meal, mostly out of tins; meat and vegetables – or dog's vomit as the troops liked to call it – but at least it hadn't been going stale in hot boxes for hours. The potatoes and vegetables were dehydrated but the cooks serving the stew from in front of a mound of opened tins wore self-satisfied looks on their faces, feeling they'd performed a miracle.

'This the bloody best you can do?' Syzling asked.

The smiles were wiped away in a flash. 'Do you release what we've been through to provide this?' the cook-corporal demanded. 'This is the third bleeding meal we've got ready. The first got blown up and the second's floating down the Liri.'

The hot food warmed them only temporarily and they were soon wet, cold and miserable again, all of them occupied with their thoughts. Yuell was still worrying about the air strike. He'd heard nothing and was by this time firmly of the opinion that he never would. He was also worried about his grenades and mortar bombs, because there was no sign of the mule train that was supposed to be bringing them. Something had clearly gone wrong and, due to weariness, weather, wounds, or plain bloody-mindedness, someone had failed to do what he ought to have done. He was still brooding when Peddy brought a message to the effect that Colonel Baron of the Yellowjackets had been injured in a jeep accident.

'Slid off the road into a ditch,' he said.

'Is he much hurt?' Yuell asked. He and Baron had been through the desert together and were old friends.

'They say not. Strained neck and three broken fingers. He insists on carrying on. Except – '

Yuell's head turned. 'Except what?'

'They're wondering if he's got concussion. He insists he's all right but it seems he gave his head a pretty hard whack.'

'I hope he's wise,' Yuell said. 'He's got a good second-in-command and, under the circumstances, he might do better to lie up for a day or two. From a purely selfish point of view, we're expecting the Yellowjackets to join up with us and if, for some reason, they don't, we're going to be pretty hard-pushed. There are already enough things that have gone wrong with this affair, and the Yellowjackets aren't the best in the business at the moment. They took a lot of casualties at Sant' Agata and they're pretty well a new battalion.'

While Yuell added Baron to his worries, Peddy worried about his wife. They'd been married for twelve years and had grown used to each other. Trying now to write to her as he always did before going into action, he was less concerned with what might happen to himself than with how she'd feel if it did.

Jago was worrying in case his nerve was going. He'd recovered from the shakes after the patrol but it was something that hadn't happened before and he was concerned that it might happen again – at the wrong time. Second-Lieutenant Taylor, being new to war, was worried that too much might be expected of him. Private Fletcher-Smith was worried about the girl in Trepiazze because it had suddenly occurred to him that he hadn't been very careful. Now he was trying to make up his mind whether he was in love or not and, if he were, should he marry her? He also had enough knowledge of war to suspect that things had started to go wrong in San Bartolomeo and couldn't resist quoting to those whose education didn't match his own the words of other more famous soldiers.

' "There is such a choice of difficulties," ' he said, ' "that I own myself at a loss how to determine them." '

'Oo said that?' Private Rich asked.

'General Wolfe at Quebec.'

'General 'oo where?' Private Rich had probably once heard of General Wolfe but, if he had, it hadn't registered. 'What's 'e got to do wi' us 'ere?'

'The circumstances are the same,' Fletcher-Smith pointed out.

'No, they're not,' Rich insisted funereally. ' '*E* was there; *We're* 'ere. That makes 'em a lot different.'

Fletcher-Smith gave up but Private Rich hadn't finished.

' 'E won't need to worry after tomorrow any road,' he said. 'By that time, we'll either be in San Eusebio, else we'll be dead.'

It was blunt and forthright but, though it disturbed Fletcher-Smith, it didn't disturb Rich. To Rich it was all the same, being alive or being dead. He preferred to be alive because it meant beer and food and getting girls on their backs in the long summer grass. He supposed being dead was unpleasant, but his mind had never explored the question very far and he was quite incapable of imagining it.

'By tomorrow we'll be in it proper,' he said.

' "And a day of battle is a day of harvest for the devil," '
Fletcher-Smith quoted.

'Why don't you shut up, you morbid sod?' 000 Bawden
growled.

Lieutenant Deacon worried about Private Syzling who, he
felt sure, would be bound to do something stupid. Deacon
was less concerned that Syzling's stupidity would halt the
attack dead in its tracks and lose the war than that it should
redound to the shame of Lieutenant Deacon. Private Syzling,
inevitably, didn't worry at all. He found a corn bin in the
outhouse of the ruined farm where they were billeted,
crawled inside and pulled the lid down on top of him.
Anybody else would have worried about mice or fleas or that
that the lid would jam and he would suffocate. None of these
things occurred to Private Syzling and, of course, there were
no mice or fleas and the lid didn't jam, and he slept, warm,
dry, comfortable and lost to the sergeants, while everybody
else was wet through, cold, miserable and chivvied.

Major Warley found he was worrying chiefly about
himself. Up to that moment, he'd never been inclined to
worry much, but suddenly he felt he needed to survive. He
was twenty-five and, after five years in the army, old age
seemed to be zooming towards him at full speed. He needed
to go back and find Graziella Vanvitelli and talk to her again.
Thinking about her, he knew he'd never now marry the girl
in Manchester he'd been engaged to before he'd left for
overseas. For some time he hadn't cared much about what
happened between them and had been largely indifferent to
her letters. Now he didn't care at all, because Graziella
Vanvitelli filled his mind.

'Must be soul mates or something,' he said ruefully to
himself.

They were all in the mood to talk about themselves and
discuss their hopes for after the war, what they intended to
do, the businesses they were going to start, the plans they'd

made. Fletcher-Smith's ambition had always been to go in for teaching and become the headmaster of a forward-looking school. Now he found it was merely to get his hands on the girl in Trepiazze again. Rich wanted to open a corner shop. Hunters felt it would be best to emigrate. 'There'll be no future in England after this lot,' he said.

'Then what the bloody 'ell are we fightin' for?' Rich asked.

766 Bawden intended to be a bookmaker. He'd been a bookmaker's runner most of his life, and once Warley had found him in a barn holding a large black book and surrounded by a circle of men. He had thought at first he was giving a Bible reading. It was only as he drew near that he found that the 'Bible' contained 766 Bawden's notes about the form of horses, betting, times, trainers, jockeys and starting prices for several years back, and that what he was giving his friends was not the Scriptures but some good advice about where to put their money.

Martindale raised a shout of derision because his only ambition was to become a regular soldier. He'd spent nearly all his days before the war ploughing. He still walked like a ploughman, and at recruit training camp they'd had the greatest difficulty persuading him to swing his left arm with his right leg. More than one corporal was said to have disappeared to the mental hospital as a result of trying to teach Martindale to walk like everybody else.

When he'd been called up, the farmer he'd worked for had tried to get him deferred on the grounds that he was needed, but to Martindale, who'd got up regularly at 4.30. a.m., the prospect of the army's six-o'clock was like a Sunday lie-in, and the arduous muscular exercises the army insisted on were nothing to humping sacks of fertiliser. So he'd fought off his employer and joined up, deciding more and more each year that it was a life of ease. Private Martindale was considered to be slow-thinking but he was no fool.

'What'll *you* do after the war, 'Enry?' Parkin asked White.

'I dunno.' Quite honestly White *didn't* know because he'd been in the army so long now he couldn't imagine being out of it.

'The welfare officer'll find you something, I reckon.'

'They didn't have welfare officers when I joined,' Henry said.

'I know what I want,' Lofty Duff interrupted and Parkin patted his head.

'Down, boy,' he said. 'Sit. We know what you want. You want to join a Punch and Judy show, don't you? You want to play the policeman.'

Everybody in the barn seemed to have offered his thoughts for the future. All except Poker Hunters who was deep in a paperback with a white cover and a screaming girl on the front. Minor publishers had long since discovered that one of the things the troops wanted more than anything else was salacious literature. It stood to reason that, cut off from girls, they'd want to read about what they were missing. The books were invariably in white covers with a lurid picture on the front, and a whole host of opportunist authors had discovered they could make money writing about sex for the troops. But, since they had to be paid for their endeavours, there were also a few opportunist publishers who'd caught on to the fact that there were some classics that also fell into the category of salaciousness but were so old there'd be no demands for royalties. Even Rabelais had found his way into paperback, complete with a girl on the cover being seduced by a soldier. The fact that the girl wore a modern dress and the soldier a wrist watch didn't matter much because there was enough of bawdy humour and rowdy words in Rabelais to please even the most demanding.

Private Hunters, however, had picked a loser for once. The girl was there on the front all right, having her clothes torn off by a bloke in tights and a blouse like a ballet dancer, but the title, *The Decameron,* didn't seem to have the same

143

connotation as *No Orchids for Miss Blandish* or *Kiss the Blood off My Hands,* to name just two that Private Hunters had read; and certainly this geezer, Boccaccio, couldn't hold a candle to James Hadley Chase.

Rich started him out of his bewilderment by nudging him. 'What's *your* ambition, Poker?' he asked.

Hunters looked up from the paperback. 'Wouldn't mind going to bed with Betty Grable,' he said.

By the evening, Colonel Yuell knew the worst. There would be no aircraft strike. The air force squadrons in the immediate vicinity were still bogged down, and in any case no one was prepared to risk valuable aircraft with a cloud base down to around eight hundred feet when the mountains behind reared up to almost two thousand and in places to five. In justice, Yuell could hardly blame them; but all the same he did, in the manner of all service men who have embarked on something dangerous and feel they're not getting the support to which they're entitled.

It was still raining and the thought that they were to leave their overcoats behind made him wonder what it would be like at the other side if the thing wasn't over quickly. Despite the fact that spring couldn't be far away, the weather seemed to be growing worse, not better. The ground outside the little farmhouse where Yuell had his headquarters was thick with mud, and the greyness of the scene was unutterably depressing. He couldn't imagine a more cheerless spot, and not for the first time he recalled a lecture he'd attended in his last year at Cambridge.

It had been given by a man called Wavell whom he'd never heard of in those days.

'Military history,' Wavell had insisted, 'is a flesh-and-blood affair, not a matter of diagrams and formulas or of rules; not a conflict of machines but of men.'

It had stuck in his mind, that lecture. Not all of it, but a few salient points: 'The man is the first weapon of battle; let us then study the soldier in battle, for it is he who brings reality to it' and 'To learn that Napoleon won the campaign of 1796 by manoeuvre on interior lines or some such phrase is of little value. If you can discover how a young unknown man inspired a ragged, mutinous half-starved army and made it fight, how he gave it the energy and momentum to march and fight as it did...then you will have learned something.'

Yuell had never forgotten those words, even though he and his fellow undergraduates hadn't thought much of Wavell or any other professional soldier at the time. In 1939 pacifism had seemed the only worthwhile creed, and young men were swearing they'd never die for England in another war.

Certainly Wavell had not impressed them with his presence. He was just a solid-looking man with a blind eye and thick legs who seemed to be rooted to the ground, a man of no apparent humour and no visible sensibility. But when he'd looked him up in the reference books the next day, Yuell had been startled to find he was a poet and a scholar of that most intellectual of public schools, Winchester College. It had probably been that discovery, more than anything else, that had encouraged him to leave Cambridge and seek a commission in the army where he'd quickly found himself ideally suited to the military life. When, after Dunkirk, the army had been reorganised and expanded, promotion had come very quickly and he'd even begun to hope that eventually he might become a general. He'd also learned, however, that rank brought its own particular anxieties and he constantly had to apply Wavell's simple teachings to them. Never forget the man. Never. Never. Never. It had brought him a few grey hairs despite his youth, but it had also brought him the respect of the soldiers who served under him.

As it began to grow dark, information arrived that the mule train had been organised at last and that the largest part of the grenades from the wrecked lorries had been rescued and were on their way again. But, since mules didn't travel as fast as lorries, they weren't expected to arrive until the last minute.

Yuell was still trying to find out exactly where they were when Brigadier Tallemach walked in, his shadow against the wall made huge by an electric light bulb powered by the battery of one of the lorries.

'I've been to see Baron,' he said. 'I think the first suggestion that he was concussed was right, so I've pulled him out and left his second-in-command to run the show. Unfortunately, that's meant moving everybody up a peg and one of their companies is going to be taken across by a chap who'd expected to be doing something else entirely. How about your people?'

'We're all right, sir,' Yuell said. 'At least, the men are all right. We're still short of grenades and mortar bombs, though. They haven't arrived yet.'

'I'll get the Baluchis to look for them. They won't be needed until morning at the very earliest.'

While they were talking, an RASC captain joined them. 'How do we get these boats of yours down to the river, sir?' he asked.

Yuell indicated Route C on the map but the captain shook his head.

'Have you seen that road, sir?' he said.

'What's wrong with it?'

'It's only a raised cart track and it runs through flooded fields.'

Yuell was looking puzzled and the RASC officer gestured as though to force his point home. 'There's nowhere to pull off the road, sir, and nowhere at the end to turn a Scammell round.'

'Why the devil are you using Scammells?' Tallemach demanded.

'Because there's a shortage of vehicles, sir, and a Scammell will carry fourteen of these boats compared with seven on a three-ton truck. Nobody at Divisional HQ mentioned that the road was narrow, and we can't "back and fill" one at a time right under the Teds' noses.'

'Not even after dark?'

That brought up another point. 'Sir, we can't wait that long. My orders are to be opposite Cassino by morning.'

'What the devil for?'

'There's a crossing being made down there in twenty-four hours' time, sir.'

'There's one being made up here – now. Or hadn't you noticed?'

'Sir –' the RASC officer looked worried ' – my orders are quite clear.'

Tallemach began to grow angry. 'For God's sake, man, you've got to get those boats down to the river for us!'

The RASC officer remained apologetic but firm. 'Even if the Germans weren't there and we could turn round without difficulties, sir, we can't get two Scammells to pass each other on that road, however hard we try. It's a soft surface, and if they go on the verge the thing will simply crumble. The next thing we know we'll have the Scammells lying on their sides in the field.'

Yuell's face was growing darker. 'We'll have to arrange to transfer the boats to three-tonners, sir.'

Tallamach frowned. 'We haven't got that number,' he said. 'Every spare vehicle we had's been taken off us for the New Zealanders' attack.' His face grew grim. 'This is bloody ridiculous. I'll get in touch with Div.'

But when he got back to the group of vehicles and tents that were his headquarters, he found 19th Division Artillery in trouble too. A modern army not only marched on its stomach, it needed petrol, oil, radio batteries, spare parts and ammunition, and to support several thousand men in combat there must also be a large number of vehicles and mobile workshops. But the villages of the Arunci Mountains were small and, backed hard up against the lower slopes, didn't provide much flat land in which to disperse them. As a result, most of the time the area was an impossible traffic jam with the Engineers trying to push equipment down to the river; trucks lurching on the narrow roads; bulldozers trying to force their way through to carve out the banks; long-barrelled anti-tank guns moving forward in the rain, one after the other, gun after gun, limber after limber; Bren carriers; cavernous, shrouded three-tonners where the glow of a match in the interior showed men's faces; ambulances; water trucks; and endless lines of supply vehicles.

In the middle of it all, the colonel of the 215th Field Artillery was trying to locate new battery positions within range of the target areas while taking into account at the same time the need to switch targets from the San Eusebio area to a German-held farm at Castelgrande opposite the Yellowjackets' attack.

His instructions ran to fifty-six pages of typing, most of them lists of eight-figure map references. For every task the detail, time, target, type of ammunition and rate of fire had been set down. A smoke screen had been laid on, some guns allocated to tanks, others to batteries. Provision had been made for guns to be surveyed in, pits dug, and ammunition convoys directed in the dark along roads whose edges were still mined. Artillery draughtsmen, clerks, Intelligence officers and others had been working on the instructions for days, fully conscious that one slip could mean death to other British soldiers.

But, though the results looked impressive, there were still occasional small errors that led the gunner colonel to doubt the veracity of the whole.

'I don't know who organised this thing,' he said, 'but the sites we've been given aren't going to be much good. We're going to hit the infantry as they go in.'

'Don't talk nonsense,' Tallemach said.

The colonel was not put off. 'The river's only fifty feet wide, sir,' he said, and then went on to bring up the other point that was worrying him. 'How long is this thing likely to go on, sir?'

'It should be over in forty-eight hours.'

'Well, I'll need to know that we're going to be able to get clear quickly when we go.'

'When you go where?'

'My orders are that as soon as you're safely established on the other side we hitch up and move to the New Zealanders' sector.'

'*My* information,' Tallemach snapped, 'was that you were here to help *us*.'

'Until you're across, sir! I've been informed that we're to be down there in forty-eight hours.'

Tallemach couldn't believe his ears. 'We're going to need support longer than that!' he said. 'Dammit, we can't hold ground with half our guns taken away from us!'

The gunner colonel frowned, bridling a little and feeling he was being pushed around. 'I understood this wasn't a holding operation, sir,' he said. 'Just a feint for the crossing further up.'

Getting through to Division, Tallemach discovered that General Tonge had been called to Corps for a conference on the plan to link his bridgehead with the one that was to be thrown over further north. As a result, he had to talk to Heathfield instead.

Heathfield was feeling well satisfied with the way things were going. Marder's report on his questioning of Pramstrangl lay on the desk in front of him, and he knew that Russians and Czechs in front of them inevitably meant an easier crossing. The soldiers of the German satellites were never as good as the Germans themselves. Most of them were conscripts longing for a German defeat to free their homelands, and none of them could see the point of dying for a country that had enslaved them.

He was still in a state of euphoria as he listened to Tallemach, until it suddenly dawned on him that what Tallemach was doing was not giving him an enthusiastic report but making a complaint, and being bloody-minded about it, too. 'Whose bright idea was it,' he was saying furiously, 'that 19th Div. Artillery's to be withdrawn after forty-eight hours?'

Heathfield came to life with a jerk. 'Not mine,' he said self-righteously. 'Not the general's either. It came down from the high altar.'

He knew he wasn't being quite honest, because what had come down from the high altar had been merely a request. The fact that it was difficult to refuse was beside the point. He had agreed to it without protest, when a protest might have caused the request to be withdrawn.

Tallemach seemed to suspect something of the sort and his retort was sharp and angry.

'Then you'd better get on to them,' he said, 'and tell them it's not possible. Suppose there's a delay here? My chaps can't hold ground across the river without full artillery backing. Div. promised everything they could muster.'

'My orders are unequivocal. I can't alter them.'

'This damn thing's becoming ridiculous,' Tallemach snapped. 'Whose suggestion was it that the infantry use the secondary road from Capodozzi?'

'I was given to understand that it would be impossible to use the San Bartolomeo approach.' Heathfield sounded calm and sure of himself. 'The general himself put forward the suggestion that you use it.'

'Who reported on it?'

'One of the general's staff. He said it was all right and, with the engineers and the tanks using the San Bartolomeo road, it seemed perfectly suitable for your infantry.'

'Well, it isn't!' Tallemach explained what the RASC officer had told him.

'Can't the men carry the boats from Capodozzi?' Heathfield asked.

'Have you ever tried to carry a boat over a mile and a half while you were laden down with ammunition, weapons and equipment? I dare bet you haven't.'

'No, that's true,' Heathfield admitted. 'But the report was that it was a perfectly good road and that lorries would be able to transport the boats down.'

'Lorries, yes. They've arrived in Scammells and you know how big they are.'

'Can't they be transferred?'

'What into? There's nothing that isn't already earmarked. How are these men expected to fight their way into San Eusebio when they'll be exhausted before they start?'

Heathfield's voice was cold. 'You'll just have to do the best you can,' he said. 'We have our orders as you do. It's not easy here either.'

'I'm sure it isn't! All those bits of paper that have to be rewritten!' Tallemach couldn't resist the jibe and it made Heathfield's temper flare.

'It's your job to get your people across the river, not pick fights with me, Tallemach!' he snapped.

'They'll be lucky to get across the river at all,' Tallemach snapped back.

'I think they'll do it,' Heathfield said. 'Given the right leadership!'

Tallemach exploded. 'Are you suggesting they're *not* getting the right leadership?'

In fact, that very thing had crossed Heathfield's mind but he realised he'd gone too far and he hastily withdrew. 'Not at all,' he said coldly. 'I was merely suggesting that it looks as if it's going to be a difficult sort of show and it's a case of make do and mend.'

'Make do and mend *what?*' Tallemach demanded. 'We've nothing to mend! We've got the wrong lorries, the wrong road, not enough boats, and as far as I can make out, no mortar bombs and hand grenades!'

'Is Yuell still going on about that?' Heathfield said, trying to side-track.

'Yes, he is,' Tallemach snapped. 'And with good reason! Nobody can fight a battle without weapons.'

'Look – ' Heathfield was patient – 'they're on their way. I've been following them every inch of the route. Yuell made it very clear he was depending on them and I've tried to make sure he gets them. We can hardly be blamed for the rain and the wet road and the accident that threw the lorries into the ravine.'

'They should have been up long before then.'

'Where were we to get the lorries? Italy's been denuded of men, machines and guns, as you well know. You've just said yourself they're scarce. And now Army have set up their own crossing, and because they're higher up the scale than we are, they've grabbed most of what was going.'

'I still consider we've been badly let down.'

'Do you wish me to pass that on to the general?' Heathfield asked silkily.

He'd expected that with this mild threat Tallemach would withdraw, but Tallemach didn't.

'Yes,' he said. 'You can. And if you like to write it out for me, I'll sign it.'

five

Yuell had by now moved to Capodozzi where the Scammells had off-loaded the boats in a wood and the Engineers were assembling them.

They were a scow-type craft with a square stern and flat bottom, thirteen feet long and more than five feet wide. They weighed four hundred and ten pounds, and held twelve men and a crew of two. They were bulky and awkward to carry, and were normally transported to the river by truck. There were also some rubber craft but they were large, easily punctured, difficult to paddle, easy to capsize and hard to beach.

Yuell examined the boats carefully. The scows had canvas sides, held in place by wooden pegs, and in some cases the paddles were missing.

'They'll have to use their rifle butts,' he growled. 'Is this the lot?'

'All we've been given, sir,' the RASC sergeant in charge said. 'We were told the boats would have to be brought back for a second load.'

Yuell frowned. They couldn't hope to succeed if they were going to cross in penny numbers. With every crossing they made the chances of being hit increased.

'Is it possible to make rafts?' he asked.

'Sir –' the RASC sergeant was pointedly polite 'with respect, I reckon you've been here longer than I have but I've seen nothing to make rafts of. If you know of anything, I'd be glad...'

'Never mind, Sergeant,' Yuell said tiredly. 'You're quite right, of course. There is nothing. This place has long since been stripped bare of wood for fuel. Everybody's been so damned cold and so damned wet for so long.'

The actualities of war, the imponderables, were taking over: the narrow road from Capodozzi, the officer – whoever he was – who had said that it was fit to use, the loading of the boats on to Scammells instead of ordinary lorries, the accident to the grenades and mortar bombs, the absence of hot food, the unbelievable amount of rain that had fallen.

Yuell made his way to his jeep and headed back to San Bartolomeo where he ran into a traffic jam so appalling he had to get out and walk. Tanks supposed to be parked in an orchard, where there wasn't room for half of them, were struggling to get off the road and holding up the bridging material which in its turn was holding up the ammunition trucks trying to reach the guns. There was also a convoy of ambulances, brought in because fresh mines had been laid on both sides of the river adjoining the bridge. The Engineers were doing their best to lift them and clear the area; but they couldn't guarantee complete success, and casualties had in consequence to be anticipated. The whole scene was one of confusion, frustration and exploding tempers.

One thing was clear. Neither sufficient time nor thought had been given to the details of the operation. Despite the problem of the boats, Yuell began to feel glad that he and his men would be using the Capodozzi route. It would be a long trek in the darkness carrying their awkward loads, but the alternative of advancing along the road to the bridge would surely lead them into nothing short of complete chaos.

The German guns were already pecking away at the rear areas as the afternoon wore on. By the end of the day they were hammering steadily at all three routes to the river.

The Yellowjackets, he heard, had already suffered casualties in Foiano, and eventually a few long-range shells started dropping in and around Capodozzi and San Bartolomeo. Two or three lorries were hit and a few men were killed.

Then, waiting impatiently for his mortar bombs and grenades, Yuell was informed that a long-range stonk had wiped out the mule train as it had approached the town. Those mortar bombs and grenades that hadn't gone up to splatter the mules all over the countryside were now scattered among the bushes and trees and undergrowth. Groups of men were trying to collect and hurry them forward, but undoubtedly a lot of them were gone for good.

Yuell's lips were tight and his eyes hard as he went to see the colonel of the Baluchis, to try to scrounge grenades from him.

The Baluchis' officer wasn't very keen to hand over the small supply he already possessed. 'If the others don't come up,' he pointed out, 'my Baluchis'll be going in with nothing.'

'So will we,' Yuell said. 'And that won't be much help against untouched troops.'

In the end they agreed to share the grenades, which left neither of them satisfied, and as Yuell set off back to his headquarters the Baluchis' colonel went off to inspect the wreckage of the mule train which had been hit and see if he could salvage something from the mess himself.

As Yuell returned to his headquarters once more, the Engineer colonel was waiting to ask for his help.

'I need men,' he said.

'You can't have mine,' Yuell said briskly.

'Look –' the Engineer sounded worried – 'if I don't get my material down to the river in time *you're* going to be stranded on the other side without support. Whoever chose that road didn't give much thought to it. We can't dump material on the verges because they're mined. We're trying to clear them now, but it's getting dark and there are a lot of them, and if your chaps could assist by carrying, it'd help.'

'They'll be carrying boats down the track from Capodozzi in a few hours time.'

'Can't you at least spare a few to help us down the road from San Bartolomeo? We've improvised footbridges but we need help to get them to the river. I'll have men there to show what's to be done, and they'll stay to handle the guy lines, but we can't do anything unless someone helps carry the planking down. My lorries are already full of pontoons and Bailey panels.'

His mind already busy with problems, Yuell considered. He knew his men had to have the bridge the Engineers were going to throw across, and to have the bridge it seemed they would have to help to carry it to the river. An operation that called for many hours of careful planning seemed to have been conceived in haste, with complicated staff work so careless that the most elementary mistakes were now creating chaos even before zero hour. He did a bit of juggling with his plans.

'I can let you have half a company,' he said. 'Will that do?'

The Engineer nodded. 'Thanks. I could have done with more but I'm grateful. I'll try to get a few of the Indian muleteers as well.'

Yuell found Warley sitting in the ruined house where he had set up A Company headquarters, writing a letter to Graziella Vanvitelli. It wasn't easy to feel romantic sitting on an ammunition box with the rain dripping down his neck from the shattered roof, but Warley was managing surprisingly well. Somehow the situation seemed to call for warmth and tenderness, if only to combat the starkness of his surroundings. Love, he decided, was a sort of self-immolation and, though he'd thought himself in love before, this time it left him dizzy and for once he didn't care and was quite happy to be swept along by it.

'Mark, I'm sorry,' Yuell said, 'but the Engineers are in difficulties. They're short of men and I've said I'll lend them half a company to get their stuff down to the river. You'll have to move off earlier than expected.'

'Oh, charming, sir.' Warley folded up his writing materials. 'It all sounds as though everything's moving ahead very normally. As the Yanks say, "Situation normal, all fouled up." '

His very willingness made Yuell feel guilty. 'A Company will have to use the San Bartolomeo road after all,' he said. 'They'll have to jump off from near the broken bridge and pick up the other companies on the other side. You'll have to move off a couple of hours before everybody else with half your men. You'll not be carrying your boats, of course.'

Warley smiled. 'I trust not, sir. Not in addition to bridging material.'

Yuell wished Warley weren't quite so amicable. 'Tony Jago'll have to bring them down the Capodozzi road and along the bank to you. He'll also have to start before the rest, but he should have plenty of time to get organised before he takes the first wave across.'

'Sir, isn't he going to be fagged out? Hadn't I better go across with the first wave?'

'A good leader,' Yuell argued, 'isn't selected for heroics, but for his ability to organise. Jago's the man to take them across, with Deacon to follow up. For the moment, go and see the Engineers and find out what they want. Then get your people fed and watered, and move off. You might have to wait forward of the three-hundred-yard line on the San Bartolomeo road for Tony Jago. We can't risk him missing you. I'll just have to leave it to your judgement.'

'*Is* there anywhere to wait, sir?' Warley asked.

Yuell shrugged. 'Not much, I'm afraid.'

'Things seem to have got a bit out of control, sir, don't they?'

'I'm afraid they have,' Yuell admitted. 'It's nobody's fault, really.' Except, he thought, for a few of Heathfield's people at Division who'd been slack. 'It's the weather chiefly, and that new crossing Army have planned further north. They've collared all the equipment and we're just having to manage with what's left.'

Warley's men were bored, fed up and far from home, and when he explained what he wanted to Farnsworth, the CSM frowned. Warley knew exactly what he was thinking. Some actions went right from the start. Some never went right at all, and this seemed to be one of the latter.

As they assembled on the San Bartolomeo road among the sweating Engineers, behind them the Yeomanry's tanks began to move. The whole area was a bedlam of noise, the sound of dropped hatches, the drum of the rain on canvas. Bundles, camouflage nets and bivouacs lashed to turret sides and engine decks softened the outlines of the great vehicles. Though they were Territorials – unpaid, Saturday-afternoon soldiers – they'd always been dead keen, with a history dating back to the days of the Napoleonic Wars. An apocryphal story about them was that when they'd been given their first tank, they'd applied to it the same zeal with which they'd once curry-combed and brushed their horses and had worked on it with emery cloth, metal polish and chamois leather so that in no time at all they'd transformed its mud-caked shape into a lump of glittering steel that blazed in the sunshine and blinded the stars.

Nevertheless, they were surprisingly good with their Churchill tanks, which everybody recognised at once from the design of the track. If Snow White were immediately recognisable by the seven dwarfs, a Churchill was recognisable by its eleven bogies, one advantage of which was that you could have a few shot off by the Germans and still be left with enough to support the tank.

Generators were throbbing and the whiff of petrol and exhaust fumes filled the air in the little orchard where they were deployed; the squadron sergeant was just completing the final adjustments to a carburettor while one of the crews finished a quick game of Brag. They seemed completely in control. They'd learned to move quickly and could cook a meal, pack their kit and be away in half an hour. And, since the early days of the desert when they'd more than once been chased away from their equipment by the Afrika Korps, they always made certain that there was at least the means for a brew-up, whatever else they left behind.

A truck that had been topping up their petrol tanks lurched away as commanders received the last details about routes and timings. Then the orders came.

'Okay, mount and start up.'

Crews scrambled into their seats, wriggling into the hulls' warm interiors out of the cold and the rain, signallers bent over radios, gunners crouched below the commanders' feet. Starters whined and the engines roared into life, the flicker of exhausts coming in the darkness to throw the next tank in line into silhouette. Pinpoint tail lights illuminated white-painted air deflectors as the Yeomanry began to move.

Warley watched them trying to get into position. Although Yuell had spread the newcomers through his battalion, there were too many inexperienced men in his company, among them Second-Lieutenant Taylor who even still showed an inclination to salute CSM Farnsworth.

If they were called on for the small extra effort that would produce results, would they fail because of inexperience?

s i x

As Warley's half-company began to move off down the tarmac road towards the broken bridge, they looked like hump-backed dwarfs threading in and out of the waiting lorries. Weighed down with timbers and girders and Bailey panels – as well as with Brens, Stens, rifles, two-inch mortars, Piats and radios – they slithered and splashed their way through the mud and puddles; grey and shadowy shapes in the mist that rose from the rain-saturated fields. In addition to everything else, they all carried ammunition but, though each rifle was loaded, there was no round in the breech in case an accidental discharge should alert the Germans. Bayonets were not fixed, but Warley intended they should be as soon as they reached the river bank.

The road seemed to be packed with vehicles and they couldn't understand why the Germans didn't shell them.

'The bastards are just waiting till we get nearer,' 000 Bawden said. 'So they have a better chance of hitting us.'

'Pity it ain't like cricket,' the other Bawden said. 'Then we could call it off. Rain stopped play.'

' "Il faut combattre," ' Fletcher-Smith said, ' "avec bon courage et gai visage." '

'What's that mean?' Hunters asked.

'That we should be going into battle with good courage and a cheerful face.'

'Up your kilt, you twit,' Hunters snorted. 'Think I enjoy contemplating having a nebelwerfer stonk drop on me?'

Warley listened to their grumbling with an affectionate warmth. Many of them had been with him for a long time now. He knew every one of the old hands, their faults, their failings, who was reliable and who wasn't. When they'd met for the first time, in a state of extreme wariness, his own nervousness had kept him too much on edge to make an idiot of himself, while they'd hidden their doubts about him behind blank faces. Thanks to Farnsworth, Warley had kept out of trouble. It had been possible in those days to conduct a whole conversation with Farnsworth answering nothing else but 'Sir!' though the wealth of meaning he could put into the word had always made it clear just what he felt.

In the end, because Warley had been willing to learn, he had won a good friend who'd been a help to him in his inexperience. How much they'd both succeeded in what they were trying to do had been shown by an incident in Bardia when, on pay day, Warley had failed to secure the fastening of the bag containing the money and it had flown open, scattering notes to the wind. Yuell had given him a hard look when he'd reported the disaster, informed him that the losses would have to be made up out of his own pay, and wished him luck. Within an hour, almost every note had been handed in – greasy little balls clasped in the same dirty hands that would shortly be held out to receive them back. Warley had felt close to tears.

Yet it was his job now to lead these men across the river, knowing perfectly well that some of them would not return. Every time orders for battle were issued, it was implicit in them that some of the men trying to carry them out would very likely soon be dead.

In the growing darkness, he could hear Syzling whining and the shrill indignation of Lieutenant Deacon. It probably wore Deacon down, but at least it was good for the morale of the rest of the Company.

The poor bastards belonged to an unlucky generation. Civilisation, Huxley had said, depended on the patience of the poor, but some of these men had been asked to endure too much. The older ones among them had spent their childhood suffering the shortages of the First War and, after putting up with the Depression of the Thirties, with unemployment, the means test and the half-witted antics of mindless politicians, they were now in another war which those same politicians had made – and almost lost for them before they'd even started. It hadn't been much of a life, when you considered it; yet now, soaked, tired, cold, deprived of hot food, despite their grumbling they showed no sign of faltering.

Plodding through the rain, he wondered how much longer the struggle for Cassino would go on. In the whole of Italy, perhaps no name implied so much sorrow. After it was all over, no doubt the histories would say it began that day in January when the Americans made their first unsuccessful crossing of the Rapido, and that it had ended on the day when the monastery was in Allied hands. To a man involved in the event, however, it was merely one more heave in the struggle and the day any battle started was the day when a mortar bomb killed a friend; its end came when they carried him from the field on a stretcher or stuck him in a hole and covered him with earth.

By this time the boats were all assembled or inflated, and had been laid out in lines among the trees near Capodozzi. As Yuell's men fell in alongside them, they were shivering with the cold and damp and looking curiously tall in the grey haze. Because they had to carry the boats themselves, they'd had to turn out much earlier than expected and start off down the road from Capodozzi before full dark. Beyond the three-hundred-yard line they were facing the prospect of another long haul when the whistles went, while Captain

Jago's men faced an even longer one to the broken bridge where the rest of Warley's men would be waiting. As he watched them, Yuell knew they were angry – not with him, but with the staff who hadn't taken enough care.

While he waited for the order to move off, he was called to the telephone. It was Tallemach. 'I understand the Yellowjackets are ready,' he said. 'Are you?'

'As far as bad weather and bad luck have let us be, sir. We can go.'

'Good. I'll be in touch with you all the time. I only phoned to give you my best wishes.' Yuell was about to put the phone down when Tallemach spoke again. 'I have to confess I'm a bit worried,' he said. 'I've learned that they got a second mule string going with what's left of the grenades and mortar bombs but some idiot sent it down the wrong road. I'll do my best, though, Edward, I promise you. I know you need them and I'll get them to you so that the follow-up wave can take them across.'

His words didn't encourage Yuell. He was already affected by the tenseness and uneasiness of his men. How the Yellowjackets were faring he didn't know, but he could only assume that their problems had been much the same as his own. They would soon find out when they linked up on the other side of the river.

He glanced at his watch. It was time to go. He hoped that by this time Warley's company were approaching their position and were not too exhausted.

'All right,' he said to Peddy. 'We'd better be off.'

It was a quiet way of starting but it was typical of Yuell not to make a fuss. He suspected his men preferred it that way. They didn't like dramatic leaders given to vivid gestures, any more than they liked signs of uncertainty. The British soldier was different from any other soldier in the world. American officers liked to put on a show of toughness and the French a spirited performance of elan, dash, panache, whatever you chose to call it. Most of the Germans he'd seen tried to appear efficient and ruthless, while the Poles believed in tempestuousness, as though, defeated in their own land, they had to prove they'd not lost their honour. The Italians were merely apologetic and lacking in backbone. The sort of officer the British soldier liked best was quiet, unassuming, able occasionally to address his men by their first names without losing their respect. They tended to puzzle the officers of other armies because, all too often, those who were most professional chose to appear thoroughly lacking in know-how.

The tanks were edging forward now, ready to take up their positions on the strips of wire matting which had been laid in loops like railway sidings in the fields that the Engineers had cleared of mines, so they could run on at one end and off again at the other as soon as the Sappers had completed their Class 40 Bailey bridge. They had still not emerged from the trees behind San Bartolomeo, waiting for the men who were to lead them to the matting with shaded lamps. As soon as the infantry were across, it was expected they would be able to support the artillery with their guns until the time came to move.

Behind the tanks, the artillery waited. It was their job to drop shells on the known German positions overlooking what would be the bridgehead and to ring the area with a curtain of high explosive to prevent counter-attacks. A Very light from the opposite side would be the signal for them to lift their fire to the German positions higher up the slopes.

From his observation post, Brigadier Tallemach was staring across the river. Directly opposite the end of the San Bartolomeo road, beyond the railway line and the road to Rome, flat ground ran inland to an escarpment which would provide some protection. Beyond this was a winding road, already torn by artillery fire. Above it, a further half-mile back, stood San Eusebio with its heavily scarred church tower. The church itself was a wreck, a mere skeleton in which Mass was now said beneath the open sky. They'd had to shell it because they suspected the Germans were using it as an artillery observation post. Even now they couldn't be quite sure that the Germans weren't still using what little was left of it; especially the tower which tottered precariously but had so far defied all their efforts to bring it down.

'Somebody,' Tallemach muttered to himself, 'has worked out a shocker for us.'

He didn't even like the width of the river. The first German positions, low down on the slopes, were not much higher than the bank and, as the gunners had suggested, it was going to be hellishly difficult with the low trajectory for the artillery to hit them without knocking out their own infantry.

Yuell's men were picking up the boats now and setting off down the dirt road to the site of the old ferry, which the constant rain had reduced to a morass of glutinous grey mud. In the growing dusk a cold and heavy mist rising from the Liri cast a silver-grey veil over everything with visibility near to zero. Not being able to see what was happening ahead hindered their progress, but at the same time gave them the advantage of being invisible to the Germans sitting up above them on the far side of the river.

For the first two or three hundred yards they moved in a silence broken only by the muttered grumbling of men finding the boats surprisingly awkward to carry; especially when loaded down with equipment, weapons and ammunition, which continually slipped from position and trapped fingers that were already numb with cold.

'I bet the bastards can see us,' someone said hoarsely.

'They can probably also 'ear you,' a sergeant rapped back. 'The way you rattle on.'

Complete darkness seemed to come suddenly. They thanked God for it because now the Germans couldn't pinpoint them even if the mist lifted. But they all knew that earlier on they must have been observed forming up in and around San Bartolomeo, Capodozzi and Foiano, and they waited tensely for the first horrific stonk from the German guns; at the same time deeply conscious of the unseen presence up ahead of Monte Cassino rearing up into the night, dark and ominous.

Standing among the trees just outside San Bartolomeo, Brigadier Tallemach had watched them go. Behind him, the little town was a turmoil of snorting vehicles that choked the narrow streets. He was unhappy at the way things were working out. The plan had been altered so often to suit the changing circumstances, he knew only at second-hand what Rankin's 9th Indian Brigade was intending to do. It was always a help to understand what the commander of the flanking or supporting formation was up to and why. It was also elementary that such details as boundaries, lateral communication, artillery support, and siting of headquarters should be co-ordinated, but he seemed to be remarkably ill-informed on all these matters. Rankin was always inclined to rush things, and his brigade was still on the reverse side of the mountains, because there was no room in the villages on this side and any attempt to move them up would have left them in full view of the Germans.

There was little he could do now but wait. He wished he could simply go to sleep or have a drink or something. He'd heard that Monty slept like a baby the night before an attack, confident that all that had to be done had been done and there was nothing else to worry about.

When he reached his headquarters, the canvas on the tents was sagging under the weight of their own dampness. The air seemed heavy and suffocating with moisture. To his surprise, Brigadier Rankin was waiting for him, a burly, crimson-cheeked man with a habit of stooping slightly so that he seemed permanently about to rush head-down at something. He was a Yorkshireman, proud of a northern forthrightness which Tallemach preferred to call plain rudeness.

'I've just learned that we're going to lose half our artillery just when the bloody battle's beginning to be interesting,' Rankin said.

'So have I,' Tallemach acknowledged. 'They want it for the crossing further downstream.'

'For God's sake, we can't hold ground across the river without full artillery backing!'

'I objected.'

'And – ?'

'They said that if I wouldn't do it, they'd find someone who would – meaning you, I suppose.'

'Surely you objected strongly?'

'You're very welcome to try again,' Tallemach said sharply. 'After all, you're to pass through us, so you'll need them as much as we do; and you can be much ruder than I can.'

Rankin gave him a sour look and reached for the telephone. He appeared to be getting short shrift, so Tallemach left him to it and went out into the rain to see how things were going. The darkness was still full of the sound of engines, and now the Engineers were moving forward. Behind them the tanks lurched nearer and he saw the vast bulk of a Churchill sidling forward between the ruined houses, the snout of its gun probing ahead like the antenna of some great insect. There appeared to be no hold-up and Tallemach went back to his headquarters. Rankin was staring at the telephone like a bewildered bull that had just butted its head against an immovable object.

'The bastards aren't playing,' he said.

'They didn't with me either,' Tallemach pointed out dryly.

Rankin scowled. 'We're just buggering about like a lot of dogs round a lamp post,' he complained. 'Waiting to see who'll be the first to lift his leg. It's nothing but a game of military suck-it-and-see.'

He was still resentful as they pored over the map, exchanging views while Tallemach pointed out the positions they hoped to hold. Rankin seemed subdued, which made Tallemach suspect he'd been given a flea in his ear and told to get on with it without arguing, and they managed to sort things out without rancour.

When Rankin had gone, Tallemach lit a cigarette and, staring at the map, drew a notebook towards him. It seemed a good idea to think a little ahead, something he'd always been good at. This attack he'd been thrust into had been set up too quickly and it made sense to provide for things going wrong.

He pulled up a chair and sat down. It was going to be damn difficult without air force support, but they'd done things before without the RAF and he supposed they'd have to do it again this time. He was thinking that they'd been badly let down when his brigade major appeared alongside him with a signal.

'I'm sorry, sir,' he said. 'Very sorry.'

Tallemach looked up. 'Sorry? What for?'

The brigade major said nothing but his eyes went to the signal. Tallemach stared at him for a second. Then his eyes dropped to the flimsy, wondering what it was. It was addressed to him and it had been routed through Division and had come originally from the RAF.

'Regret to inform you that your son, Flight-Lieutenant R. M. A. Tallemach, DFC, has been reported missing, believed killed, from operations over the Ruhr.'

For a long time, Tallemach stared at it, disbelieving. Then gradually it sank in. He looked again at the date of the operation. It was three weeks ago, so there could be little doubt. If his son had survived, by this time the International Red Cross would surely have discovered it.

The brigade major quietly withdrew while Tallemach still sat staring at the signal, trying not to believe it, forcing himself not to believe it. It wasn't possible! It couldn't have happened! Not both his sons within three months of each other!

He gave a tremendous sigh and pushed the signal to one side. He had a job to do. The war was still going on and he was responsible for the lives of a lot of men. Indulging his personal grief was not part of the job of commanding.

He looked at the map again and reached for his pencil. But the map suddenly made no sense and he couldn't make his mind work.

On the slopes behind San Bartolomeo, 19th Division Artillery had at last got into position, and the adjutant of the 215th Field Artillery, which was to start the barrage, sat in his command post vehicle surrounded by maps and the apparatus of calculation and power, watching the fingers of his watch.

He had twenty-four 25-pounder guns under his control and every weapon in the two divisions was to take its lead from him in a vast weight of destruction and terror. His network of radio and telephonic communications covered the whole front, backwards to the senior artillery officer at divisional headquarters and sideways to the other artillery regiments.

Watching the front covered by the North Yorkshires, his forward observation officer was reporting targets he'd already pinpointed. There weren't as many as he would have wished because the Germans had gone to enormous trouble to conceal their strongpoints, but for the moment his chief concern was the eight guns of C Battery which, in direct support of the Yorkshires, lay concealed beneath nets in an irregular line on the forward slopes of the hills, the great weapons twenty-five yards apart, their cartridges and shells stacked within reach. Nearby, lorries and limbers stood ready to dash forward and hook up the guns as soon as their task was finished the next evening.

The hands of the adjutant's watch moved closer to zero hour.

'Stand by,' he said quietly.

'Take post!'

The gun crews jumped into position, one man in the layer's seat, the ammunition numbers behind the breech, another man holding a handspike for traversing, his free hand in the air to notify the troop officer he was ready.

'Battery target, stonk,' the troop commander said. HE 177. Charge 3. Angle of sight, 15 minutes. Elevation, zero 17 degrees, 20 minutes. Stand by to fire...'

As the guns announced their readiness, the minutes dragged slowly by.

In the cellar of the house on the outskirts of San Eusebio, Captain Reis glanced at his map and wondered what was coming. Something certainly was. On the Russian front he'd learned a great deal about defensive fighting, the one thing these days that occupied the German army above all else. Transport was at a premium and the possibility of any help from the Luftwaffe had long since been written off.

His orders had contained a trenchant note of warning. 'A special degree of alertness is ordered. The enemy is expected to attack the San Eusebio position within forty-eight hours and no one should allow himself to relax.'

He seemed to have been living in the cellar for days, eating the sausage and black bread and drinking the ersatz coffee which made up his meals. He was aware of a suffocating feeling of helplessness and was even anxious to escape. But he knew he couldn't. His orders were as unequivocal as Yuell's. 'You will hold San Eusebio.' They were as simple as that and allowed no variations.

The telephone buzzed and he lifted the receiver to hear Lieutenant Thiergartner on the other end.

'Further to my earlier report of 1600 hours, another group of tanks observed at the end of the San Bartolomeo road. Also gathering of heavy vehicles, which could be carrying bridging material.'

'That's the second lot we've seen,' Reis said. 'There's obviously something coming.'

He considered for a moment. There were sufficient weapons and ammunition for immediate needs stored by the weapon pits and he could call on armour if need be. Though it was within reach, however, it could hardly manoeuvre in numbers on the steep slopes and rocky valleys round San Eusebio.

He was tied to a static defence and he was relying largely on mines, machine-guns, two anti-tank guns, two self-propelled guns which he'd hidden in a valley behind the village, and one or two old tanks he'd been given which had been sunk in the cellars of houses with only their guns protruding.

'Think they're aiming at any particular spot, Thiergartner?' he asked.

'There appear to be three approach routes, Herr Hauptmann,' Thiergartner replied. 'One from Foiano to Castelgrande, one from Capodozzi to the old ferry and one from San Bartolomeo to the bridge.'

'How about you? Are you all right?'

'But, of course, Herr Hauptmann.'

Thiergartner sounded too damned cheerful to be true, Reis decided.

He grunted and replaced the receiver. As he did so, 215th Field Artillery's first shell arrived. It removed the roof of the house above him, knocked down the chimney stack and, shaking the cellar to its foundations, filled the place with black soot and grey plaster.

Reis scrambled free, spitting out dust. He was lucky. The exits might be blocked, but he was still alive, and he jumped to the telephone again and called Thiergartner.

'Here we go, Thiergartner!' he said.

'We're ready, Herr Hauptmann.'

'By God,' Reis shouted above the growing din. 'I hope you are!'

PART THREE

The Sharp End

'The front line is a very small club.'
Lt Gen Sir Brian Horrocks

o n e

The crash in the darkness, the scream and then the sudden silence, was shattering in the shock it delivered.

Warley's company were approaching the river, still struggling under the weight of the Engineers' timbers and Bailey panels, when they heard the mine explode.

Because of the need for the bridging material and the dwindling time at their disposal, Warley had long since decided, as Yuell had anticipated, to press beyond the three-hundred-yard start line the artillery's worn guns had necessitated, considering it wiser to risk an odd 'short' to make sure they were in position at the right moment. Jago's men, working along the bank with their boats, were taking a chance and Warley had felt that he must too. But down here, near the river, the white tapes that had been laid to show where mines had been cleared seemed to have been removed and the thought that was in Warley's mind was that this could well have been done by a German patrol the night before.

There was a cry of 'Stretcher bearers!' behind them, and all movement down the long straight road stopped dead until everyone knew exactly where it was safe to go. Then the word came down to them as they huddled, heads bent against the rain.

'Lorry. Tried to pull off the road because of a jam. It got bogged down on the verge and when the driver got out to see what could be done, he trod on a mine.'

They all drew breath again, lifting their heads, spitting away the rain that gathered on their lips. As if to indicate how futile their battle was compared with the vastness of nature, it had started to come down in torrents, dripping off the ends of their gas capes, their eyebrows and chins; off the weapons and equipment they carried, and the planking and Bailey panels they struggled with. Occasionally, when a shaded light appeared in someone's hands, it picked out the wavering lines of water and made the drops running down the timbers and girders sparkle as they moved. Heavy feet splashed and shuffled through the puddles.

'Lord,' 000 Bawden lifted his face to the sky – 'I know we have to have rain now and then, but this is bloody ridiculous!'

They were just about to move off again when they heard a pop from the other side of the river.

'Mortar!'

They waited in agony for the first bomb to land. The crash came from up ahead near the river bank. Immediately there was another and another and another.

'Oh, Christ,' Rich said in his dark, ghoul's voice. 'This is goin' to be bloody marvellous.'

Warley moved among them, pushing at them, urging them forward.

'Go on,' he kept saying. 'Don't stop. The sooner we're down there, the sooner we can dump this lot and start thinking of finding shelter.'

'And the nearer we'll be then to them bloody mortar bombs,' 766 Bawden said.

'More like the nearer, my God, to Thee,' his namesake added.

The guns on the slopes behind San Bartolomeo were hammering away at full bore now and, looking back, Warley could see the flashes. So far, the Germans had not retaliated with counter-fire – nothing more than light and heavy machine-guns which were spraying the river bank and the roads that led back into the hills.

Then, as he watched, he saw the mist on the hillside opposite glow with a white light as the German batteries finally opened fire. Shells began to fall on the flats, smashing equipment and killing men. Engineers, lorry drivers and signallers began to scatter for cover, dropping what they were carrying. Some of them stumbled into undiscovered mines, and the tapes which had been so carefully laid were trampled into the mud or dragged out of position by muddy boots. One or two of the more fainthearted of Warley's men disappeared, and it was hopeless to think of trying to round them up because the mist and rain concealed them.

Suddenly the road was scattered with bodies and abandoned bridging material. All round Warley the darkness was filled with curses as men fought to keep their feet on the slippery mud and avoid crashing into Engineers who, occupied with the task of preparing to throw a bridge across the river, struggled with wire hawsers, tackles, ropes, anchors and pontoons. Then another flurry of shells landed in the fields nearby, exploding to fling mud, water and earth in a filthy slash across the road.

'Come here often?' one of the Engineers asked sourly.

'Only Sat'day nights mate,' Parkin responded no less bitterly. 'The dancin's better.'

News and rumour began to trickle back. Some of the bridging material dumped along the road had been damaged beyond use by the shells, and out of the four planned footbridges one had already been destroyed by mines and another found to be defective.

'And there's a bloody good chance,' an Engineer officer said, 'that this bloody shelling will polish off the other two before we get 'em erected.'

Sweating now despite the cold and the rain, they passed a little blockhouse which had once been German. Then a mule went by, carrying two wounded Engineers, their trousers glistening with fresh blood. Farther on there were more casualties resting by the side of the road.

There was another long halt. Then, from ahead, there were urgent calls to get a move on as though something had gone wrong. The assault area, now they were approaching it, seemed to be right on top of the German positions. There was an eight-mile-an-hour current swirling past and Warley planned, as soon as the boats arrived, not to wait but to rush them straight down the bank and into the water. He was suddenly appalled at the idea. The tanks were too far away to give their support with their guns, while he and his men would be far too close for the artillery to keep the Germans' heads down. The very thought of it put the fear of God into him.

When at last they were able to rid themselves of the bridging material, one of the Engineers looked quizzically at Warley. 'Your men ever done this job before?' he asked.

'No,' Warley said angrily. 'They're getting on-the-spot training.'

As they left the road and started looking for shelter, two men, a corporal and a private, appeared out of the darkness carrying what looked like a theatrical property basket.

'North Yorkshires, sir?' the corporal asked.

'Yes,' Warley said. 'What's that?'

'Told to report to you, sir. Corporal Carter. Pigeons. We've got half a dozen in here. They're going across with you.'

Warley managed a smile. 'Poor little buggers,' he said. 'I hope they can swim.'

Now they were below the level of the road, Warley felt a small breeze touching the side of his cheek, and realised that the mist which had been helping to hide them was dispersing. In the flash of shells, he could see it breaking into wisps and, beyond it, the dark shape of the opposite bank. A machine-gun opened up and slots of light shot out of the blackness directly towards them. In the darkness a man cried out, and someone started swearing steadily in a low voice that could nonetheless be heard above the lorry engines. Never repeating itself, the voice let forth a vicious stream of oaths and abuse directed not against the Germans but against the people sitting in offices who had got them into this mess.

They were hiding along the bank now. It varied in height and they were crouching behind little mounds covered with rough marram-like grass where the river had eaten into the soil. Their shelter wasn't more than three or four feet deep at any point and they had to cower on the mud, heads down, slithering and slipping on the black slime until they were all soaked and filthy.

'Pity I wasn't born a mule,' Martindale said bitterly.

'Never mind mules, mate,' Parkin retorted. 'You remember what your mum said when you joined up and don't get your feet wet.'

'Oh, bloody funny,' Martindale said. He was kneeling in six inches of water and smoking his pipe upside-down to keep the rain out.

They heard the sudden hysterical screech of a Schmeisser and the steady thump of an answering Bren, then the low burrp of an MG42, and all the time a sizzling noise as giant shells sped swiftly above them to burst ahead with a searing flash and a clap of thunder. The German artillery was going full throttle now, and they heard a lorry blow up behind them. There was a low 'whump', and the night was lit by a towering flower of flame. Against its yellow glow, they could see figures moving backwards and forwards, running for shelter. A man began to scream in the darkness again and again, as though he didn't know what to do with himself or how to hold back his agony.

'For Christ's sake,' Hunters muttered between gritted teeth, 'shut the bastard up, somebody!'

There was no sympathy for the injured man, only a selfish fear for their own safety that showed itself as hatred for the man who was causing the noise. Then, as they listened, the cries slowly dwindled and finally died.

It left them shaken, and almost at once the heavy counter-barrage from the opposite side of the river shifted and the shells began to whack down on the road. As Yuell had predicted, the Germans didn't have to aim. They had a battery opposite the end of the road and all they had to do was raise or lower their sights.

Another lorry went up with a crash, and vehicles were trying to back away out of the holocaust. Other shells began falling alongside the dirt road from Capodozzi to the disused ferry. With their usual efficiency, the Germans hadn't overlooked that one either.

Warley tried to keep in contact with each group of huddled men. He found it difficult because the shelling had scattered them into the darkness. But as far as he could make out, almost all of them were still there, and the shrill voice of Lieutenant Deacon, nagging at Private Syzling to get his head down, even took on curiously reassuring quality.

Corporal Carter, the pigeon handler, was sprawling next to him with his basket of birds, the mud smeared across his face.

'They all right?' Warley asked.

'Yes, sir,' Carter said. 'They don't like the water though. It's coming through the bottom of the basket. They're nervous little things, sir, and I always think it's a bit hard taking 'em into a battle.'

Warley moved on, talking to his men, making sure they knew exactly what to do. 'As soon as the boats arrive,' he kept shouting above the racket, 'get them down to the water's edge. You'll be safer down there. They won't be able to see you against the blackness of the bank. And no taking off in ones and twos. The first wave's got to arrive on the other side all together.'

He had a feeling that, however hard they tried to avoid it, the second wave would be ragged because boats would have been holed by bullets and there would probably be wounded or dead to remove from them before their second crossing. God alone knew what the third wave would be like.

The artillery was laying a smoke screen now, and to Warley there seemed too damned much of it. It was blowing back towards them, and the artificial haze produced by the oil droplets choked the soldiers and was beginning to handicap the Engineers and cause confusion on their own side of the river.

For a moment, he thought despairingly of Graziella Vanvitelli. He had no idea where the thought came from because she certainly didn't belong in the madhouse that the river bank had become, but it suddenly occurred to him that Creation must be crazy when it could separate two people who were obviously made for each other, just because a cabal of semi-lunatics in Berlin wanted to rule the world. He wondered why he was so certain they were intended for each other and even whether there really was a God. He'd noticed all along that it was always the best, the bravest, the most level-headed, the most kind who seemed to be killed, while the shits lived on to a ripe old age, full of honour and loaded with rewards. He'd heard his father going on about the same thing after the last war, and so far in this one he saw no reason to disagree with him. Perhaps the ones who died were merely stupid. Certainly the grass grew as green over the graves of the shits as it did over the graves of the gallant and good.

He glanced about him, wondering what his men were thinking but the only two he could see were Corporal Gask and Henry White on either side of him. and they were no help whatsoever. Gask's pale bony face was totally unemotional, as if he were waiting to cross a busy road at a rush hour. White's leathery visage was equally blank, his jaws moving all the time like a cow ruminating over its cud. The born soldier and the experienced soldier. They weren't the ones he was worried about.

He looked at his watch. They were going to be late starting, and he called up the artillery on the radio and asked them to continue the preparatory barrage for another ten minutes. Nearby, cursing Engineer officers were managing to put together a complete footbridge from the pieces of two damaged ones and a defective one.

'You'll have to hang on,' one of them told Warley. 'It won't be open for foot traffic for some time.'

As the last of the smoke curled away, the first of the boats arrived, carried by Engineers and men from the other half of A Company. They had found the struggle along the bank a nightmare. Already two boats had been lost. A man trying to side-step a bush had trodden on a mine just off the footpath, and the boat had slipped from the hands of the others as they'd rushed to help him, and been swept away by the current; a second had been hit by bullets and holed. They were staggering and stumbling, and one of them was soaked to the waist as though at some point he'd slid from the bank into the water.

'There you are,' he snarled as he dropped his load. And you're fucking welcome to it!'

Jago appeared out of the darkness and started barking at them. 'Come on, then, let's have you! Don't hang about! We've got things to do!'

Out of sight in the shadows, someone told him to get stuffed and Warley saw at once that the men were exhausted to the point of rage and were in no state to set about crossing the river.

'Hold it, Tony,' he said. 'These chaps are whacked. Give them a chance to get their breath back. Deacon, are you ready?'

'Yes, I'm ready.'

'Right, then get yourself across! Find somewhere to dig in and wait until Tony Jago arrives. We'll have the two waves together for the push up the slopes.'

By this time, the road was a scene of confusion in the darkness and smoke. Overhead shells raced, the 25-pounders sounding as if someone was tearing a curtain, the 4.5s and 5.5s churning through the air like express trains. The noise grew harsher, reminding Warley of the noise the iron shutters on Parisian bars made when they were dragged down at night. He glanced up, half expecting to see the sky streaked with rocket trails, and was surprised, as he always was, to find that the barrage was invisible.

It was no longer a matter of maps and charts, he thought, but of flesh and blood – *his* flesh and blood, and the flesh and blood of his men.

With one eye on his watch, Warley kept the other on the far bank. The two companies at the end of the track from Capodozzi must have already started. As the extra minutes he'd requested drew to a close, against the deafening sound of the barrage, he yelled 'Go!' and they all grabbed the boats and started to drag them down to the mud.

Immediately, the launching assumed the proportions of a disaster. Boats put into shallow water bogged down at once and refused to budge, and Deacon started screaming frustratedly.

'Get out!' he yelled. 'Get out! You'll have to wade further out! Syzling, get out of that bloody boat!'

Struggling and splashing in the shallows, they carried the boats into deeper water and pushed them out again. Once more, Syzling climbed aboard and sat down on the starboard side. But when two other men joined him, the boat upended and the river began to pour in. In no time, it was on the bottom again and they were waist-deep in water.

Warley appeared among them. Having a boat of his own at Bridlington, he knew something about them, which was more than his ham-fisted clodhoppers from the hills did. Some of them even came from the south-west tip of the county, which was about as far as you could get from the sea in England, and they had no experience whatsoever. One boat, caught by the current, went wandering off with only three signallers on board, paying out the wire of the field telephone, and Deacon began to shout at them to bring it back. But as the signallers dug at the water with their rifle butts, the boat merely swirled round in helpless circles, and continued to drift downstream until it was lost in the darkness. Another boat, held steady until everybody was aboard, simply sank under them. There were a dozen splinter holes in it.

The confusion was appalling. Watching with dilated eyes as his boat vanished beneath him, 766 Bawden gulped and cried out, 'I can't swim.'

As he found himself struggling in the water, 000 Bawden grabbed him by the collar and hauled him towards the bank. Scrambling to safety, they looked round for other transport. Such was the discipline instilled in them, it didn't occur to them for a moment that they'd done all they could. They found Warley pushing off another boat and climbed in. Before they knew where they were, they were in midstream again, terrified it too would sink and they would drown under the weight of their equipment.

In those boats which were under way, men tried to row with paddles, rifle butts and hands. Already wet through from the rain and liberally daubed with mud, the spray from the slashing paddles and rifle butts now drenched them again, so that they crouched with heads down as if battling their way through sleet. Only Gask sat upright – bolt upright – as if he were riding on a Number 11 bus and didn't expect any problems.

They were half-way across when the smoke began to break up and the Germans found them. The gun-fire was intense and concentrated, mostly heavy machine-guns and mortars, coming from the slopes just above the bridge. Glancing back, 000 Bawden saw that the Engineers were already in position on the stonework, apparently indifferent to the fire, dragging up girders and planks to throw across the broken span. He felt like a sitting duck, and was just turning to say so to 766 Bawden, sitting next to him, when he saw his head whipped off by a shell. Spattered with blood and brains, he leaned over the side of the boat, weak and sick with terror.

From the shore, Warley watched the shambles in silence. It was horrifying to see the unprotected boats driving on in a sidling movement against the stream towards the other side. Huge spouts of spray kept shooting up as shells exploded, and the small arms fire churned the water until it looked as if it were boiling. The flames were catching the movement of the river, so that it seemed alive with copper-coloured lights. Then he saw a shell score a direct hit on a boat, and when the smoke had cleared he could see nothing but one arm – one arm reaching up out of the water, black and stark against a patch of flame-tinted river, with clawing fingers reaching for help that didn't come.

Shrapnel was ripping into the little flotilla. 'For Christ's sake,' someone screamed from the near bank. 'Somebody direct those bloody guns on to the Germans!'

But the shells were German. The British artillery and the tank gunners had had to stop, now that the boats were approaching the opposite shore, for fear of hitting their own men who could see the Germans standing up to aim at them, an officer in a steel helmet directing the fire.

In Hunters' boat they were crouching down, keeping their heads as low as possible, aware that the frail canvas sides gave them no protection whatsoever. Then the Engineer at the rudder touched Hunters' arm. 'Take the tiller, mate,' he said, and flopped forward into Hunters' arms. Pushing him aside, Hunters reached over him, trying to steer by staring over his shoulder, his backside in the air towards the German lines.

'I must be the only bloody man in the world who's crossed the Liri on all fours backwards,' he thought wildly.

Up in the bow, Corporal Carter, clutching his basket of pigeons, was trying to direct him, but a shell exploded in the water nearby and Hunters felt something hit him in the side. For a moment, the boat swirled round, out of control; then, uncertain whether he were badly injured or not, dying or not, Hunters managed to grab the tiller again and steer towards the bank.

A lifting breeze had blown the remains of the smoke screen to shreds of white mist, and the Germans could now see well enough in the glare of the flames to turn their attention to individual boats. Trying to avoid the fire, Hunters steered the boat in a circle. There was another crash, and he realised it too had been hit and was sinking. Amidships, a man was yelling at him something he couldn't understand, and as the boat vanished from under his feet he found himself standing in water no more than waist-deep and knew he'd reached the other side. Without waiting to see what had happened to his companions, and certain he was dying, he scrambled up the bank and cowered under a muddy tufted knoll that was being clipped by machine-gun fire. His uniform was soaked – he had no idea how much of it was water and how much blood – and all he could feel in his side was a numbness which turned into a sharp pain every time he moved.

As the boat had sunk, Corporal Carter, his Number Two vanished in the confusion, had grabbed his basket of pigeons and lifted it in his arms. He had no idea how he was supposed to swim with it but his job was to save the birds if he could. He was just about to forget the pigeons and think of himself when, like Hunters, he realised his feet were on the bottom and, holding the basket high above his head, he waded ashore, dripping water. As he looked up, another boat beached alongside him, every man in it dead but the man at the tiller. It was Corporal Gask, still blank-faced and unemotional, who yanked him from his seat and literally threw him into shelter.

As the tanks began to lay a fresh smoke screen, two more boats arrived. In one of them Deacon kicked at Syzling to get him on his feet, gave Puddephatt a shove which stirred him to life, and then began to climb up the bank, determined to do something even if it were wrong. Hunters crawled from his shelter to follow him, curiously exhilarated to find himself still alive. The pain in his side didn't seem to be bothering him much, so perhaps it was just a cracked rib and he hadn't been properly wounded at all. Somehow or other more boats were arriving all the time, and out of them more men were landing to follow Deacon.

Hunters had never been very fond of Lieutenant Deacon and his shrill voice, but he had to admit that at least he was no coward.

There were further casualties as they crossed the open ground, before reaching a small hollow where they flung themselves down and turned their weapons on the slopes just above. Behind them the river bank was now littered with dead and wounded men. Among them moved the stretcher bearers, trying to pull them into the shelter of the tufted knolls, stretching them out on the mud in the only places where it was safe from the flying metal.

From where he crouched on the opposite bank, Warley had been gathering his scattered group together. What was happening at the end of the Capodozzi track, he didn't know. He'd already had several of the waiting men wounded, but the German small arms fire was beginning to slacken a little, as if Deacon's weapons were beginning to take effect. Now that the Engineers had got their vehicles down to the river bank and were unloading them, the tanks had been able to follow up on to their little sidings of wire matting, and their fire was also helping the struggling infantry.

Nevertheless, he had a suspicion that everything possible had gone wrong. War was never easy, but battles had a feel about them and Warley had been in enough to know that this one was going to give them the horrors until their dying day.

The rain was still drifting down, thinner now, coming in grey waves that seemed to wander down out of the darkness and then turn into a coppery haze in the light of the flames; only to disappear in the smoke that was beginning to drift across the river again as the smoke shells from the tanks took effect. He could see the boats heading back now, sidling across the river like black water-bugs against the red-tinted ripples. Glancing about him to make sure his men were ready, his eyes fell on the strained face of Jago. He looked more worn out than Warley had ever seen him before.

'You all right?' he asked.

Jago had once been offered a job on the staff by an uncle of his who was a brigadier with Montgomery and had promised to do what he could for him. Feeling that no real man could sit at an office desk and push flags about over maps, Jago had turned the offer down but now, exhausted by the long struggle north from Sicily, he wished to God he'd accepted.

'Yes,' he managed. 'I'm fine.'

Warley didn't agree and made up his mind at once. 'Look, Tony,' he said. 'It looks to me as though this is the biggest balls-up since Hastings, and I think I ought to be across there to help Deacon; he seems to be doing very well. So I want you to stay and organise the final dribs and drabs. There are bound to be a few who'll hang back.'

Jago nodded, his face taut. Once – years ago, it seemed – he'd been fresh and had found in war some of the basic exhilaration of the hunt, the pitting of his own wits against other men's wits. But it had gone on too long and the winter had taken too much out of him.

By this time, the remaining boats were approaching the bank in a ragged wave. Most of them were way off course, and Warley saw at once that they were going to arrive a hundred yards further down. Calling to his men, he led them along the bank to meet them. The Engineers had already got girders across the broken span of the stone bridge, and he was staggered at the speed with which they'd worked. But at that moment another clutch of shells came down and, as the smoke cleared, he saw that the span beyond the one they were repairing had now collapsed.

A groan went up from the men around him but he tried to shut his ears to it. It wasn't his job to worry about the Engineers. He knew they wouldn't let them down if they could help it, and even now he could see a group of them lying flat on their faces at the far side of the partly repaired span and staring at the newly broken one, trying to decide if the pillars were still strong enough to support their work.

Watching from the other side, Captain Reis realised he had to move fast. The British seemed to have a foothold across the river and it was up to him to see that they were thrown back before they could enlarge it.

'Thiergartner,' he yelled into the telephone above the din. 'Can you see where they are?'

Thiergartner said nothing and Reis yelled again.

'You all right?'

Thiergartner's voice came at last. 'Yes, Herr Hauptmann,' he said uncertainly. 'I'm all right.'

'Then for God's sake, find out where they are! We're probably going to need help!'

'I'll do what I can, Herr Hauptmann.'

'Never mind "I'll do what I can." Your job's to feed me reports about what's going on. Above all, it's to hold that post. Understand?'

Thiergartner still sounded uncertain and, slamming the telephone down, Reis called Pulovski towards him. Writing out an order, he handed it over. If it were in writing, Thiergartner wouldn't be able to claim the right to use his own initiative. There was no such thing at that moment, and Reis was making sure that Thiergartner wasn't given the opportunity to back away.

'Take this down to Lieutenant Thiergartner,' he said. 'You know where he is?'

'Exactly, Herr Hauptmann.'

'Then be off with you. As soon as you've given it to him, come back here. Understand?'

'Jawohl, Herr Hauptmann.'

Pulovski glanced at the shells flashing on the plain below and seemed to hesitate. Reis gave him a shove and he began to move off.

'Not that way, you damned idiot!' Reis yelled as he drifted to the left. 'They're covering the road with their machine-guns. The other way. Down the front slope.'

As Pulovski vanished, Reis wondered again if he dared leave the defence of the river bank in Thiergartner's hands. He'd have liked to have gone down there himself but it was his job to stay where he was and co-ordinate the defence from a position where he could see everything that went on; from where, if it became necessary, he could easily retreat to the stronghold they'd constructed in San Eusebio.

Thiergartner had sounded distinctly shaky, and that quiet humour that had always seemed to support him appeared to have vanished. If there were the slightest hesitation in what he did, the British would be quick to take advantage of it because they were now as experienced in attack as the Germans were in defence and had developed a great gift for spotting the weakest points.

JOHN HARRIS

The Engineers were already pushing their Class 40 bridge out from the bank, floating out their pontoons, attaching the bows to the hawser they'd strung across and hauled taut with tackle, and throwing out anchors to hold the sterns in place. As they worked, more men hurried the Bailey panels forward and were bolting them together like a child's construction kit.

As the returning boats grounded on the mud, Warley blew his whistle and the men around him rose up from among the knolls and hillocks of earth, daubed with dirt, wet-through and half-frozen from the rain.

Among them he saw the medical officer and Father O'Mara.

'Not yet,' he shouted above the din. 'You come over with Tony Jago!'

The doctor smiled and shook his head, and O'Mara gave one of his expansive Irish gestures, waving cheerfully with his walking stick. He carried no weapons but he was loaded down like the commonest soldier with rations, medical supplies and even ammunition.

'Me eyes may be on the next world, my son,' he said, 'but I'm aware that it's the work of a man of God in this one to smite the ungodly.'

'But not to get yourself killed, Padre.'

O'Mara smiled. 'You miss the point of me belief, my son. That comes from not listening to the sermon in church.'

Though the German barrage had slackened a little, it was still churning up the mud on the river bank, and, going from boat to boat, upright in spite of the flailing fire, Warley made the men fall in properly on either side, knee-deep in the swirling water; then, while the boats were held securely in place, he made them climb in carefully, and had the last man push off. This time there were no sinkings through haste or lack of knowledge. After having survived one crossing, the men in charge had grown more careful.

The undergrowth and brambles along the bank were catching fire in places from the shelling, but the darkness and the rain made it impossible to see more than a few paces in front. As Warley moved across a stretch of shingle with Henry White, a shell exploded on the very spot where he'd been sheltering. Bowled over by the blast he saw White disappear in the other direction. As he scrambled up, he saw him on his feet but bent double, muttering curses, one hand to his mouth, the other with the fingertips pawing the ground.

'You all right, Henry?' he asked.

'No, sir,' White mumbled. 'I'm not. I've lost me fuckin' false teeth.'

Every bit of artillery on the German side was ranging in now, and Warley saw another boat capsize. Wounded men clung to the wreckage or tried to swim back to the near bank. With Warley in charge, however, there was no panic. One man, sole survivor from a sunken boat in the first wave, staggered ashore wearing nothing but a shirt and underwear. Somehow, he'd managed to divest himself of clothes and equipment, though he still clutched his rifle and wore his steel helmet.

'I got across, sir,' he grinned.

'Don't talk so bloody daft, man,' Warley said. 'You're still on the same side.'

There were a few men still crouching among the bushes and undergrowth. Jago moved among them, kicking them to life. 'Get going, you bastards,' he was yelling. 'You're needed! Get cracking!'

As he turned towards his boat, Warley fell over a group of bodies. What had happened to them and why they all came to be dead together he couldn't imagine. Then he saw men taking advantage of the darkness and confusion to dump the canvas identification panels they'd been given for the air force strike and he made them pick them up again, feeling that sometime, somewhere – even if it were only in the event that they had to retreat – they might be glad of them.

His own boat was the last to push off, and he huddled in the bow along with his signaller and the company runner. The river was jet black but it was caught here and there by sparkles of light. Overhead, tracer bullets flashed in streams. On his right, Warley could see the loom of the bridge with its empty span stark against the flames, Engineer officers standing, indifferent to the firing, on the edge of the newly-broken stonework.

Then a spatter of bullets stirred the water alongside them and the signaller's eyes dilated.

'Can't say I like this, sir,' he said.

'I'm not enjoying it much myself,' Warley admitted.

In midstream, the German fire seemed to lose them and they were able to make the last twenty yards to the other side without too much trouble. The boat grounded on the mud, and he was slapping at the shoulders of his men and following them as they bounded ashore, splashing and slithering their way up the bank to the footpath. They had drifted twenty or thirty yards further downstream from where Deacon had landed and one of the men, wandering off course a little, found himself in a minefield. There was a crash and a scream, then nothing.

'Keep going,' Warley yelled. 'Keep going! And bear left for Mr Deacon's group!'

Mortar bombs were coming down on them now, exploding by the water's edge, throwing up great gouts of mud from the shallows. But they were across. How many, Warley had no idea. But they were across.

They were across.

three

On the track from Capodozzi, Colonel Yuell stood in the drizzling rain staring towards the mountains beyond the river, identifiable only by the twinkling of lights that betrayed the positions of German guns on their slopes. What was happening to his men he had no idea because they'd hardly had time yet to get across and establish themselves.

Then Major Peddy called to him and, entering his command post, he saw that the second-in-command's face was grim.

'The Yellowjackets are in trouble,' Peddy said at once. 'They seem to have had a chaotic march down to the river. They had a lot of stragglers who took advantage of the smoke, and the guides lost their way and wandered into the minefields. Some of their rubber boats were holed by shell-fire and they thought the Engineers were bringing up replacements and waited. They also got into a sunken road near the crossing site, and that delayed them too.'

'Are they across?'

'Just. The Teds brought nebelwerfers down on them but they got one company across just after 2000 hours. They got up the banks but they came under accurate small arms fire from concealed posts, so close the artillery couldn't give 'em support. They're digging foxholes and they report hearing tank engines.'

Yuell glanced over his shoulder into the darkness, suspecting that the report might well fit his own men's crossing before the night was over. 'Go on,' he said.

'Heavy casualties. Mortars pinned them to the edge of the river. Some of the company officers killed or wounded were men who'd been given special jobs to do. They're yelling for help and want us to push on quickly to relieve them a little.'

'I wish to God we could,' Yuell said. 'Why the devil haven't we heard from Warley? Have you kept trying?'

'Yes, sir, I have.'

'Shells must have severed the telephone wires.' Yuell slapped at his leg with his walking stick and made up his mind.

'Get my jeep up,' he said. 'I'm going down to the river.'

'You'll probably have to walk,' Peddy pointed out. 'I gather the San Bartolomeo road's jammed with vehicles and the track from Capodozzi's under heavy fire now.'

'Very well,' Yuell said. 'I can always do that.' He frowned. 'I wonder why we haven't heard from them?'

The reason was simple. There wasn't a single working link. All the 'Eighteens' had been lost or damaged in the disasters of the crossing, and the field telephone line, unreeled as they'd advanced, seemed to have been cut by shellfire somewhere near the river. The regimental signallers, ordinary soldiers who got no extra pay and only crossed flags on their sleeves, had set off in pairs, with their knives and insulating tape, to find the break. Until it could be repaired they were out of touch. There wasn't even contact with other companies.

Deacon had showed remarkable initiative and had continued to push inland, leaving guides behind to direct the second wave. He'd reached the uneven ground beyond the road and the railway line and had found a larger hollow surrounded by rocks, which he was busy fortifying when Warley joined him, pushing men out to right and left to dig slit trenches. On the German side of the dip, sheltered by the

196

slope, there was a small stone building probably once used as a cow byre to which they were carrying the wounded.

'We've got to get in contact with the colonel,' Warley said. 'Let's try a pigeon.'

But, in the din and confusion of mortar fire, the bird merely circled slowly above them and they saw it come to rest on a broken wall just ahead of them out of reach, shaking its head and fluffing out its wet feathers.

'The bastard's allergic to the dark,' Farnsworth snarled.

'It'll probably go at daylight, sir,' Corporal Carter said helpfully.

'Let's hope so,' Warley growled. 'Got any more?'

'Yes, sir.'

'Better wait a bit then. It'll soon be daylight. We'll try again then.' As Warley turned, he saw his signaller sitting against a rock with blood on his face and a dazed look in his eyes.

'What happened?' he asked.

'Bits of stone, chiefly, sir, I think. It's made me go deaf. I can hardly hear a bloody thing.'

'Think you can help the doctor and the padre set up an aid post, and get the wounded to it?'

'I reckon so, sir. You'd better use another signaller in my place.'

'Right. See what you can do to help. We seem to be a bit short of men.'

As the signaller crawled away, Warley stared round him. Deacon had surprised him with his ability. Up to that point, he had thought of him merely as a dubious disciplinarian who sought to conceal an inner lack of self-confidence by his constant harrying of the wretched Syzling. But he had clearly got an eye for country, and the dip he'd chosen couldn't have been bettered by a man with fifty years' experience of fighting. It gave them more shelter than they could have expected and had even provided somewhere for the doctor's dressing station. Nevertheless, they were struggling against an overwhelming barrage from the hills. The German gunners weren't entirely sure where they were yet, but it was quite clear that until the artillery damped down their fire A Company were going to be unable to move forward. The British shells exploding just in front didn't seem to be dropping in the right spots, yet they were unable to redirect them without radios.

'Have we heard from the Yellowjackets?' Warley demanded. 'They ought to be moving down here to help us.'

'No, sir.' Deacon answered. 'There's been nothing. Nor from B or C Companies.' He turned back, 'Syzling, for the love of God, keep your stupid head down! It might not worry you if you get a bullet between the eyes, because I don't suppose there's much behind them, but it'll worry me. I need you.'

Warley began to move round the dip, checking his men. In the stone byre, the medical orderlies, the doctor and O'Mara were crouched over the wounded. Only one of them had been hit by enemy fire since they'd reached the dip. All the rest had been brought down in the rush from the river and been dragged along by their friends.

As Warley checked, a whole new group fell into the hollow, their weapons and equipment clattering. Jago was among them.

'Christ!' His voice was thin and edgy. 'Is this all we've got? Where's B and C?'

'They haven't arrived yet,' Warley said. 'And we've had no word from the Yellowjackets. We'd better get D across. How many did you bring?'

'I set off with about forty men but I seem to have lost a few en route. I heard firing further downstream, so some of them probably drifted down there. I expect we'll pick them up as we move on.'

'If we move on,' Warley said grimly. 'There's firing on our left, so I suspect B and C have got lost over there somewhere. We'll know as soon as it's daylight.'

When Yuell reached the river bank, he discovered that three of his companies had managed to establish themselves across the river, even if only in small groups; but opposite the point where Warley had crossed, only one of the three footways the Engineers had managed to put up on kapok bales near the stone bridge was still standing. The German fire was extraordinarily heavy and extraordinarily accurate, and his signals officer had been badly wounded.

He called Peddy to him. 'Sit on the rear link radio in case we re-establish contact with Warley,' he said. 'I'm going across with D.'

Another flurry of German shells landed along the river bank, sending slashes of mud sweeping across the scrubby undergrowth. As Yuell plunged on to the swaying footbridge with D Company, yet another salvo landed just behind them. The last man heading across the bridge cried out and fell into the water, and one of the Engineers waded out and dragged him ashore. Looking back, Yuell saw stretcher bearers were also busy round the hollow where he'd left Peddy and Mr Zeal. And even as he flung himself down with D Company, a shell severed the thin thread of steel and wood so that, like the rest of the battalion, D Company was now also effectively marooned without the support of tanks.

At first it seemed impossible in the dark to decide just where Warley was but, finally, Yuell stumbled into the hollow where he and his men lay.

'Where are B and C?' he demanded.

'We've seen no sign of them yet, sir,' Warley said, shouting to make himself heard. 'I've managed to pinpoint all my chaps, though, and we're all in contact.'

'This is a bad business,' Yuell said. 'I think Peddy was hit as we left the bank. Zeal as well, I suspect. I'd better go and see if I can find B and C. Are you all right here?'

'Yes, sir. We're all right, especially now D's arrived. They won't be able to throw us back, but I'm afraid we can't do much about moving forward for the moment.'

Yuell found the remnants of the other two companies huddled among the ruins of a farmhouse near the disused ferry. It had been turned into a strongpoint by the Germans, and they had had the greatest difficulty in silencing it. Yuell was staggered to see how few of them were left.

'Is this all there are?' he said, and then set about gathering them together before sending them stumbling through the darkness in small groups in the direction of Warley. The stretcher bearers had carried the wounded down to a cellar that smelled of mice, onions and damp. There seemed to be an extraordinary number of them, including B Company's commander who was lying on his back, his face covered with blood, making snoring noises through his mouth.

'Back of the head, sir,' the corporal in charge said. 'I'm afraid he's had it.'

Yuell glanced about him. 'Think you can manage for a while?' he asked. 'We'll get back to you as soon as we can.'

'We're all right, sir,' the corporal said. 'There should be reinforcements across at daylight.'

'Yes,' Yuell agreed, but neither of them believed it.

By the time he had brought the remnants of the two companies up to Warley, Yuell guessed he had perhaps three hundred and fifty men out of the battalion, either in the hollow or dug in near the stone walls of the cowshed, still capable of fighting. But there wasn't the slightest hope of them moving forward. The rest of the battalion had been scattered by the current and lost in the darkness, and by this time, with the night almost over, he could see ahead of him a belt of barbed wire that was heavy and thick enough to hold off anything without the assistance of artillery or tanks. Forced to dig in, they were unable to reinforce or communicate with the far shore. They couldn't even retreat because most of their boats were sunk or smashed, and they could only cling to their pitifully small gains, praying help would come soon in the shape of the Baluchis, to save them from death or captivity.

The German fire started again and a lot of it was mortar fire. One of the first landed at the feet of the man Yuell had chosen as his runner, just as he set off to contact Deacon away on the left. Only because someone saw it happen did they know who it was, because until his name tags were found it would have been impossible to identify him.

The mortaring and counter-mortaring went on for some minutes. Evans' bombs were being fired at intervals but the German fire was almost continuous and their aim was only just off, so that the bombs were bursting close to their positions. Then the fire stopped abruptly, and at once they saw heads emerge from the positions opposite.

'They're trying a counter-attack!' Warley yelled.

As the last explosion rang out, the Germans jumped up, only to be caught by the full blast of the battalion's weapon strength. Dodging from group to group, Warley saw Henry White and McWatters tossing grenades in a steady stream – White's face grave and full of concentration as if he were in his usual position fielding at deep extra cover for the battalion cricket team, McWatters grinning as if he were throwing bricks at the police. The 'Sieg Heils' crumbled into confused shouts. One section tried to break to the right for a gap in the wire but CSM Farnsworth spotted the move and, as he redirected the fire, the Germans scattered like leaves in a gust of wind. A shower of stick grenades came out of the air, one exploding close to Warley, but McWatters dragged him down just in time and the hot blast passed over his head.

When he looked up again the Germans had vanished and he realised they'd beaten them off. But he also knew that suddenly it wasn't the Germans who were the defenders but themselves. They were isolated in their hollow and, though they'd beaten off the counter-attack – even if they beat them *all* off – without tanks they couldn't move an inch forward.

'We need help,' Yuell said. 'Either to go forward or to extricate ourselves. Haven't we a single damn communication working?'

'We have carrier pigeons, sir,' Warley said.

'Then let's have one sent off with our approximate numbers and state.'

The call went out once more for Corporal Carter. He arrived soon afterwards, crawling forward with the pigeon tucked in his battledress. It didn't look very airworthy and Yuell stared at it grimly.

'Is that the best you've got?' he asked.

'Yes, sir. One of the wounded fell on the basket and smashed it, sir. He was a big man. This is the only one I could save.'

Yuell wrote out the message and handed it over. Attaching the message to the bird's leg, Carter threw it into the air. Immediately, a German with a Schmeisser machine-pistol spotted it and fired several bursts towards it. Bewildered and shaken by the noise, the bird flew in circles over the dip for a while, watched by dozens of eyes, then launched itself off – in the wrong direction.

'It's all the noise,' Carter said, almost in tears. 'They were never bred for taking part in a battle.'

'Neither was I,' Jago growled. 'They ought to send the buggers over an assault course.'

Then someone noticed that the pigeon they'd sent off during the night had disappeared from the wall where it had settled. Whether it had been caught by a burst from a Spandau or defeathered by blast, or had finally taken off for its loft, they had no idea. They could only hope it had made it across the river.

Fletcher-Smith heard them talking and spoke to Farnsworth.

'If they want a message taking, Sar'-Major,' he said, 'why not let me go? The runner's been hit and there's nobody else.'

Farnsworth studied him warily. He still didn't have much time for Fletcher-Smith, whom he considered too clever by half. Farnsworth had been brought up in the days when cleverness in common soldiers was not encouraged and he was suspicious of Fletcher-Smith's motives.

'You trying to dodge back?' he said.

Fletcher-Smith looked indignant. 'Christ, I'm offering to swim the bloody river!' he snorted. 'Would *you* fancy that?'

Considering it carefully, Farnsworth decided he wouldn't.

'Okay, son,' he said. 'Let's see the major.'

Warley listened to Fletcher-Smith's offer and took him to Yuell.

'Could you get across?' Yuell asked.

'I'm a good swimmer, sir,' Fletcher-Smith said.

'Good enough for that?'

Fletcher-Smith almost laughed. 'I've swum Windermere, sir. In 1938 I had a go at the Channel. I was only sixteen. They pulled me out only four miles from Cap Gris Nez.'

Yuell knew Fletcher-Smith well by sight but he'd never heard anything like this.

'There's nothing in your records about it,' he said.

'I never told anybody, sir. They wouldn't have believed me.'

Yuell still hesitated. 'The Germans are covering the river with machine-guns,' he said.

'Sir,' Fletcher-Smith replied firmly, 'I used to be able to swim two lengths of the baths without coming up for a breath. If I can get into the water, they'll only see me for a couple of seconds at a time. The worst bit will be getting down there.'

Yuell studied Fletcher-Smith. Despite his glasses and moon face, he was built like a barrel and certainly looked like a swimmer.

'All right,' he said. 'Major Warley will tell you the position.'

Warley took Fletcher-Smith to one side. 'You'll be doing us all a favour if you can make it,' he said.

'If I can get down there, sir, I'll get across.'

Warley indicated the water meadows behind them. 'There's what looks like a ditch just down there,' he said. 'It seems to run all the way to the river. If you can get into it, you might make it without being seen. It looks like a drainage ditch. It might even be for sewage. I don't know. Would you like someone to go with you to help?'

Fletcher-Smith shook his head. This, he had decided, was his affair and nobody else's.

In his headquarters in San Bartolomeo, Brigadier Tallemach was struggling with the information that was coming in. It was scanty enough in all conscience. A machine-gun had been knocked out here. A tank had been reported there. The German 431st Regiment had been identified. The very scantiness of the reports indicated the scope of the disaster on the other side of the river.

He frowned and tried to produce ideas to cope with it, but he was not being very successful because his son's face kept intruding.

His fears for Yuell's North Yorkshires and the Yellowjackets were very real. Certainly they had attracted plenty of attention and it was obvious from the din – field guns of all sizes, tank guns, mortars and machine-guns – that the Germans were pushing in everything they'd got. While he was brooding, a message arrived from the signals section –

'Both battalions across.' Tallemach stared at it, finding it hard to believe. What he didn't know was that both battalions had reported that *elements* were across, and in the confusion the message had been fined down by an over-zealous signals officer.

He was unable to confirm his doubts, however, because since the message had been received, contact with the river had been broken just after he'd heard that Peddy, Yuell's second-in-command, and RSM Zeal had been killed by a shell. Signallers were trying at that moment to restore the link.

He moved to the Intelligence truck. The information about the opposing forces was marked on the transparent talc that covered the big map that hung on one wall. The hatching showed the flooded areas of the river, the trees and orchards, even the farmhouses and their outbuildings. The black crosses marking the minefields stood out like an ugly fence; the Germans were experts at minefields, and leg wounds and amputations showed how many there were.

Once more he studied the message that indicated that both battalions were across. Alongside it were other messages. One from the artillery complained that it was impossible to help Yuell because he was too close to the German positions. One from the Engineers reporting that footbridges had been thrown across was followed closely by other messages reporting, one by one, that the bridges had been destroyed. Vivian had reported that he'd had to withdraw his tanks behind San Bartolomeo again from their wire matting stands by the road, for the simple reason that they couldn't possibly stay there in full view of the Germans all day.

He turned to the 19th Division gunnery officer. 'We need more smoke,' he said.

The Gunner looked worried. 'Artillery doesn't usually lay down smoke, sir,' he pointed out. 'It's normally left to the mortars.'

Tallemach frowned. 'The mortar bombs haven't turned up yet,' he said. 'They're missing, like the grenades. We're still trying to find them. You've got to do what you can.'

'The number of smoke shells at a gun site's pretty small, sir, and we fired off a lot during the first assault.'

Tallemach turned to his brigade major. 'How about smoke pots? Can we get them up-river to lay their smoke over the bridgehead?'

'We have no smoke pots, sir. We got a signal from Div. to say there were six hundred of them in San Bartolomeo but I haven't been able to find them. I've been trying ever since the mortar bombs went missing. No information came down from Div. HQ about them.'

Heathfield again, Tallemach thought. He turned to the Gunner. 'Use what shells you have,' he said. 'It'll give us time to find the smoke pots.'

'They won't last long,' the Gunner pointed out. 'We were short when we started. They collected them all for the crossing at Cassino and there's been a shortage for months.'

'Where are the nearest reserves?'

'Naples.'

'Then someone had better go and fetch them.' Tallemach again turned to his brigade major. 'Get hold of the RASC.' He swung back to the Gunner. 'How many shall we need?'

'To keep the screen going all day, thirty thousand.'

'Very well, let's get on with it.'

Turning back to his map, Tallemach tried to concentrate. It wasn't easy, because he was not only thinking of his newly-dead son but also of his wife and what she must be feeling. They'd only just got used to the loss of one son. Now they had to go through the whole thing again over the second. Suddenly he felt desperately tired and knew he wasn't far from a crack-up.

With an effort, he forced his mind firmly back to the job in hand. They had reached the most dangerous point of the operation. The most critical period of any crossing was not the passing of infantry across the water but of maintaining them on the far side against artillery attacks on their bridges and counter-attacks by armour. It was a vicious circle because the infantry needed the support of tanks, but the tanks couldn't cross until the bridgehead was so big the crossings couldn't be swept by close-range fire.

Since Yuell's crossing opposite San Bartolomeo had seemed at first to be a disaster, the Baluchis had been lorried upstream to support what had seemed a better option by the Yellowjackets, advancing on Castelgrande by way of Route B, the road from Foiano. Then, as the messages had begun to come in, it had become clear that of the two crossings, only Yuell's showed the slightest promise at all and they'd been brought back again. Now, the increasing light revealed the same flooded meadows with nowhere to hide, and with the bridges smashed the Baluchis had had to withdraw to the safety of their original jumping-off point in San Bartolomeo before the German guns could destroy them. Only Yuell's small group was now having any real effect on the battle.

A few wounded had managed to get back before the last footbridge had gone and from them they'd estimated Yuell's casualties at around a hundred and fifty to two hundred, which was heavier than most units could stand. But at Castelgrande, the battle had produced an even worse mess.

Out of one group of the Yellowjackets, not a single man had got across; out of the other, elements of only one company had managed to reach the far side, but their casualties were even higher than Yuell's and German mortars had pinned them to the edge of the river. Behind them, two more companies had waited as Engineers had tried to locate equipment which guides were unable to find or tried to repair bridge parts damaged by shellfire. The night had been an interminable period of fear, pain, confusion and delay, and only a few men had reached the shelter of a farm near Castelgrande.

As the day grew brighter and the radio link with the river was repaired, a message came from the senior surviving officer of the Yellowjackets. The Germans had begun to attack with tanks and self-propelled guns and, in face of complete annihilation, he was asking permission to withdraw what men he could get out by the one remaining but now damaged footbridge.

'No,' Tallemach snapped. 'Tell him to stay where he is! We'll try to get support up there.'

Calling for his jeep, he drove as hard as he could from San Bartolomeo. The rain was coming down heavily again and the skies had a funereal look about them. The highest points on the mountains opposite were out of sight in the clouds, but Tallemach was under no delusion that there weren't plenty of other points lower down from which the Germans could see everything that was happening.

When he arrived at Foiano, he was already too late. Only the few Yellowjackets who had got into the farm near Castelgrande were still across the river. The rest had started recrossing not long after sending their request and they were now arriving in Foiano, wet, muddy and exhausted. A few had returned by the footbridge, placing their feet on timbers just visible under the swirling water, but most were without their uniforms and equipment because they'd had to swim. The icy water had numbed them to indifference and their morale and self-confidence had been badly shaken. As a battalion they had virtually ceased to exist and it was quite obvious that everything now depended on Yuell. To Tallemach it seemed to be time to organise a second attempt for the coming evening, not so much to support Yuell as to rescue him with whoever could still walk.

Weighed down with weariness and worry, he was just conferring with the colonel of the Baluchis by the light of a hurricane lamp whose flame jumped and flickered to the banging of the guns, when Heathfield arrived. Both Tallemach and the colonel were soaked by the rain, their clothes splashed by the liquid grey mud. In contrast, Heathfield was immaculate, his buttons polished, his boots shining, and immediately he and Tallemach began to disagree violently.

'There's no point in bringing them back,' Heathfield snapped. 'Having got them across, surely it would be much better to reinforce them.'

'You don't reinforce failures,' Tallemach said. 'And this is failure.'

'Yuell's still there,' Heathfield snapped.

'The Baluchis aren't,' Tallemach said. 'And they're supposed to be.'

While they were arguing the telephone went. Tallemach answered it, listened, then handed it silently to Heathfield. Heathfield looked curiously at the other two, spoke briefly, then replaced the receiver.

'That was the Divisional Intelligence Officer,' he said. 'He was with General Tonge. Their jeep was in collision with a six-wheeler belonging to the US 10th Corps. The driver was killed and the general has a broken arm. He's been taken to hospital. It seems he was quite conscious, though in pain, and was able to say that the attack is to go on as if he were here. He'll return as soon as he can. He wants the support troops across the moment we have a foothold.' Heathfield shifted his shoulders in a kind of shrug. 'It seems to me, gentlemen, that it's up to me now to sort this thing out.'

Although he was Tonge's principal confidant at HQ, Heathfield's job was primarily to co-ordinate the divisional artillery. As senior brigadier, it was Tallemach's job to take Tonge's place. But in the chaos existing, it was quite clear that Tallemach should stay where he was, and Heathfield was not a man to be argued with, anyway.

Tallemach made no comment and for a while there was silence, before they got down to work again, leaving the position of the second crossing to be decided by events and conditions.

'We need an all-out attack,' Heathfield pointed out. 'Preferably before noon while the Germans are off-balance.'

'They don't seem off-balance to me,' Tallemach said.

'They must be by now,' Heathfield insisted. 'They're only Russians and Czechs anyway, and we've just had a message from Army to say they're putting their men across tomorrow at Cassino. The Germans must already be sending their reserves in that direction.'

'Chiefly, I suppose,' Tallemach said dryly, 'because it'll already be clear that they won't be needed here.'

Heathfield was silent for a moment – the silence of affront. 'We could do them a great deal of harm by continuing the attack,' he said eventually. He was still irritated by the way his well-planned attack had been relegated to the status of a feint, and had begun to see it now as a success that could earn him apologies and praise in equal quantities. It would be damned funny, he thought, if his attack succeeded while the bigger one further north failed.

'If we reinforce this farm the Yellowjackets have got into,' he said, 'the Germans are going to have to withdraw men from Yuell's front to stop us moving out of it.'

'I favour supporting Yuell,' Tallemach said. 'Judging by the weight of the shelling at Castelgrande, nobody's going to be moving forward anywhere in that sector.'

'I disagree! The Yellowjackets are behind bricks and mortar. Yuell's still out in the open and too much under observation. We'll never get another bridge across in front of San Eusebio.'

'Pity you didn't think of that before,' Tallemach growled.

Heathfield ignored the remark. 'The artillery claim they're on top of the opposition at Castelgrande,' he said, 'and that's certainly not the case opposite San Bartolomeo. So Castelgrande's where we should push men across. We'll switch the tanks up there in support.'

'Crossing on what?'

Heathfield frowned. 'War isn't a game of snakes and ladders,' he said icily. 'There are no rules. We have to react to events. Get the Engineers to push their Class 40 bridge over up there.'

'It'll mean shifting all their equipment.'

'Then tell them to get on with it! If they do, they can finish it while the sun is in the Germans' eyes.'

Tallemach's head jerked round. 'That's a ridiculous suggestion,' he snapped. 'There probably won't be any sun and it only leaves us three hours to prepare!'

'It's got to be done,' Heathfield said. 'And Yuell must be supported to keep up the pressure in this sector as well. So let's have two companies of the Baluchis across with ammunition and supplies. The other two can go in to help the Yellowjackets at Castelgrande, supported by one of Rankin's battalions, the other two to be kept in reserve.'

'Yuell will need more than two companies,' Tallemach pointed out sharply. 'And that's impossible with the Baluchis as disorganised as they are.'

'If we're disorganised,' Heathfield snapped, 'then we shouldn't be! What's wrong with the Baluchis, anyway?'

'They're scattered all over the place. They were brought up in a hurry under intermittent fire and were pushed down to the river from Capodozzi to wherever there was shelter for them. When the bridges went they had to be brought back to San Bartolomeo.'

'Then collect them, get them fed, and have them reorganise themselves. How soon can you get things moving?'

'Not before noon,' Tallemach said. 'That's for certain.'

Heathfield gestured irritably. 'By the time you finally get down to it,' he said, 'the Germans will have reinforced. They move pretty fast. You'd better get on with it.'

As he picked up his cap and left, Tallemach noticed grimly that he'd left the details to him.

Though Heathfield's fears of German reinforcements were well founded, it was also clear that the early reverse had been more complete and demoralising than General Tonge had realised. The Yellowjackets no longer existed as a coherent organisation and if Yuell had lost as many men as appeared to be the case, he must also have lost many other things too – weapons, equipment and ammunition – that would make it hard for him to hang on. Time was needed to reorganise and regain control, while to repeat the failed night attack in daylight seemed to be making things just too easy for the Germans.

Certainly the Germans thought so. To Captain Reis' surprise, Lieutenant Thiergartner was doing very well. He was containing the British with remarkably few men, and Reis' suggestion that he should push forward reserves to him had been rejected.

'We're holding them quite safely Herr Hauptmann,' Thiergartner had told him over the telephone. 'It only appears to be an armed reconnaissance.'

Reis wasn't so sure. From where he was, and judging by reports on the prisoners who'd been brought in from near Castelgrande, it was very much bigger than that.

A movement opposite caught his attention, and he frowned and used his free hand to put his binoculars to his eyes.

'Surely they're not going to come again – in *daylight!*' he said.

'Yes, Herr Hauptmann,' Thiergartner answered calmly. 'They must be mad. If I'd started such a movement, I'd not expect to be treated kindly either by you or the people above you. To persist in this fashion's crazy.'

'Never mind the military psychology, Thiergartner,' Reis snapped, 'What about help? Are you sure you don't need any down there?'

'Of course not, Herr Hauptmann,' Thiergartner said. 'We need no reserves. We're holding without trouble. We even know their numbers because we captured a pigeon they sent off. It was a little bewildered and its direction-finding equipment seemed to have broken down. It arrived just outside our position and Pulovski enticed it in. He might be dim in some ways but he has a way with living things. I've sent him back to you with its message and returned the bird. He talked it into recovering a little and it flew off exactly where it was originally supposed to go.'

'Doesn't it occur to you, Thiergartner,' Reis snapped, 'that even a pigeon has its uses? They can use it again and it's our job to deny them the use of *anything* that may be of value to them. Even pigeons!'

'All the same – ' Thiergartner's chuckle came down the line ' – we ought not to lose our sense of humour, Herr Hauptmann. There's little enough of it in wartime. I couldn't resist it. I attached a message – "Herewith pigeon returned. We have enough to eat and look forward with pleasure to your next attempt." '

f o u r

It had always been hard in training exercises in England to persuade men to dig. Here, however, wherever it was possible, they had dug for all they were worth and, where it wasn't possible, they'd thrown up sangars of stones. They'd learned a lot in North Africa and advancing up Italy. Once Yuell had had to threaten them with punishment to make them go down two or three feet. Now, wherever the rocky nature of the soil permitted, they were already much deeper than that.

It was a good job, too, because the Germans had brought up a nebelwerfer, the multi-barrelled mortar which fired six bombs at once. In flight the clusters emitted a noise that was a cross between a shriek, a whine and a sigh, and was no help to the nerves of those at the receiving end. Shaped like a small cannon, it had been dug into the hillside higher up the slope and the officer directing the fire was obviously doing his observing through a narrow notch chipped out of the rock.

The Germans knew now where they were and the first cluster came in to burst with a series of shattering explosions. They heard the bombs coming and dived for cover, huddling at the bottom of what had become known as Deacon's Dip. The barrage lasted only two or three minutes, but by the time it finished they had lost seven more men killed and wounded.

Nobody was firing back much because instructions had gone round to reserve ammunition for the night, but one or two did and the German machine-guns retaliated and the heavy mortars started again. If one of their bombs landed in a hole where a man crouched it would save the need for a burial party.

'If only t'bloody rain would stop,' Rich wailed.

But it didn't. It still fell, not heavily now but steadily, and already the holes they'd managed to dig were full of water and grey ooze into which bloody scraps of clothing and ammunition clips had been trampled by heavy boots. A German light machine-gun chattered hysterically and the bullets clacked and clapped overhead. Evans the Bomb tried retaliation with his two-inch mortar, setting it up just behind the lip of the hollow. As the loader slid a bomb into the muzzle, ducking sideways to avoid the blast, Evans waited for it to explode, made a small correction and tried again. Then two lights soared up into the gloom, and almost immediately three German mortar bombs exploded in red-yellow flashes just in front of them. The loader's steel helmet was whipped off by the blast and he rolled into the bottom of the dip with a wound in the head.

'They must be able to see us from San Eusebio,' Yuell said, his head down as mud and small stones spattered down on them. 'If we could only get an air strike on the place, we might get somewhere.'

But, even if they'd had the means to direct one, there could have been no help from the air with the cloud level below one thousand feet. Their position was growing desperate. Fletcher-Smith had been gone some time, but whether he'd succeeded or not nobody knew, and all they could do was hang on.

Crowding the tumbledown cowshed, the wounded lay side by side in the mud without benefit of stretchers or blankets. The doctor and the orderlies were giving morphia injections and writing in copying pencil on the injured men's foreheads the time and size of the dose they'd given. O'Mara had been moving among them the whole of the night, his spectacles shining, his smile always present. Because of his calmness, men who'd schemed like foxes to avoid church parades had asked him to say a prayer for them, and more than one had gone to his Maker with Latin phrases falling on his fading hearing. Warley could only suppose it was because O'Mara was unafraid of death.

'The apprehension of personal danger can be mastered,' O'Mara said. 'Once you accept that nothing worse than death can be expected.'

'It's a useful faith to have, Padre.'

O'Mara smiled. 'Faith's not just a guess at what lies beyond the clouds, my son. Sometimes I think that's something that bishops and cardinals don't always appreciate. To someone with faith, death's only a step into a better world.'

'It's not the better world I fear, Padre,' Warley admitted, his voice a croak because, after all the shouting of the night, it had finally whirred away into nothingness like a broken watch-spring. 'It's the step itself, the pain of the mortal wound.'

As they crawled across the bottom of the dip, the doctor was just putting a man's arm in a splint while an orderly gave him a sniff of chloroform. One of the corporals had also just been dragged in, with one leg half-severed. The shock seemed to grip him, however, and he appeared to feel no pain. The morphia he'd been given hadn't yet begun to take effect, but his leg was bleeding badly and the dressings had slipped. The doctor told Warley to hold a pad on it. Then, to Warley's surprise, he opened his jack-knife and quickly cut through the fragment of sinew and flesh that still attached it. The corporal didn't seem to feel a thing.

A great many of the injured were suffering from head or eye injuries because the fragments of shells and bombs

216

bursting on the rocky slopes flew further. As O'Mara continued to move among them with his dwindling supply of water, he became increasingly conscious how essential it was that those men still lying in the open should be brought in.

'I'm going to try to get the wounded in,' he announced suddenly.

Yuell swung round. 'Don't be damn silly, Padre! It's impossible.'

'I'm going to try, nevertheless, Colonel, sir. Perhaps the Lord will cause the Germans to act with mercy.'

Yuell was about to reply when he was called to the other side of the dip and in the urgency forgot about O'Mara. Frowning, the padre stripped to the waist, finally removing his white vest. Then he replaced his shirt and tunic and attached the vest to his walking stick. Before anyone realised what he was doing, he had raised this impromptu flag and slowly begun to edge himself above the lip of the hollow. A burst of machine-gun bullets threw earth in his face and he blinked; then the gun stopped. Beyond the wire, they could hear shouts and gradually all the firing ceased and there was an almost unearthly lull in the battle.

'You wish to surrender?'

The voice came clearly across the open ground.

'I do not wish to surrender,' O'Mara shouted. 'I claim the security of the Red Cross, though I have no Red Cross flag. I am a Roman Catholic padre and I wish to bring in the wounded and give absolution to the dying.'

There was a long silence. Seeing O'Mara's flag, Yuell had crawled back across the bottom of the dip.

'Come down, Padre!' he snapped. 'There'll be no surrender here.'

'I'm not surrendering, Colonel, sir,' O'Mara said calmly. 'I'm a Christian appealing for mercy to men who are also supposed to be Christians.' And with that he slowly straightened up and stepped outside the dip.

'The buggers'll shoot the sod,' Puddephatt gasped.

'Dry up,' Warley said, his heart in his mouth.

The silence seemed interminable, and then a voice came from the German lines. It was Reis. By good fortune he'd joined Thiergartner to check that he was as secure as he said he was.

'I, too, am a Catholic,' he said. 'You may collect your wounded, Father, but I have not the authority to allow you to evacuate them to the river. You have one hour and you must not approach our wire.'

O'Mara lifted his hand in a blessing, two fingers upraised; then he called briskly over his shoulder to Warley.

'One hour, me boy! Better get cracking!'

'Pick the smartest men, sir,' CSM Farnsworth hissed. 'Don't let the buggers realise what it's like here.'

'You're right,' Warley said. 'Corporal Gask, Rich, Martindale, Bawden, Duff, Parkin. You'll do for the first party. Sar'-Major, round me up some more.'

Twice the stretcher-bearers went out from the dip, lifting the inert figures while O'Mara continued to stand bolt upright in No Man's Land holding up the white vest on his stick. As the second party struggled back to the dip, Reis' head appeared.

'I could just knock yon hoor off from here,' McWatters said, cradling his rifle.

'There'll be no shooting,' Yuell snapped. 'Not with the padre out there.'

'You are a brave man, Father,' Reis called.

O'Mara managed a smile. 'I hope I'm a compassionate one, my son,' he observed.

'You have twenty more minutes,' Reis said.

'One more journey,' O'Mara pleaded.

'One only,' Reis conceded. 'After that you must not make any more.'

By the end of the hour, they had carried in everyone within reach who had survived his wounds and Reis fired a flare which soared above their heads.

'*Genug,*' he called. 'That is enough.'

O'Mara waved. 'We can ask no more, my son. The Blessing of God be upon you.'

'And upon you, Father. Go now. I must order my men to fire.'

As O'Mara slipped back into the dip, Warley stared at him. 'I never expected to see that, Father. It was very brave.'

O'Mara blinked. He looked a little startled at what he'd done. 'The strength of any religion,' he said slowly, 'lies in the behaviour of those who practise it. It was nothing, my son.'

The firing didn't start again at once, but after a while one of the German Spandaus let off a short burst, which another one took up. Eventually they were back to normal, nobody being particularly aggressive but nobody missing any chances either.

'They're a long time throwing in another counter-attack,' Yuell said.

'Perhaps they don't think it's necessary to risk lives, sir,' Warley pointed out. 'After all, it's obvious we're not going anywhere and that we can't get back to the river. They've only got to keep up the pressure and we'll run out of ammunition.'

There was nothing to do but wait. The hours passed slowly. By mid-morning there had still been no fresh counter-attack, and even into the afternoon the Germans had not gone beyond the use of gunfire and mortars. Then the lorries returned from Naples and the gunners at the other side of the river began to thicken up the smoke screen, confident now they could keep it going indefinitely. It proved a double-edged weapon, and soon after three o'clock the ominous grating of tanks was heard beyond it. First came the roar of engines followed by a clanking noise and what sounded like someone throwing gravel against a tin fence; then the crack of a high velocity gun. The shell burst just beyond the dip.

Everybody fell silent as soldiers must have done when Hannibal had appeared with his elephants, two thousand years before, or Murat had borne down with his glittering squadrons of horsemen.

The first tank lurched round a clump of rock, moving slowly, its gun swinging in search of a target. With everyone in the dip, there wasn't much to fire at and the tank commander seemed uncertain what to do. Then a second tank approached, partly hidden behind the first. As they both drew closer, vanishing temporarily into a fold of ground, the man with the Piat anti-tank launcher laid down his weapon, scrambled out of the hole he was occupying with Syzling and Deacon, and ran towards the river.

'You rotten bastard,' Syzling yelled after him. 'You bloody rotten yellow bugger!'

He and Deacon were manning a Bren just ahead of the dip to give support to the Piat team; but of these, one had been killed, a second wounded, and the third had just bolted. However, there seemed to be plenty of bombs and Deacon stared at the three-foot-long tube with its pistol grip and firing mechanism. There was a bomb alongside the open-ended trough, its detonator in place. As he well knew, infantrymen with Piats were difficult to spot and their tactical effects were profound, their mere presence inducing caution in tank crews who immediately started calling up infantry support; something that would not be easy here because the dip he'd chosen was a sound base and he and Warley and Jago had worked throughout the night to strengthen it.

Deacon continued to stare at the Piat with growing fascination, realising as he did so that it could cause a considerable slowing down of operations which normally thrived best on speed. He turned towards Syzling.

'Shut up swearing,' he snapped, 'and get hold of the bloody thing!'

'Oo?' Syzling said. 'Me?'

'Why not, for God's sake? You've been trained.'

'I've forgot it all.' Syzling scowled. 'Besides, I'll get killed. You ain't got a chance of getting a 'it at more than a 'undred yards. I'll 'ave to wait for 'im to get closer and I'm not that daft. That bugger's got another one be'ind 'im and they'll be on the look out for me. Anyway,' he went on aggrievedly, 'I saw one 'it by a Piat down in Sicily an' all it did was blow the bloody 'atches open. The crew just shut 'em again and went on like nothing 'ad 'appened.'

Deacon shifted uncomfortably. What Syzling said was only too true. Not only did the bomb sometimes fail to stop a tank, sometimes it also disproved the theory that the blast from an internal explosion was lethal. After further badgering, however, Syzling eventually had to admit he could just possibly still remember how to use the weapon.

'Well, look slippy, you idiot,' Deacon bellowed, despairing even now of ever getting Syzling to call him 'sir'. 'The bloody thing'll be on top of us soon.'

Syzling lifted the Piat and peered anxiously over the edge of the hole. The leading tank was just coming into view again, and Deacon felt himself shivering. It looked as big as a house – huge, dark and angular – its great gun probing ahead of it. His face twitched and he tried in vain to stop it.

'If you don't get on with it,' he hissed, 'the bloody thing'll run us down!'

Laboriously – incredibly slowly, it seemed to Deacon – Syzling managed to check the missile.

'And this time,' Deacon went on, his nerves twanging with tension, 'don't lower the muzzle or you'll lose the bloody bomb as usual.'

'I'm trying, aren't I?' Syzling said.

'Okay.' Deacon struggled to hold on to his temper in case he panicked Syzling. 'Give it a bit longer till he's nearer, but for Christ's sake don't leave it too long!'

'I wish you'd shut up,' Syzling wailed. 'You're putting me off! I can't concentrate!'

'You never could.'

'I'll bloody well aim it at you soon!'

Deacon was so startled at this little mutiny he fell silent while Syzling took a deep breath and stood up in full view of the Germans. The range was around sixty yards and the explosion seemed to be on the tank's starboard track. They saw the flash and the puff of smoke, then a curling metallic snake as the track ran off the bogies. Deacon's eyes almost fell out of their sockets.

'You hit the bloody thing!' he cried, like Syzling standing bolt upright in amazement.

'Well, you shut up for once,' Syzling explained patiently. 'That's why. Nobody ever gives me time to think.'

The tank's gun fired and the shell burst just to their left in a huge cloud of smoke, scattering mud and rock.

'Give it another for luck!' Deacon yelled excitedly.

This time Syzling's shot landed just in front of the tank, raising another huge cloud of smoke. Once again the tank fired, but the shot whistled over their heads and sailed down towards the river. Then they saw the crew climbing out. As they jumped down, they opened up with Schmeissers but they didn't appear to be certain where the Piat was and, as Deacon fired the Bren, they all disappeared from sight, either dead or wounded. There was a roar of enthusiasm from the dip.

'Now the other!'

'Other what?' Syzling demanded.

'The other tank, you gormless idiot! It's coming up!'

'Well, shut up then,' Syzling said peevishly. 'And pass me one of them bombs.'

It was a new experience for Deacon to be told what to do by Syzling instead of the other way round, but in the excitement of the moment he didn't even notice. As Syzling fired again, the second tank was just turning as if to retreat and it immediately burst into flames. Beyond the smoke they saw the crew running, their clothes on fire. Deacon shot them down, and then he and Syzling grabbed each other and shook hands, grinning.

'Better give the first 'un another for luck,' Syzling said. 'In case they come back an' get it.'

Deacon helped with the bomb again, but this time it went off in the tube. There was a tremendous clang and Deacon was flung against the earth wall of the hole. When he came to, his head was ringing and his lungs felt full of acrid smoke. He pulled himself upright, coughing and retching, the sweat standing out on his face, the bile dribbling from his open mouth. Then he saw that Syzling was huddled in a corner with two enormous black eyes and small pieces of metal sticking in his face.

He looked dead, but Deacon realised he was breathing and decided he'd better try to get him to the stretcher-bearers. Their vicious little attack seemed to have shaken the Germans and, hidden by the smoke from the burning tank, he was able to get Syzling out of the hole and heave him on to his back. There was one more burst of firing, but even that stopped as Deacon fell into the dip where the orderlies took over.

'Who is it?'

'Syzling. Frying Tonight.'

'What happened to him?'

'Piat blew up in his face.'

Collecting two men and several Bren magazines, Deacon squirmed back through the smoke to his hole, feeling curiously bereft. He'd been nagging at Syzling so long that to be without him was like losing a limb. He hoped there'd be no more tanks.

'Oy!' The voice made him turn and he saw Syzling running bent double towards him. 'Catch 'old of this 'ere!'

'This' was another Piat and it almost flattened Deacon.

'Where did you get it?' he demanded.

'They had one wi' nobody to fire it.'

'You've got a couple of lovely shiners, Syzling. You all right?'

Syzling looked dazed. 'Me 'ead's spinnin' a bit,' he said. 'It's addled me brain.'

'You never had a brain, Syzling,' Deacon grinned. 'Nobody with a brain would have dared to do what you did.'

For once, Syzling failed to react with a protest.

'Well, you 'elped,' he admitted.

'I'll get you a medal for this, Syzling, if it's the last thing I do.'

'You ought to 'ave one as well, sir. You stood up wi' me.'

Deacon was overcome. Sir! Syzling had finally managed it. At last he seemed to have got through to him. At last they were on the same wavelength.

'I think we've got this business taped,' he said.

five

Carefully examining Warley's radio, the signallers had come to the conclusion that, with a cracked panel and the veins of the condenser shot to hell, they weren't going to get much out of it, and they were too far from the river by this time to use the field telephone. But, with B and C Companies finally rounded up and the parts of another damaged set available, late in the afternoon they were able to announce that they'd managed to make one of them work. Yuell immediately ordered them to contact the Yellowjackets. 'If we can get 'em to move up to us,' he said to Warley, we might hang on and, if we can, they might get the tanks across.'

Warley thought the colonel was being bloody optimistic and, in any case, the Yellowjackets seemed to have disappeared off the face of the earth. By this time, however, Tallemach had pushed a group of Baluchi signallers and one of their sets across the river, and it was now possible to relay a message to the other bank and receive assurances that help was coming.

Giving the position of German mortar and machine-gun posts, they were also able to ask for artillery support and had the satisfaction soon afterwards of seeing the first shells landing among the wire just ahead. The guns were firing well, just clipping their position to land their missiles among the Germans. But then a new battery joined in, firing to instructions given in the fifty-six page orders where a weary clerk had misread the numbers, and three shells arrived far too close for comfort. They left shallow craters that were still smoking from the tremendous heat of the explosion when a moment later another salvo arrived, showering them with dirt and stones and wounding two men with fragments of rock.

'For God's sake!' Warley was staring towards the other side of the river, as though by sheer will-power he could compel a change of range. 'Haven't we got enough shooting at us without those silly buggers!'

The radio squawked as Yuell sent off a series of angry messages, but the artillery didn't appear to believe him and more shells arrived, still fortunately just ahead. It was twenty-five minutes – during which they all hugged the earth, sick with fear – before they could get the shooting stopped. Morale, raised by Syzling's feat with the Piat, had slumped badly.

As the offending guns became silent, the German fire began to increase again, hammering at a point by the river. Turning his binoculars in that direction, Yuell was just able to pick out movement in the greyness round Capodozzi and at Foiano further east.

'Must be the Baluchis supporting the Yellowjackets,' he said.

The new attack had started in the early evening. The air was already thick with smoke, and though the sun had appeared briefly, it gave no warmth. With the clouds rapidly closing in again, it became impossible to make out what was happening, but the firing in front of them slackened a little as though the German weapons had had to be diverted. Then, as the breeze cleared the smoke for a moment, they saw the outline of the bank, scarred with craters, and boats ferrying men across.

'The Yellowjackets must have done better than we did,' Yuell observed. 'They'll be pushing towards us before long.'

But by the time it was growing dark, there was no sign of relief and the rain had started once more. They were wet, tired and more than a little frightened. Hunger, and the shadow of a prisoner-of-war camp hovering over them, added to their misery.

The Germans kept firing flares, as if expecting them to try to advance, and the battlefield was lit up in a series of fleeting glimpses. They were all thinking about their own artillery now because it had suddenly dawned on them that until they moved, the guns were as likely to hit them as hit the Germans.

'I wish they'd shell the bloody general,' Hunters growled.

A few of them managed to snatch a little sleep in catnaps, while others counted noses in the dark and tried to find out what had happened to everybody.

'Where's Pedlar Parkin?' White asked. It was almost as if he missed Parkin's baiting.

'Ain't seen 'im since we got down to t' river,' Rich said. 'Musta got lost or copped it down there somewhere.'

There was a sudden silence because it wasn't like Parkin to get lost.

'Peace in our time.' 000 Bawden spoke next and as though he'd been brooding on something for a long while. 'That bastard with the moustache and umbrella. When he came back from Munich. Remember? Fat lot of bloody peace we've seen since then.'

'I notice 'e didn't join up and pick up a rifle,' Martindale said, sucking at an empty pipe.

'They never do, them lot,' Henry White said, his mouth as empty as a cavern. 'They're good at declarin' war, but they never join up an' fight it.'

'They did at Waterloo, 'Enry,' Rich said, as though he considered it his duty in Parkin's absence to take over the baiting. 'Napoleon was there. You musta seen 'im.'

'I 'eard,' Puddephatt said solemnly, 'that the Argylls caught a chameleon in North Africa.'

'What's that got to do wi' it?' Rich asked.

'Nothing. They put it on one of their kilts. It settled it champion. It couldn't manage nothing more than a mucky brown, they said.'

'Well, could *you?*'

'I'm not a chameleon.'

'Even if you were.'

The argument dragged on as army arguments always did, pointless, witless, following no particular line, getting side-tracked whenever they lost the gist of what they were talking about. But it took their minds off their misery, the hunger and the cold, and the dead and wounded in the bottom of the hollow. As darkness finally enveloped them, every single weapon seemed to stop firing within a matter of minutes and there was one of those strange lulls that occasionally fall on a battlefield.

And then, someone started to sing in a foxhole over on the left. The voice came out of the darkness, shrill, almost falsetto, the accent ill-educated but quite plain. They could all hear it and knew that the Germans could hear it too.

> 'Now the day is o-over, night is drawing nigh,
> Shadows of the e-evening flit across the flippin' sky.'

'It's Pedlar,' White said, his empty mouth grinning.

The arguments stopped and men smiled, pleased that A Company's fool was still around. Even Yuell, crouching with Warley near the radio, stopped and listened.

The voice came again, doggedly.

> 'When this bloomin' war is over,
> Oh, 'ow 'appy I shall be,
> When I gits me civvy clo's on,

No more soldierin' for me.
No more church parades on Sundays,
No more askin' for a pass,
You can tell the sergeant-major
To stick it up 'is bloomin' arse.'

There was a dead silence as the song finished; then from the German lines they heard a faint cheer and someone shouted. 'Encore! *Noch einmal!* More, please!'

The invisible Parkin was silent for a while, then his voice came again. 'Thank you. Thank you, one and all. And now from my extensive repertoire – '

'The monkey and the baboon sat upon the grass,
And the monkey stuck its finger up the baboon's...'

'That'll do!' Yuell was still smiling as he shouted. 'We've all enjoyed it, but they might be trying to find out where you are. You'll probably get a mortar bomb on you.'

'No!' A voice came from the direction of the Germans. 'It vas beautiful. Perhaps you would like us to sing for you.'

'This is bloody ridiculous,' Warley said. 'Stopping the war to collect wounded and singing serenades while we try to kill each other.'

But there was no more singing because suddenly a German Schmeisser opened up, ripping off a burst like the tearing of a giant sheet of linen. Other weapons followed it. They could see the flashes and tried to make out what the Germans were shooting at. They soon found out because the remnants of two companies of Baluchis, who had crossed the river during the afternoon, fell into the dip. Tall, good-looking men with smooth faces and glittering black eyes – and well known to the Yorkshiremen who'd shared more than one nasty moment with them – they were loaded with ammunition and carried rations in sandbags.

'Tik hai, Johnny,' Corporal Gask said in his frozen-faced way.

'Tik hai.' The lance-naik he addressed beamed at him. 'Very nasty war, sir.'

The officer in command was a captain, his major having been badly wounded in the crossing. 'We've been clinging to that bloody bank all afternoon,' he said bitterly. 'I thought we'd never get going.'

Yuell stared round at the Baluchis beginning to disperse into the dips and holes to right and left.

'Is this all there are?' he asked.

'What's left of two companies, sir. They sent the other two over at Castelgrande to reinforce the Yellowjackets. Whoever it was who sent us across in broad daylight must have been mad. We could hardly move for the ammunition and the grenades.'

Yuell's head jerked up. 'You've brought grenades? Who sent them?'

'We just helped ourselves. I think they were part of a load that went missing somewhere. We found the muleteers wandering round in the dark asking where they should go and we decided the best place was here because we heard that our other two companies at Castelgrande are still pinned down close to the river. When do we move forward, sir?'

Yuell looked at Warley. 'I doubt if we do,' he said.

They were not to know how small the gains at Castelgrande had been, or that the other two companies of Baluchis, thrown across there in support, had proved of little value against the intense German fire. The Yeomanry had tried once again to work their tanks down to the river, but the shelling was frustrating every effort made by the Engineers and a vehicular bridge had not even been started. The Engineers were now merely fighting to stay alive until the next effort could be made; while the tanks had been obliged once more to move back behind the hills, and the Baluchis, their colonel wounded, were pinned down in the low, wet water-meadows, utterly naked to enemy observation.

To confound the scene further, Brigadier Rankin, in an excess of bull-headed zeal, had committed not one of his battalions but two – the Birminghams and the Rajputs – and seen them both decimated. His last battalion, the Punjabis, who might have helped Yuell, had also been sent up to Castelgrande but, with disaster already in the air, had not been committed. Like the Baluchis the previous day they had taken part in neither action, wasting the whole of the daylight hours in the wet hen tactics of moving backwards and forwards. A desperate attempt to move from Castelgrande towards San Eusebio to link up with Yuell had been completely defeated, and in no time the whole group, including the remnants of the Yellowjackets, were back on the river bank.

The extent of the disaster was made clear by the message that was handed to Tallemach. It had been brought to his headquarters by an Engineer sergeant in San Bartolomeo who had seen Yuell's pigeon returning home and had watched it all the way across the river to its loft.

The last of the pigeon handlers was lying face-down on the grass verge half-way along the San Bartolomeo road, where he'd been caught by a shell burst, and since there was no one about and because he was a pigeon fancier himself at home, the sergeant had entered the hut and examined the bird. Unclipping the message from its leg, he had shown it to his officer who had sent him at once by jeep to Tallemach's headquarters.

'*Herewith pigeon is returned. We have enough to eat and look forward with pleasure to your next attempt.*'

Tallemach stared at the message, written in English on a scrap of paper torn from a German message pad, then handed it in silence to his brigade major. Obviously they had barely scratched the surface of the German defence. He made a great effort to get his tired brain to concentrate, even now unable to accept that he no longer had any sons.

Without General Tonge, the fight seemed to have got out of hand and Heathfield was still demanding that they strengthen the Castelgrande attack. Rankin was up there now, raging that it was impossible, that those of his men who'd got across had found no survivors from the previous day's fighting, and that he wasn't going to commit his last battalion for any bastard. By butting his head again and again at the German defences, he'd almost destroyed two of his battalions and, uncertain now what to do, was blaming everything on Heathfield. Much of it was certainly Heathfield's doing, Tallemach knew, but he suspected Rankin wasn't without blame either.

'The man's inefficient,' Rankin had stormed on the telephone. 'He shouldn't be in a position to destroy men's lives.'

Coming from a man of Rankin's methods, the words were pure irony, but Tallemach said nothing and the angry voice went on. 'He's artillery, anyway, so what does he know about infantry tactics? And the bastard's behind us in the Army List, you know, Tallemach. He's just bloody lucky to be where he is. When this bloody thing's over I'm going to raise the biggest stink you ever heard.'

Tallemach let him rant on. He'd known Rankin a long time and had never been particularly fond of him. It was one of the chances of war that he was obliged to work with him, but it was not something which roused much enthusiasm in him.

As he struggled to produce order out of the chaos that confronted him, Rankin himself appeared from Foiano, black in the face with fury.

'Did you know 19th Div. artillery's leaving already?' he stormed.

'Yes,' Tallemach said. 'They're booked to give support fire at Cassino.'

'That bastard Heathfield promised it. He promised it after the first day. Typical staff college nonsense. Staff college always constipates field soldiers. I got on the blower to him and told him that if he took the guns away from my sector before I'd got my chaps back, I'd go up there and shoot the bugger.'

'What did he say?'

'He said I was mad.' Rankin rubbed a big red hand over his face. It left his moustache lopsided. 'Probably I am. Italy makes us all a bit barmy. All the same, I said I'd do it. I told him, "What's one life against the dozens you'll destroy if you shift the guns?"'

Tallemach looked at him sadly. Rankin was all shout, and he knew – as doubtless Heathfield did – that it was an empty threat. All the same, it showed that to Rankin command wasn't just pushing little flags about on a map as it was to Heathfield, unaware that they represented beings of flesh and blood, with thoughts and feelings and an awareness of pain and fear.

'You'd never have done it, George,' he said quietly.

'No,' Rankin admitted slowly. 'I don't suppose I would. But I was so bloody angry. I just hope it frightened him a bit.'

They were still gloomily wondering what could possibly be their next move when a message from Foiano arrived. *Under heavy fire,* it announced. *Bridgehead untenable. All senior officers killed or wounded. Units disorganised. Bridges and boats gone. Am ordering remnants back east of river.*

Rankin sighed. 'I'd better get back there,' he said.

As he reached for his hat another message arrived. It was from Division this time and had been originated by Heathfield.

'Keep up pressure. Attack at Cassino started. First reports indicate success.'

Tallemach handed it to Rankin. 'I'm pleased he's pleased,' he said quietly.

Tallemach was still pondering the imponderables when Fletcher-Smith was brought in.

Rankin had long since disappeared to the Castelgrande sector and the reports that had come in had indicated a disaster there even worse than the one in the early hours of the morning. Rankin's men had made their way back under extreme difficulties, leaving their dead and wounded behind them, and he was occupied at the moment with attempts to bring out the last few isolated groups. Those who had made it had lost clothes, weapons, everything. The whole thing was a mess, one of the worst foul-ups since Tobruk.

Tallemach was studying the map when his brigade major appeared. 'They've just brought in a chap who's got across the river from Colonel Yuell, sir,' he announced.

'Got across?' Tallemach lifted his head. 'How?'

'Seems he swam, sir.'

'Did he, by God? Bring him in.'

Fletcher-Smith was blue with cold and wrapped in a blanket, beneath which he wore nothing but a pair of ragged underpants.

The crossing had been more hellish than he'd ever expected but, having succeeded, he was possessed by a feeling of elation that at last he'd found his proper niche. Never in his wildest dreams had he expected to be able to use in the army the one thing he was really good at – swimming

– but now he felt he wouldn't mind swimming back and forth across the river all day.

Getting to the water's edge had taken him hours. The German machine-guns had chased him from one rock and hollow to another until he'd had to dive for cover into a shell crater and crouch there for what had seemed years. It was almost as if the Germans had suspected what he was up to because, in addition to the machine-guns, they seemed to have put a sniper to watch him, and every time he tried to move, a bullet clipped the earth to send flecks of mud into his face. As evening approached and the light had gone, however, he had seen his chance and, dodging from the crater, his heel clipped as he went by a last shot from the sniper, he had dived into the ditch Warley had indicated. It was full of filthy brown water and weeds and smelled of sewage, which he'd decided meant that the Italians, in their slap-happy fashion, had used it to get rid of the effluent from San Eusebio. Nevertheless, it was a lot better than being in the open, and, with the German machine-guns still clipping away, he'd crawled along the muddy sloping side most of the way, slithering helplessly from time to time into the water. At one point where the bank was bare and he couldn't find a damn thing with which to pull himself out, he'd thought he was drowning – him, Francis Fletcher-Smith who'd swum the length of Windermere and bloody nearly made it to Cap Gris Nez! In the end, he'd got a grip on himself and stopped panicking, and had continued down the ditch, half wading, half swimming, until he'd found a tree with which to drag himself clear.

Soaked, half frozen and plastered with mud, he'd reached the river bank as it grew dusk. He'd seen groups of dark-faced Indian soldiers crouching on the mud by the bridge – clutching weapons, ammunition boxes and sandbags – and was staggered at the number of bodies, both Indian and British, that were sprawled about. Here and there a man still moved feebly, and a medical orderly with a bandaged head had dragged one or two of them into the shelter of the bank. When he discovered what Fletcher-Smith intended, he gave him a tired smile.

'You'll be lucky even to get to the water,' he said.

As he spoke, a man sheltering among the tufts of grass not far away jumped up and tried to run to where an assault boat was lying lopsidedly by the water's edge. Immediately, a machine-gun churned up the mud around him, throwing it up in little black splashes until he sank down and sprawled on his face.

Fletcher-Smith knew this was going to be the hard bit and he stripped slowly to his underpants. They were a little on the grubby side but this didn't seem to be a time when he needed to worry about who was going to see him. As a boy his mother had always insisted on clean underclothes – in case he was run over, she'd said, and was taken to hospital. In the precise, dogmatic way which marked him now and was already emerging even in childhood, he'd never been able to understand why it was more important to be dead in clean underclothes than alive in dirty ones.

As he dropped his shirt to the grass, he took off his glasses and handed them with his wallet to the medical orderly. 'That's my money,' he said. 'It isn't much, but some time I'd like it back.'

There wasn't much money in the wallet but there was a photograph of the girl in Trepiazze. In his heart of hearts, Fletcher-Smith knew his interest in her was only physical and that it was purely fortuitous that she was interested in reading like himself. Nevertheless, it had been nice to think of her at times, and as she had provided him with his first experience of the warmth of a woman's body, he felt he owed her a debt of gratitude if nothing else.

'I'm off,' he said and began to move along the river bank, his head down, looking for the best place to cross.

There seemed to be a lot of debris floating about, but most of it had been cleared by the current. Deciding that the safest place was near the bridge, which would at least give him protection on one side, he made his way to the mud between the abandoned equipment and holed boats that lay about. Finally, standing upright, he set off towards the water at full speed.

When he was shown in to Tallemach by the Brigade Intelligence Officer, it was dark. He had a bandage round his foot where he'd cut it as he'd run to the water, and his teeth were chattering furiously.

'Has he had anything to drink?' Tallemach asked.

'Rum, sir,' Fletcher-Smith managed between the shuddering. 'From the Engineers when I arrived.'

Tallemach reached for a bottle of whisky, sloshed out a tumblerful and pushed it across.

'Better drink that,' he said. 'Where've you come from?'

The whisky was taking Fletcher-Smith's breath away more than the swim had. 'Colonel Yuell sent me, sir,' he panted. 'I'm a good swimmer and I volunteered to try to get across.'

'You were damn lucky some sniper didn't get you.'

'The swimming wasn't too difficult, sir,' Fletcher-Smith said. 'It was getting to the river that was the worst. I thought I'd never make it.'

To Tallemach it seemed he was totally unaware that what he'd done was brave; as if he'd done it merely because it had to be done, like polishing a barrack room floor or enduring a freezing night on sentry duty. He glanced out into the night. There was a suggestion of sleet in the air, and he realised just how cold it must have been.

'Find him a mug of tea somewhere,' he said to the Intelligence officer. 'Hot as you can get it.' He turned again to Fletcher-Smith, his brain functioning properly now that there was something concrete to grasp. 'What's happening across there?'

'Colonel Yuell's in a dip, sir, just to the east of San Eusebio. We got to our first objective but we're pinned down now, and running short of ammunition.'

'Haven't you received any more? Two companies of the Baluchis were sent across with as much as they could carry.'

'When I left they were still pinned down near the bridge, sir, but they've probably reached Colonel Yuell now it's dark.'

'What else can you tell us? How about casualties?'

'Thirty per cent, sir, Colonel Yuell told me to say. He also said to say he's all right at the moment but can't move anywhere without reinforcements. With help something might be done, but we need all we can get, sir.'

'Can you read a map?' Tallemach asked.

'Yes, sir.'

'Think you could pinpoint the German machine-gun posts?'

Fletcher-Smith rose from the chair they'd found for him. As he did so, the blanket swung open and he was horribly aware of his tattered, mud-stained underpants. His mother was right – the thought came crazily into his head – it was always best to wear clean underwear. You never knew when you might have to report to the brigadier wearing nothing else. He jabbed his finger at Tallemach's map.

'Sir, Colonel Yuell said if we could only get an air strike – '

'I wish to God we could,' Tallemach admitted. 'But not only can they not fly in this stuff, but half of them are bogged down on their own fields.' He looked at a sergeant standing behind the brigade major. 'Get him somewhere warm, Sergeant, and see he gets a good hot meal.'

'I'll go back, sir,' Fletcher-Smith offered. 'If I could be fitted up with a uniform and a rifle, I'll go back.'

'You've done enough.'

'I'd *like* to go back, sir. They need me. They might need someone to swim across again.'

Tallemach put his hand on his shoulder. 'I think you'd better stay here,' he said.

Fletcher-Smith was insistent. 'I'd *rather* go back, sir, if you don't mind. If anybody's crossing tonight I'll go with them.'

Soon afterwards, Rankin telephoned with news of the New Zealanders' fight at Cassino to the north-east.

'Same balls-up as here,' he snorted. 'They actually got bombers over but now the tanks are held up by the craters they've made. It seems to me somebody's appreciation of the enemy's strength was a bit out. I think all we can do is get our chaps back to safety.'

Tallemach was still staring at the map when Heathfield appeared. 'The crossing at Cassino seems to be going well,' he said.

'My information's to the contrary,' Tallemach said coldly.

'No, you're wrong.' Heathfield was enthusiastic, slapping at his leg with his stick. 'They're on to Highway Six and heading for Castle Hill.'

'Perhaps the imponderables were in their favour up there.'

Heathfield's head jerked round. 'What do you mean?'

'Well, they certainly weren't in our favour here, were they? The loss of those grenades and mortar bombs when they were needed. That damn bad recce of the track from Capodozzi. Whoever did that ought to be sacked.'

'In fact, he's in hospital,' Heathfield said coldly. 'With malaria.'

'Then perhaps he should have been better briefed, because he obviously didn't know what was wanted. Then there was the absence of boats. We hadn't half enough.'

'Anything else?'

'There are quite a lot of things, and I intend to make them known in my report.'

Heathfield ignored the comment. 'I'm getting Rankin to try again at Castelgrande,' he said.

Tallemach gave him a hard look. It was the duty of a leader to chivvy his commanders and control the tendency among them to plan for every conceivable contingency when speed and boldness were called for, but there had to be a compromise between forceful leadership and the acceptance of practicalities such as difficult terrain, winter weather, the tiredness of overworked men and the expertise of the enemy. 'My impression,' he said, 'is that he's got nothing left to try with and that it would be a dead loss in any case.'

'*My* impression is that it would *not* be a dead loss,' Heathfield snapped. 'We're wearing down the Germans.'

'I thought attrition went out with the last war,' Tallemach snapped back. 'We're wearing *us* down, too.'

Heathfield went doggedly on. 'I've ordered him to erect two footbridges and I've told the Sappers to press on with getting the tanks across.'

It was Tallemach's impression that there was a certain amount of spite in Heathfield's insistence. It was enough to shake anybody to have somebody offer to shoot you – especially someone on your own side and it must have shaken Heathfield. He was never the sort of man to take things lying down, and he seemed to have decided to break Rankin for his bluntness.

'I've ordered another smoke screen,' he was saying. 'There are six hundred smoke pots we can use in Foiano.'

Tallemach's head jerked round. 'Why were we told they were in San Bartolomeo?'

'You weren't.'

Tallemach didn't argue, because he knew his brigade major well enough to be certain he would have filed the signal that said they had been.

'How much does it take to convince you that the defeat up there's a final one?' he asked.

241

Heathfield stared coldly at him. 'Are you arguing with the general?' he asked.

'If the general's insisting,' Tallemach said, 'no, I'm not. If it's you who's insisting, then, yes, I am. This persistence with Castelgrande's nothing but wishful thinking. The Germans aren't groggy and their morale's not low – especially up there, where we haven't a single man on their side of the river capable of doing a damn thing. They haven't shown the slightest signs of withdrawing anywhere, least of all up there.'

The argument went on for some time, with Heathfield continuing to insist and Tallemach at one point even offering to write out his resignation. The matter ended with neither of them satisfied, but clearly Heathfield wasn't backing down.

Tallemach watched Heathfield leave in silence. He was still trying to decide what to do, with all their reserves committed except for Rankin's single remaining battalion of Punjabis to which he was clinging like a leech, when General Tonge appeared. He wore his left arm in a sling and there was a piece of sticking plaster across his forehead. He looked pale and in pain and he also looked, Tallemach thought, in a damn bad temper.

Tonge had left the crossing to Heathfield, thinking that, since he'd done all the planning, he ought at least to be able to handle the actual event. He'd also been inclined from the first reports he'd been sent to lie back in the hospital where they'd taken him and let them get on with it, but then he'd begun to hear rumours that things had gone very wrong indeed.

Heathfield, he supposed. He'd always admired Heathfield's drive but he'd long suspected he was slapdash in his methods, and so dictatorial he wouldn't listen to advice from more experienced men.

Discharging himself, he'd been driven up to the Castelgrande sector and had arrived just in time to see

SWORDPOINT

Rankin's Punjabis forming up with the remnants of the Birminghams and the Rajputs for a new attack. He had also seen with some surprise the senior surviving officer of the Birminghams shaking hands with his subordinates.

'Why are you doing that?' he had asked.

The officer, a very young captain, had at first refused to answer, and it was only when Tonge insisted that he'd sheepishly admitted that he was saying good-bye.

'Why?'

The captain drew a deep breath. 'Sir, I made the strongest possible representations to Brigadier Heathfield. I was not prepared to lead my people across the river again. I consider it certain destruction. He insisted, however, and said that if I wasn't prepared to do the job, then he'd have to find someone who was. Because I could see no sense in committing them to the attack under someone who was a stranger, I said that in that case I'd go. But I explained to my officers what I'd done and I was just saying good-bye to them.'

'Hardly a way to instil confidence in them,' Tonge observed tartly.

'No, sir.' The captain, who seemed about twenty, looked faintly ashamed.

'The attack will not go in, nevertheless.'

As he'd left, Tonge managed to acquire the captain's name. His sympathy lay with him entirely, but officers who made dramatic gestures of that sort weren't the type for promotion to command of a battalion. Gestures were all very well but they usually achieved nothing and very often merely put the fear of God into other people.

All the same, he was disquieted by what he'd heard. In addition to mistrusting officers who made pointless gestures and argued about their orders with senior officers, he didn't like senior officers who wouldn't listen and used threats. British soldiers weren't a bunch of Hitler Youth, blindly

243

obeying the diktats of a megalomaniac commander. Men who were being asked to risk their lives had a right to state their views if nothing else, and Heathfield not only hadn't bothered to listen, he'd been prepared to push the matter to the point of intimidation.

He glanced at Tallemach. He looked tired, he noticed. 'I'm sorry about your son, Tom,' he said. 'I've only just heard.'

Tallemach nodded, grateful to Tonge for his sympathy. It made it a little easier to bear. Tonge's son had disappeared in *Hood* just when his father had been engaged with the Germans in Crete. Both young men had no known graves and neither father had been vouchsafed the time for mourning.

'Thank you, sir,' he said. 'It was a bit of a shock. I only lost the other a month or two back.'

'Yes, I know.' Tonge didn't dwell on the event. It didn't help, and it would never bring the boy back. 'This crossing of yours,' he said. 'Tell me what went wrong.'

Tallemach paused, then decided there was no sense in beating about the bush. It was up to Heathfield to look after himself. There was often a great deal of infighting in the higher echelons of the army and it wasn't all with the enemy.

Tonge listened quietly, making no comment, no recriminations for things that had gone wrong.

'I suspect it might be my fault,' he said finally. 'The reports I received were that two battalions were across.'

'*Elements* of two battalions, sir,' Tallemach corrected. 'I was also told two battalions were across but I knew it couldn't be two *whole* battalions, and I took care to check it and correct the message before I passed it on to your headquarters.'

Tonge said nothing, deciding that Heathfield had been deliberately clouding the issue for his own satisfaction. Heathfield was a man who liked to win, Tonge remembered. Even at bridge. And this affair was entirely his baby. It had always been Tonge's practice to encourage his subordinates. How else could they gain the experience to become leaders? But he suspected that, having made his appreciation, Heathfield was determined to prove he'd been right. It seemed he'd even falsified reports – perhaps not with the outright intention of misleading but because he hadn't yet learned to be dispassionate.

His planning, too, it seemed, had been misguided and, because of his personality, inflexible, and the two, together with the imponderables of war, had added up to confusion. War and battles were always confused and victory went to the general who could first sort out order from the chaos; Heathfield had not only failed to do this but, by his rigidness, his willingness to believe what he wanted to believe, had actually added to it. Heathfield would have to go.

'A pity it hasn't helped them opposite Cassino,' he said.

Tallemach's thoughts were bitter. If it hadn't even achieved that, the thing had been pointless from the beginning.

'I think I'm going to call it off, Tom,' Tonge said. 'I'm sure it'll be understood, and I'm keeping the 19th Division artillery here a bit longer. So keep them hammering at Jerry to keep him busy. I shall have to explain, but it might help Rankin at Castelgrande. When they're all out, try to evacuate the men in this sector.'

Tallemach was still considering ways and means of extricating Yuell's men when Yuell himself appeared. By dint of shouting, the men on the other side had managed to convey their need for boats to evacuate wounded, and the few that were left had been pushed across in the dark. Yuell had been in the last boat, with a gaping hole in his thigh.

He refused to be put in an ambulance and insisted on being rushed to Tallemach's HQ. He was deathly pale and in a lot of pain so that his words came slowly, but he was making an effort to make his brain function intelligently.

'Warley's hanging on,' he said. 'He's done damn well and I want to make sure he gets something out of this, because he deserves it. We were just starting to evacuate the wounded when I was hit. But the German fire's slackened a bit, and the Baluchis brought across a supply of ammunition and what appears to be some of the grenades we lost a couple of days ago. I think now it might be possible to make a move forward instead of backward.'

Tallemach sighed. The bloody grenades *would* finally arrive when it was too late. 'Unfortunately,' he said, 'the general's just called it off.'

Yuell frowned. 'At any other time, I'd have agreed, sir,' he persisted, 'But, at the moment, I think we should try just a little longer. Haven't you noticed the weather?'

Tallemach's eyes lifted. 'What about the weather?'

'It's clearing, sir. You can see stars to the east.'

Tallemach turned to his brigade major. 'Get Intelligence to check with the RAF,' he said quickly. 'Then get hold of Division. I also want to speak to the general and to the artillery. Finally, find out if we have any information about any movement towards Cassino by the Germans opposite.'

When the brigade major reappeared, he held a fistful of reports. 'The general's not at Division,' he announced. 'But the Germans *are* moving north. Army have let Div. know because they believe they're moving out of our sector. The Germans have had heavy casualties at Cassino and they seem to think they can contain our attacks here.'

As the brigade major vanished, the intelligence officer appeared. 'RAF Met says the sky's clearing, sir,' he said. 'They predict high cloud for tomorrow, probably even sun. I took the liberty of asking them what the chances of flying were. They said pretty good. Air Observation will be able to get spotting planes up.'

As the Gunner colonel appeared, Tallemach turned to Yuell. 'Think you're capable of pinpointing the German strongpoints for us?' he asked. 'We've had it done once but I'd like them confirmed.'

Yuell jabbed at the map with his finger.

'I'd like stonks putting down on them,' Tallemach said to the Gunner. 'We're going to try to move and I want those strongpoints swamping if possible.'

The artilleryman was about to put forward objections when Tallemach bit his head off.

'Don't argue,' he snapped. 'See it's done! I'll give you the times later.'

As the Gunner vanished and Yuell was helped out, Tallemach picked up the telephone and called Rankin.

'George,' he said. 'I want your Punjabis.'

'You can't have 'em,' Rankin fumed. 'I need 'em here.'

'George, they're doing no damn good up there! They've just been shuttling backwards and forwards all day like a set of yo-yos. I want 'em here as fast as you can get 'em.'

Rankin tried to object but Tallemach interrupted.

'Listen, George,' he said sharply, 'we've had a report from the North Yorkshires. One of Yuell's men swam the river and then Yuell himself was brought across wounded. They're still hanging on there and they think that with help they can move forward. Especially if we can get an air strike.'

'You'll be lucky in this weather!'

'George, we've had a Met report. The RAF think they'll be able to fly tomorrow. And it's been raining so long the chances *must* be in favour of it breaking. George, you know damn well I never liked this crossing, but there's suddenly a chance. It's worth taking.'

'Then why not here?'

Rankin seemed more bull-headed than ever and Tallemach suspected he was worried. Doubtless Tonge had had a few words with him and he was concerned about his future and wondering if he couldn't pull a few things from the fire.

Tallemach decided to stand no nonsense, sensing that Rankin would back down if he insisted.

'Because the general's called it all off up there,' he pointed out. 'We're only reinforcing failure and you know as well as I do that that's something we don't do.'

There was a long silence; then Rankin's voice came again, still doubtful. 'Has the general okayed it?'

'I haven't been able to contact him yet and we can't wait. I'll have to justify myself when it's over, I suppose, but I'm going to chance it.'

There was another silence, followed by Rankin's grudging consent. 'I'll get 'em in lorries straight away.'

As he put the telephone down, Tallemach looked up at the brigade major. 'Get hold of that chap, Fletcher-Smith,' he said. 'But get one of the docs to have a look at him first to see if he really is fit to go back.'

'He looked it, sir. And perhaps he is. I gather he once almost swam the Channel.'

'Did he, by God? Well, let's not have anybody say we sent him when he wasn't fit. If he is, bring him here. As soon as the Punjabis arrive, he's going to lead 'em to Warley via that ditch he used. Then get hold of the Engineers. We're going to have another go at throwing footbridges across. If they're wide enough for one man, it'll be enough to feed supports to the Yorkshires. Once they're safely across, I shall want that bridge putting over for the tanks. Tell 'em to get on with it. We've wasted enough time as it is.'

Warley lay on the lip of the hollow, peering ahead of him. His eyes were prickly with lack of sleep and red-rimmed with staring. A strange, almost eerie lull had fallen over the battle and he could even hear a bird singing.

He listened for a while, thinking. According to casualty figures, they were defeated and as good as prisoners of war. But good soldiers trusted their instincts, not figures. They tried to understand silence on a battlefield, they tried to define tanks or cannon behind camouflage, they sensed the movement or non-movement of troops.

Despite his preference for civilian life, Warley was a good soldier and his mind was moving swiftly.

'Hear that, Tony?' he said.

Jago listened, his head cocked. He was a city-dweller and knew nothing about birds. 'Sparrow?' he asked.

Warley gave a short bark of laughter. 'It's a nightingale, you bloody idiot,' he said. 'The first this year.'

Jago was unimpressed. To him it sounded like a sparrow that couldn't sleep. 'So?'

'You couldn't have heard that a little while ago. I think the fire's fallen off all round. Would you say something's happened in front there?'

Jago was a good soldier, too, and now his own acute senses were alert. 'Think the buggers fancy they've got us licked?'

'I bet they gave the padre his truce because they thought they had. It'd be nice to prove 'em wrong, wouldn't it? I was wondering if we couldn't have a go at enlarging this bloody bridgehead. The wire's cut over there on the right where those Teds came through this morning, and I notice the artillery's made a gap on the left as well. If we split our force and go for 'em at a rush, we might just do it.'

Jago shrugged. 'The colonel said he'd drum up some more men when he got to the other side. Hadn't we better wait for them?'

'You know,' Warley said slowly, 'I'm inclined to think not. If we can get through that wire before daylight, we can get into those bloody machine-gun posts that have been bothering us before they know we're there. They've quietened down a lot, and I notice there haven't been any flares lately. I wonder if some of their people have been pulled out as reserves against the crossing at Castelgrande.'

'It'd help if they had.'

'You could take the right side, I'd take the left.'

'What about the Baluchis?'

'This one's up to *us*,' Warley said. 'If we're quiet we ought to be able to get well forward. Then I'll give everybody ten minutes and fire a Very light. How does it sound to you?'

To Jago it sounded terrifying, and he felt his body turn cold at the thought of it. He'd already survived taking more chances than he deserved, and he didn't fancy taking another. But he'd been with Warley a long time and anything was better than sitting in the dip all next day while the Germans dropped mortar bombs on them.

'I dare bet the Teds' positions are deeper than this bloody dip of Deacon's,' he said. 'And I'll bet also that they're better proof against mortars. After all, they've been there long enough to make 'em strong.'

'Right. We go in with the Baluchis right behind us. If they keep close we can swamp those Ted posts in front. They can't be held all that heavily or they'd have set about us, wouldn't they? The Baluchis are agreeable to us running the show.'

'All right,' Jago said uncertainly. 'Let's give it a go.'

'Good. You take everybody to the right of here. I'll take everybody to the left. The Baluchis follow up in support. You'd better get round and warn your men. We start when I fire a red Very light. Okay?'

'Okay. Any special methods?'

'No. Just go like the clappers.'

'You can't sprint eighty yards and hope to arrive in good shape,' Jago said. 'We shan't be able to hit a bloody thing.'

'We shan't be doing that sort of shooting,' Warley pointed out. 'And the quicker across the safer we'll be.'

Jago nodded, aware that normally he was the one who advocated speed and dash.

Warley grinned under his dirt. 'See you back here in an hour,' he said. 'We start ten minutes afterwards.'

Crawling flat against the earth along the lip of the hollow to the outlying positions, Warley and Jago readied their men. It was easier in the dark, though there were still a few machine-gun bursts to set their hearts beating faster. The ammunition and grenades the Baluchis had brought were distributed, and the men lit last fags, wiped their mouths with the backs of their hands, spat, cleared their throats and emptied their bladders; all the things they would have done if they'd been entering a race.

'The safest place against enemy shelling's always in the enemy positions,' Jago told them.

There were a few silly jokes in whispers, and cigarettes were passed round for a last drag.

'Gie's one of thi cigarettes, Gasky,' Rich asked.

Corporal Gask studied him in his expressionless way. 'It'll stunt your growth,' he said.

Rich looked up at Gask's lean six-foot-three. 'It doesn't seem to have stunted thine,' he pointed out.

Deacon's heart lifted as he heard them. Their spirits seemed to have revived at the prospect of moving forward.

'We're expecting big things from you, Frying,' he told Syzling. 'They might send tanks at us, so just let's have a repetition of this morning.'

'So long as you pass the bombs, sir,' Syzling said and Deacon felt cock-a-hoop. Syzling seemed to have got hold of the 'sir' business at least. It was going to be all right in the future. No more curses. No more snarling. No more bad temper. No more sullenness.

They were going to use every man they had. Only O'Mara, the doctor, the orderlies and the wounded were to hold the position in the hollow. If they failed, it would be God help them all, but Warley was hoping they wouldn't fail.

He got the remaining officers round him. 'There's only one order,' he announced. 'Get through those gaps and into the Ted positions before they wake up. They're as tired as we are and I suspect they think they've got us pinned down. Let's show 'em they haven't. Information about the enemy: There isn't any. They're Nazis and that's enough under the circumstances, I think. Any questions?'

There weren't, and Warley continued, 'You have a quarter of an hour to get your men as far forward as you can. This bloody country's full of dips, so you ought to be able to get up close. And see there's no noise. Tell your people to tie handkerchiefs round the Bren mags and things like that, so they don't clatter. I want you in their lines within half a minute of the whistle. Get cracking.'

The order group broke up. It was the shortest and simplest briefing they'd ever experienced but by this time they all knew exactly where they were going and suspected that if they didn't arrive quickly, they'd end up dead or prisoners of war.

As they met again, Warley and Jago consulted their watches.

'Ten minutes from now,' Warley said. 'You ready?'

'Ready as I'll ever be.'

O'Mara joined them. 'If this doesn't come off, Padre,' Warley told him, 'try to go on holding this place until help comes. Or is that against your beliefs?'

'I don't think Almighty God's going to count the whys and wherefores in an affair like this,' O'Mara observed. 'As they did at Pearl Harbour, let us praise the Lord and pass the ammunition.'

'Say a prayer for us, Padre.'

O'Mara moved his hand in a blessing. 'God go with you,' he murmured, an infinite sadness in his eyes.

'Right,' Warley said. 'Here goes.'

He hitched at his belt and climbed out of the dip.

The Very light soared up, dragging a long tail of grey smoke, until it was out of sight in the darkness; then it burst into a red glow. As Warley's whistle went, they clutched their weapons and followed him.

In the light of the flare, Warley could see men already running for the gaps in the wire. His heart thudding, Jago leapt into the trench but Gask had arrived ahead of him and appeared to be beating up on his own the two or three Germans who were manning it. At home, the instructors had always insisted they should go into the attack yelling furiously and pulling fierce faces. Being an unimaginative type, however, Gask had been given up as a bad job and told he'd never be much good in an attack. The instructors couldn't have been more wrong because he was using his rifle and bayonet in the best drill manner – up, two, three; six inches of sharp Sheffield and no more – but all still in his usual expressionless manner.

Over on the left, a little behind Jago's group, Warley's foot caught in a looping strand as he passed through the wire and he did a nose-dive into a German machine-gun position. The top of his helmet crashed against a German helmet and slithered off into a German face and the two men collapsed in the bottom of the foxhole. Warley sat up to see CSM Farnsworth alongside him, clubbing the life out of the German, and as he struggled to his feet they caught in a charcoal brazier that had scattered hot coals. His trousers began to smoulder, and he slapped at the sparks to extinguish them.

'Christ,' Farnsworth panted. 'A fire to keep you warm! That's something our lot never think of.'

'Come on!' Warley sounded equally breathless. 'This is only the beginning. The real position's further on.'

As they scrambled from the hole, another machine-gun started and someone screamed. Then the gun stopped abruptly and didn't start again. Just in front of Warley, yet another one took its place, but it was firing to his right towards Jago's men and he heard the bullets swishing through the undergrowth past him. The next moment, he and Farnsworth and a few more found themselves hard up against a concrete pill-box with the gun firing over their heads out of a slit.

It was Henry White who moved first. He knew exactly what to do because he'd done it before in the mud at Passchendaele in 1917. Reaching for a grenade, he pulled the pin and slipped it silently through the aperture. The machine-gun still went on firing in short bursts; then, just when they were wondering what had gone wrong with the grenade, there was a tremendous crash and it stopped.

'Round the back,' Warley yelled.

As they reached the rear of the pill-box, they saw a German soldier scrambling away up the slope, screaming, his clothes on fire. Grinning, McWatters shot him in the back.

The inside was a shambles with a wrecked gun and four bleeding bodies. Running off to the right, they fell into a covered timber-lined trench, and Warley realised with surprise that there were now twenty-odd men with him whereas originally there'd only been three or four.

'Two of you stay here,' he said. 'The rest come with me.'

They set off up the covered trench, and saw a torch coming towards them. Duff fired his Sten at it; it went out and they were in darkness. Somebody was moaning in front of them, '*Mutter! Mutter! Hilfe mir!*'

'Got the bastards,' Farnsworth said with satisfaction.

He struck a match and just ahead they saw three men lying on the ground, one of them still alive. The Germans had been rushing down the trench to investigate what was happening. At the end was a door, and a German who looked about sixteen was just trying to jam it shut. Rich pushed his rifle in the gap but there was a burst of firing from inside and he fell away, crying out in pain, the flesh shredded from his calf. The German was still trying to push the rifle out so he could close the door when Henry White pulled the pin from another grenade and slipped it through. Then, dragging Rich clear, they flung themselves flat.

The German hadn't noticed the grenade and he threw out the rifle and slammed the door just as it went off. In the enclosed space the sound was like a firework in a tin can, a metallic roar that seemed to combine the crash of an explosion with the striking of a gong. There was no further movement from inside and they kicked open the door. The boy who'd finally closed it lay in bloody rags, and two other men were sprawled at the far side. The bunker smelled of smoke, cordite, charred wood, blood and fresh excreta.

Coming up for air, Warley realised they were now in a series of connecting trenches. The sky was full of flares as the Germans further up the slope tried to make out what was happening, and they could see everything about them in the trenches quite clearly.

They seemed to have gone as far as they safely could; to go any further would take them out into the open again. As they waited, getting their breath back, setting up the Brens and swinging the sandbags into a new position that would protect them against fire from the slopes, another group of men stumbled round the corner. Jumpy as a cat since the death of his namesake, 000 Bawden almost hit the first one with a spade, holding his hand just in time as he saw it was Deacon, closely followed by Syzling.

'We knocked out a couple of machine-gun posts,' Deacon said gleefully. 'And old Frying hit one of the Teds with the Piat tube.'

They seemed to have control of the situation and became quite certain of their victory when they began to bump into men of the Baluchis who had followed up. They were all grinning but Warley set them to work at once, turning the defences to face the other way. Among the prisoners they had taken was an effeminate-looking young officer clutching a violin case. He handed over his pistol without fuss.

'Thiergartner,' he said. 'Maximilian Thiergartner. Lieutenant.'

'What are you going to do with that?' Deacon asked, pointing at the violin.

Thiergartner smiled. 'I think I shall need it to while away the long hours in a prison camp,' he said. 'Don't you?'

As they crowded together in the trench, the first mortar bomb came down. The Germans higher up the slope had evidently made up their minds at last where they were. As the second bomb dropped, a wounded man appeared on the lip of the trench, hobbling frantically for shelter. They were just reaching up to help him when there was another crash and he slid sideways and crumpled up at their feet, his face torn open by a splinter.

Farnsworth fumbled for his field dressing but Thiergartner was quicker. Laying down the violin case, he was already producing bandages and lint. Without a word, they knelt beside the injured man and dressed the wound together. As they straightened up, Farnsworth eyed the German; then he reached into his battledress blouse and produced a packet of cigarettes.

'Have a fag,' he said.

They had seen Warley's Very light go up from the other side of the river and heard the renewed fighting after the lull.

The wounded were coming back in a trickle now, first the stretcher-bearers and then the walking wounded, pale with shock and pain, their bandages bright with blood. One or two of the leg and arm injuries were able to say what Warley was doing, and immediately Tallemach pushed the Engineers forward.

'Footbridges,' he insisted. 'Footbridges only for the time being! Let's get the men across!'

The footbridges were flung over the river, rickety swaying affairs on boats, pontoons and kapok bales that allowed only one man at a time to pass. The Engineers had also put a girder across the broken span of the road bridge, and here Rankin sent over most of his Punjabis, balancing precariously, clutching their weapons, in mortal terror of falling into the river below. But Tallemach had thought of that one, too, and he had the remaining assault boats in the water ready to pluck out anybody who did fall in.

'You can take your pick, Johnny,' the Engineer sergeants were yelling at the Indians. 'It's either Blondin crossing Niagara Falls on a tight wire or Oxford and Cambridge at Putney Bridge. And when you go at that bloody girder, run at it, and you'll be across before you know it.'

Most of the Punjabis made it across the girder. Out of those who missed their footing and fell, only one vanished from sight under the weight of his equipment before he could be rescued. Meanwhile, Fletcher-Smith was one of the first to reach the other bank and was already directing the major in command of the first company towards the ditch he'd previously used to approach the river.

'Keep moving, Johnny,' the Engineers were yelling. 'Keep moving! If you stand still, you're dead!'

Suddenly there was a confident sense of urgency about them, and it was a rewarding moment for Tallemach to realise they had their tails up again. You could feel it in the air. It was a battle-winning factor that only experience could gauge and, watching them, he began to feel better and really alive again.

Hidden by smoke, the tanks rumbled out of San Bartolomeo once more, the snouts of their guns pointing towards the river. German flares kept going up, but the wind had dropped at last and this time the smoke was just right. In San Bartolomeo there finally seemed to be room to move, and up above the clouds had broken up so that beyond the smoke it was possible to pick out stars. At last the imponderables were in their favour.

Fletcher-Smith was the first to fall into Deacon's Dip.

'The holy saints protect us!' O'Mara's accent grew broader in his excitement. 'You made it, me brave bhoy!'

'I was scared stiff, sir.'

'Bravery's being afraid of being afraid, my son. What have you brought?'

'The Punjabis from 9th Indian Brigade, sir. There's an air strike at dawn.'

'Holy Mother of God! Then get ahead to Major Warley and tell him, boy.'

The padre watched Fletcher-Smith go, humble at the courage he'd seen in the last forty-eight hours, never thinking in his humility that his personal calmness was its own kind of courage. He put it all down to Yuell. Yuell had a good battalion, and it showed not only in the way they behaved on parade but in the way they behaved in action. Most men were far too sensible for heroics, yet men who were brave in a body usually managed to be brave on their own as well.

The Germans were beginning to put mortar stonks down on their own former positions now, but Fletcher-Smith made it from Deacon's Dip. Pushing through the press of men huddling against the bank of the German trenches and foxholes, he found Warley and Jago just as they were wondering if they could push their luck and try for San Eusebio at first light.

'Fletcher-Smith!' Warley's reaction was the same as O'Mara's. 'So you got through!'

'Yes, sir. And the Punjabis are coming up behind me. The padre said he'd send 'em on.'

Warley grinned, haggard with tiredness and filthy with mud, but suddenly elated and optimistic.

Fletcher-Smith's words were still tumbling out. 'The brigadier said to wait for an air strike, sir. It's coming at first light. I heard him tell the CO of the Punjabis to let you know.'

'Did you, by God?' Warley grinned again. 'Well, that's wonderful news.' He turned to Jago. 'All right, Tony, we'll let the fly boys have a crack at 'em for a change and go in as the dust settles.'

The English colonel in command of the Punjabis arrived shortly afterwards. He was a thin languid man but he seemed to know his job and was in no hurry to take over from Warley.

Warley produced a map and indicated the road up to San Eusebio. 'I suggest we make a start up here, sir, but while they're keeping their eye on us, there's nothing to stop your lot going up the slope in front. It'll be a stiff climb, hands and knees stuff, but it'll shake 'em while they're looking one way for us to find you coming from the other. Perhaps you'd better take over now, sir.'

The colonel was an amenable man and, while he was willing to accept responsibility, he insisted on Warley running the show. 'You know the ground better than I do,' he said. 'Natural hazards, bunkers and so on. Have you got anybody you can trust to direct the attack up the road?'

'Yes, sir. Tony Jago here.'

'Then he'd better have the Baluchis.' The colonel turned to the captain commanding the Baluchis. 'Keep in close touch with Captain Jago. Give him his head and support him.'

As the first faint light began to appear, they could just pick out the spurs and peaks of the land in front. Then, against a clearing opal sky, they saw San Eusebio and the tower of the church emerge from the shadows and, soon afterwards, the bulk of Monte Cassino and the dark silhouette of the Monastery. Behind them, in the river valley, there was an incredible racket going on. The fields were covered with smoke because Tallemach had brought up every smoke shell he could get hold of and the thick haze was drifting down the river on the faintest of breezes, moving infinitely slowly, obscuring the valley from view.

The Germans were dropping everything they could round the broken bridge, but Tallemach had sent the Engineers down the farm track from Capodozzi this time and a new bridge was going across near the disused ferry where Yuell's B and C companies had started. The Engineers expected to finish it shortly and the tanks were gathering on the slopes of the hills behind San Bartolomeo for the dash down. God alone knew how many they'd get across before the road gave way under their weight, but Tallemach was determined to try it. If they could get enough across to support Warley, there was a chance of getting into San Eusebio. With that in their possession, they could move vehicles down the tarmac road from San Bartolomeo.

The sound of the shelling had become like a monstrous iron foundry by now, and Warley was explaining carefully what he wanted, confident his men would endure anything so long as they knew the reason for it.

'The only safe place round here's in San Eusebio,' he told them. 'That bluff behind'll protect us from the German guns. So see that we get there.'

He'd just lit a cigarette when he snatched it from his mouth again and threw it away. Standing with his head up, his eyes were fierce and elated under his helmet. He looked a hundred years old with the strain and the dirt that smeared his features. The colonel of the Punjabis and the captain of the Baluchis were staring upwards, too, listening as the sound Warley had heard increased rapidly, swelling until the whole sky seemed to be full of it.

Someone laughed and there was a thin cheer because they all knew by now what it was. It began to fill the whole of their existence, and Warley glanced round him for the pink identification panels and saw they were in place.

'Where are they?' Jago said, staring round him. 'Where are the bastards?'

He was moving with certainty again now. The fears that had been growing on him had vanished. The excitement and the noise and the willingness of the men around him had carried him forward. But the layer of courage was thin and brittle and he knew it would last only as long as the forward movement lasted. Like Warley, like all of them, he needed rest – a long rest. A man had only so much to give and when it was gone he was nothing but a husk.

He jerked a hand. 'There they are! End of the valley! Coming in from the north!'

They became silent again as the roar of aircraft continued to echo backwards and forwards between the hills. Then they saw the aeroplanes pass between two crests, small dark machines laying over in a steep bank as they wheeled into position, coming in, in a long slanting run, as though they intended to knock off the top of the church tower with their wing-tips.

Captain Reis was in the church. Since he'd received the reports of the British breakthrough and the disappearance – dead or captured – of Lieutenant Thiergartner, he'd had a premonition of disaster and had gone to the church to light a candle and attend Mass. Though the tower of the church was tottering and the nave open to the sky, the rest of the building was still in use. Since there were hardly any villagers left, the worshippers were all soldiers and, because most of his men were not Catholics but Lutherans, there weren't many of them.

It was the clearing sky that troubled Reis most. He'd noticed as he'd wakened before daylight that it was full of stars, and it had seemed an omen, for without doubt the low clouds and rain had been a great factor in the defence so far.

As the old priest stood before the altar, invoking the blessing of the Madonna, the sound of the aeroplanes came to Reis' ears. Almost immediately, the walls shuddered and gusts of air blasted through the church as a succession of explosions grew into one cataclysmic roar. As the first whorls of dust curled in through the broken stonework and the soldiers jumped to their feet, the old priest turned automatically and gave them absolution.

The explosions were increasing. The earth quaked, walls cracked and bulged; and as the rafters came down, Reis saw a great oak beam fall in a shower of plaster to crush two men hurrying for the door. Struggling up, his lungs filled with dust, he saw several more men caught in the open, hugging the ground, their faces drawn and pale with shock. One of them got to his feet in a panic and started to run, only to be flung against a wall by blast in a smashed bundle of flesh, bone and clothing.

For a second or two there was a lull and Reis struggled outside to dash to his strongpoint, only to stumble into a welter of smoking craters. Then, as the next salvo of bombs arrived, it seemed as if the gates of Hell had opened and he could see right into it. As San Eusebio erupted in destruction, he was aware of his body being struck by fragments of stone and wood and a shower of fine dirt. The walls about him seemed to dissolve and he saw what was left of the church tower lift, going upwards like an elevator before it crumbled, fell apart and came down in pieces on the ruins.

The place was still full of flashing light and his ears were hammered by the smack of the bombs, his body flung in a series of jerks against the revetments of the trench where he now crouched. The ground in front of him was filled with bouncing stones and bricks and fragments of timber, and a great drifting cloud of dust and pulverised soil. A blackness like that of night enveloped him, and on his tongue was the taste of scorched earth. He climbed from the trench and groped his way forward through the fog, crawling, falling and stumbling until eventually hands reached up and he was pulled head-first into another trench by his men. Lifting his head again, he saw the church had gone completely, the stumps of pillars sticking up like broken teeth, and he wondered what had happened to the priest.

Then, suddenly, there was silence except for the fading sound of engines. San Eusebio was a ruin. It had been damaged before but now it was nothing but a tumbled heap of stone, its splintered timbers sticking out of the rubble like shattered bones; stones, tiles, woodwork were all flung in incredible confusion like a child's playthings scattered in a temper; flames were appearing already, and he could see soldiers dragging themselves into the daylight.

Feeling dazedly about as he climbed into the open again, trying to find survivors among the broken rafters and masonry, Reis bent low to avoid presenting a target, thankful that the bombardment had stopped but knowing perfectly well that it was only the prelude to another kind of horror. He had lost all sense of time but, as he moved about, slowly recovering his wits, the responsibility of command began to act as a stimulant and reduce the impact of fear.

A few more soldiers appeared and he managed to instil in them some of his own determination, so that they stumbled off in some semblance of order to the strongpoints on the outskirts of the village. Then a corporal, his uniform torn, his face covered with blood, came staggering towards him, his eyes staring. But as Reis reached for him, he heard the sound of a British Bren, and the air became full of bullets swishing and cracking above his head.

He knew at once what it meant and, releasing the corporal, he jerked a hand at the men still struggling from the trench he'd shared with them and set off running down the street.

As the RAF bombers vanished, the British artillery opened up from the other side of the river, hammering every known German artillery position. For once the spotting aircraft could see, and Yuell's information had been sound. To the men just scrambling from the captured enemy positions, it seemed an unbelievable concentration of fire. As they ran forward, San Eusebio was still hidden by smoke and dust, and for a moment the German guns were silent. Then, as they recovered, they began to put down a counter-barrage; but the running men escaped the worst by the speed at which they crossed the stretch of land to the steep slopes below the village.

It was quite unnecessary to issue orders. Everybody knew exactly what to do because they'd done it a dozen times already on the way up Italy. There was only one way to go –

forward – and they scrambled up the hillside, leaving the wounded where they fell. But the climb was very steep and a whole shower of mortar bombs was dropping on them, while crossfire came from machine-guns higher up the slopes. As Warley had said, there was only one safe place to be, and that was in San Eusebio itself where there were cellars and buildings to hide in.

Slinging their weapons across their backs, they struggled up on hands and knees with the German machine-guns spitting over their heads because they couldn't be depressed sufficiently to hit them. The grim bit came when they had to rush the machine-gun positions which should in theory have been blotted out by the artillery. As usual, however, the infantry had to finish the job by demolishing them with hand grenades.

They came at last to a stretch of wire by a broken wall, but there were plenty of gaps in it and they were through them at once. Their first sight of the defenders of the village was of the backs of German machine-gunners, facing and firing steadily down the road towards where Jago's men were approaching. Farnsworth threw a grenade. The German gunners fell sideways, and a whole line of other Germans popped up like rabbits from their trenches to find out where the bomb had come from. Gask got the lot with a Bren he'd set up, and then they stood panting and exhilarated, aware that they'd reached their objective.

'I think I've mislaid a lung somewhere,' Warley said.

As he spoke, there was a colossal crash that sent them diving for cover at once, their bodies battered by a shower of dirt and stones that also obscured the view.

'That's an 88,' Farnsworth said. 'And bloody close, too. Point-blank range, I reckon. They'll have got the bastard dug in somewhere.'

Warley looked about him. The bombing had had a cataleptic effect on the Germans for a while, but they were recovering quickly and unexpected points of resistance were already beginning to appear.

'We've got nothing to touch an 88,' he said. 'I think we could do with one or two tanks up here.'

eight

As it happened the tanks weren't far away, and they were itching for a fight.

They had moved forward slowly under low-revving engines, their main armament loaded with high explosive. Armour-piercing shot would come later as they prepared to meet German tanks and self-propelled guns, but for the moment they'd been told to help the infantry. Signalling would doubtless be by shouting when they got into position, because nobody placed much reliance on the infantry radios and they all preferred the old well-tried methods such as tracer ammunition or Very flares.

Loaders swung open the main armament breech blocks and thrust home a round of ammunition until the rim tripped the extractors and closed the breech automatically. Belts of ammunition were dragged from their boxes and threaded into the machine-guns. Then, as the guns were cocked, the orders came from the leader of the first troop.

'Hello, Tiger Two. Our friends are in San Eusebio and it's our job to support them, so you go like the clappers as soon as you're across. I shall lead and the rest of you will come as fast as you can after me. And keep a bloody sharp look-out for this road as you move down to the bridge. The edges are soft so you'd better stay slap in the middle.'

Under the smoke screen, the Engineers had finally spanned the river by the disused ferry and the Yeomanry's first tank came hurtling towards it down the long narrow track from

Capodozzi. At the end, it slowed and edged on to the bridge and crossed without a shell being fired against it. The road behind it had been churned up by its tracks, but the troop leader radioed back encouragement to his next in line.

'The road's holding, but it's a mess, so don't stop. It ought to support half a dozen of us.'

The second tank made the journey, like the first, in record time, rattled over the bridge to the far side and, still under cover of smoke, began to edge after the troop leader towards the slopes of San Eusebio. But Germans were obviously suspecting something – or else from high up on Monastery Hill in the clearing weather they had seen the tanks moving in Capodozzi – and shells began to drop through the smoke near the bridge. None of them struck it, however, and the third tank came down at the same speed as the others. Half way along the road, it seemed to slither sideways and the sergeant in command yelled in alarm.

'Slow down, driver! You'll have to take it more carefully.'

They made it to the bridge, and crossed with the splinters from the German shells rattling against their armour plate.

On advice from the third tank, the fourth tank took the road at a gentler pace, because the edges were beginning to crumble and it looked a bit dicey. As it crossed, the fifth tank followed.

Six tanks made it, and Tallemach was just about to ask for more when a German shell carved a chunk out of the road, scattering its muddy surface all over the fields. It was obvious there would be no more tanks across for the moment and it was possible that the bridge itself would be destroyed before long; but six Churchills *were* on their way up to San Eusebio, and with the smell of success in the air at last, it seemed that the situation needed urgently reinforcing.

As he reached for the telephone, Tallemach saw General Tonge standing alongside him. Heathfield was just behind him but Tallemach noticed that he was saying nothing, so quiet he might have been attending a convocation of bishops.

'What the devil's going on?' Tonge demanded abruptly.

'We're into San Eusebio, sir,' Tallemach said. 'We've had a message from the Yorkshires. The Baluchis and the Punjabis are with them, but they've come to a halt at the moment and they've asked for the tanks.'

'And the tanks?' Tonge said.

'We have six across, sir. Now the road's gone and I'm afraid that's it for a bit. But the six we've got across ought to be a help and we've still got the vehicle bridge intact, together with a footbridge. We ought to be able to get more across soon.'

Tonge didn't waste time asking any more questions. 'Let's have the 11th Indian Brigade up,' he said briskly. 'Give me a telephone. There's talk of sending them along to Cassino, but I doubt if they need 'em and we could do with them here. And, Wallace, get in touch with Rankin and tell him we want every man he's got up here. He can forget Castelgrande for good. We're not going to make any gains there.'

The fighting in San Eusebio had become a mosaic of grim little encounters over small distances, a game of hide and seek in craters and the ruins of buildings, each of which could and often did conceal a man with a gun. In addition, the Germans higher up, aware that they'd lost their strongpoint, were dropping shells on the outskirts of the village now, and the British soldiers were seeking out cellars and digging in, preparatory to the next move forward. Until they could reach the far end, where the road swept into it from the river, they couldn't feel safe. Once there, the bluff behind the village would protect them; but until then it was a yard-by-yard fight through the rubble, with unexpected points of resistance appearing in the shape of self-propelled guns which had been sealed inside houses with only their snouts protruding.

Sniping had also come into its own because the rubble was a sniper's dream. Although mortaring and machine-gun fire was a general hazard, the personal menace of someone who was able to pick you off without being seen seemed infinitely more dangerous and terrifying. There was a particularly troublesome German concealed in a house above the road where Jago was watching from behind a bank, and he was glad to hear the rumble of tank engines. Running back down the road, keeping out of sight behind the curve of the land, he met the leading Churchill as it approached and waved it to a stop. As the turret lid lifted, he raised his voice and bellowed.

'Don't stick your head out. There's a sniper. In the tall flat-faced house in front of you. Can you stick a couple of shells into it for us?'

'No sooner asked than done, old boy,' the tank commander said, clanging the lid shut again. 'Gunner, flat-faced house in front slightly to the right. Give him a couple of rounds when I say and make no mistake about it. Bring the bloody thing down. Take her forward a bit, driver.'

The tank's engine puffed exhaust smoke as the driver put his foot down, and it nosed into the road, tracks clawing for a grip.

'Traverse right,' the commander ordered. 'On. Now to give that bugger one in the breadbasket.'

The Besa rattled in rhythmic harmony to make the hidden German keep his head down, just in case there was a panzerfaust waiting for them with a rocket bomb.

'Okay, gunner. Fire!'

The gun banged and lunged on the recoil, smoke oozing from its open breech until the loader rammed home another round. The first shell had plonked solidly into the front of the house and exploded, gouging out two walls with the result that the building now appeared to be balanced on the corner of the two remaining ones.

'Stick the next right on the corner, gunner.'

The second shell brought down the rest of the house in a cascade of bricks and tiles, leaving a dead man in a grey uniform, his feet trapped among the timbers, hanging head down above the settling dust and drifting smoke.

'Got the bastard,' Jago said but, just as he rose to his feet, Corporal Wymark stepped from cover ahead of him and a shot from the ruined house stopped him dead in his tracks. Shocked, they watched as he dropped his rifle, one hand groping forward like a blind man feeling his way. Then his knees buckled, the hand went down to break his fall, and for a moment he squatted on his heels, before sinking back as his legs slowly stretched out and he finally lay sprawled, his arms wide, staring at the sky.

Jago was still wondering what to do about him when Duff dashed forward, bent double and dragged him to cover. Bending over the injured man as the stretcher-bearers arrived, Jago turned to Duff.

'That was a bloody daft thing to do,' he said. 'Why didn't you leave it till the armour had sorted the bastard out? He might have got you too.'

'Well – ' Duff's small face puckered with the effort of thinking – ' 'e's got four kids. I've only got two, so it's only right, innit?'

Jago looked at him wonderingly, then turned to the tank commander peering through his half-opened hatch.

'Can you see an opening to a cellar from up there?' he asked.

'Yes.'

'Give him one in the eye then, will you? He must still be in there.'

Whether the third shell killed the sniper or not, it effectively blocked his view because the rest of the walls fell down over the hole and Jago's men were able to move forward once more.

Warley was having similar problems on the other side of the village. Without tanks, a man was constantly having to show himself for a fleeting instant to draw sniper fire, while others with Brens sprayed the marksman as soon as he revealed his position by firing. Working together, Gask and Henry White had already disposed of three in this manner, but nobody could call it an easy way of doing things.

As the Germans were killed off one by one, they made their way into the centre of the village by a series of quick dashes across open ground, from one cellar to another, from one ruin to the next. Then Warley was puzzled by the sound of a tank engine turning over quietly nearby. It appeared to come from the building next to the one they were occupying, but no tank was visible and, crawling round the back, CSM Farnsworth returned with the information that it was sealed inside.

'Seems to be a job for the Yeomanry,' Warley said.

They waited for what seemed hours until the Churchills appeared, lumbering through the debris. The leading machine had been brewed up by an anti-tank gun, but the gun had been knocked out at once and the other five tanks were now roaming through the village, waiting to be given targets. As the new leader fired on the house where the concealed Germans were waiting, it collapsed like a pack of cards and Warley's men stormed forward. The tank, still intact, lay beneath the debris, its engine running, covered with bricks, timbers and rubble. One surviving member of the crew climbed out and gave himself up. Only the fact that the commander had had to run his engines to charge his radio batteries had enabled them to discover it.

By this time, they were all hungry because they'd had no hot food since long before crossing the river. The radio sets were also out of action again, because the minute one of the long aerial antennas was put up it brought sniper fire or mortar bombs down on them. By this time, also, several of the houses were burning and the place was full of acrid yellow smoke which added to the difficulties. And then there were the rats. The bombing had disturbed whole colonies of them and, instead of being stunned by the blast, they seemed more active than usual, scattering in dozens every time the men made their way into a cellar.

Near the Piazza Roma in the centre of the village, they were held up again from the ruins of a small hotel. CSM Farnsworth worked his way forward to have a look at it and pinpointed the German strongpoint. Bellowing in his iron voice, he directed the fire of one of the Churchills and, as the building collapsed, a handful of Germans appeared with their hands in the air. He lined them up against the walls of the building where he crouched, and handed them over to 000 Bawden.

Farnsworth had an idea that there were more Germans in the ruins, only waiting for them to move away before setting up the strongpoint again. Turning to see who was with him, he caught Martindale busily lighting his pipe for a quick, soothing puff during the lull in the fighting.

'Put that bloody thing away,' he snapped. 'You think the Teds are blind? It's worse than a radio antenna. They can see the smoke and they know when you're coming.'

Martindale stuffed the pipe away, but it was still alight and he was itching to put it back in his mouth. It was always a pity to waste a good glowing bowl of tobacco, and he decided to wait until he was out of sight.

There didn't seem to Farnsworth to be enough of them to tackle the ruins by rushing them, so he decided on bluff. Spreading his men out, he sent them ahead among the ruins on either side. Martindale was with them, his hand already moving towards his pocket. Watching them vanish, Farnsworth rose to his knees and lifted his head.

'You lot in there,' he bellowed. 'I hope to Christ there's one of you understands English and knows what I'm saying because, if you're not out in two minutes, you're for it.' Raising his voice, he bellowed. 'Corporal, bring up that flame-thrower! But keep it out of sight in case the bastards spot you. Let it go when I give you the word.'

There was no flame-thrower but in the silence that followed Farnsworth shouted again. 'It'll be bloody funny being burned alive first and then having the fire put out when the sewer fills the cellar.'

There was another long silence. Then a voice came from the ruins.

'Stop! Stop! We come out!'

Twenty-five more men crawled out, their hands in the air, their eyes circling the square for the non-existent flame-thrower and the leaking sewer. As they were marched away, Farnsworth paused, listened, then pulled the pin from a grenade and tossed it into the hole through which they'd appeared. As it exploded there was a scream and he gave a nod of satisfaction.

'Thought so,' he said.

They were just moving off again, keeping well to the walls, when, just ahead, a figure stepped into the road. Half way across, a burst of Spandau fire stopped it dead. It was Martindale, his pipe in his mouth once more, and they all saw his stare of disbelief and heard the protest – unidentifiable but quite clear – that came from his throat as the pipe dropped away and clattered on to the road. As he fell, they knew he was stone dead. He had been hit in the chest and stomach, and as he rolled over, the blood glistening in the sunshine, they saw his insides spilling out.

The hatch of the leading tank lifted a fraction. 'I'll find the bastard,' the commander said.

But as the tank moved slowly up the street it suddenly stopped dead with a violent metallic clang. His head down,

Warley thought it had fired its gun. Then, looking up, he noticed there was something odd about it and saw that all the boxes of spare ammunition, the jerricans of water, bedrolls and bundles of camouflage netting on its sides had vanished. It had been hit. A man rolled out of the turret and with quick jerky movements fell into the ditch. It looked odd and almost comic until a second figure appeared from the turret, covered with blood and minus a leg. At the same time, the man crouching next to Warley sagged back and sat down, his head lolling. At first Warley thought he was the victim of a sniper, because there was a small hole in his temple, but then he realised he must have been killed by a fragment from the 88 mm shell that had hit the tank.

The man who had lost a leg was frantically demanding to know when the stretcher-bearers were going to come, and when Warley said 'Soon' he gave a bitter laugh. Evans the Bomb found a scrap of abandoned blanket and put it over the dead infantryman's face, and tried to lay another over the tank man; but the tank man seemed fascinated by the dreadful injury he'd suffered and pushed it aside, staring at the blue-white splintered bone among the bloody flesh and trying to brush away the flies that had appeared from nowhere.

The other tanks had backed away behind the ruined buildings.

'It's a self-propelled gun,' Farnsworth was saying. 'The bastard's just between those two houses.'

'Frying,' Deacon said to Syzling. 'Now's your chance. Come on. Let's get the sod.'

Moving to the side, crawling over the rubble, the two of them managed to get within fifty yards of the gun and Deacon gestured.

'Let him have it, Sizzle,' he said.

He wasn't ready when Syzling fired, and the bang as the gun was hit startled him. The turret seemed to swell and change shape, and smoke came from it in slow oozing coils.

275

'Give him another,' Deacon said.

This time, men leapt from the rear of the gun and began to run down the street. Deacon's Bren brought them down and he slapped Syzling on the shoulder, amazed at the amount of affection he felt for him. Syzling's reaction was a dull stare and a slow, spreading grin.

All morning, they fought through the ruins in a confused nightmare of small actions, from craters to rat-infested cellars, and from rat-infested cellars to ruined houses; sometimes even grateful for the shelter of a stinking sewer to escape a stream of bullets. One or two of them distinguished themselves. Deacon and Syzling, operating together in a strangely joyous sort of union, used the Piat again and again as a miniature field gun, gleeful at their own success.

Nevertheless, the Germans were still fighting back with the military professionalism that had sustained them through nearly five long years of war and eighteen months of defeat after defeat. Long after their flanks had been by-passed, small parties were still resisting, and a last stand took place in the cemetery. Headstones and weeping stone figures lay chipped and crooked and vaults lay open, smashed by mortar bombs. In some of them were uncoffined bodies, one on top of another, the remains of the poor, shrunken in death. The stench was appalling.

Farnsworth turned to Warley. 'I think we've got 'em on the run at last, sir,' he said.

But, as he spoke, what must have been the last German tank in the area appeared. It was covered with dust and rubble, looking as though it had been concealed inside a house and had finally come out to be used for its proper function. As it nosed round the corner, they all ran like hares, diving behind walls and into craters.

'Syzling!'

Once again Syzling and Deacon went into action, but this time their efforts were an anti-climax. Syzling did what he'd always normally done but had failed so magnificently to do during the whole of that day. He overlooked the angle of trajectory and, just as the tank appeared, the bomb slid out of the tube and dropped among the rubble just out of reach.

'Run,' Deacon yelled, and the two of them took to their heels and leapt into a bomb crater on top of everybody else to watch mesmerised as the huge tank swung into the street.

As it turned, the turret lid lifted and a German appeared, holding a stick grenade ready to throw. Why he was throwing a grenade when there was a gun available nobody ever knew because at that moment the lanky figure of Corporal Gask appeared from the ruined houses beyond the tank, raced up behind it, leapt on to its back as if he were hurdling, shot the German, pushed a grenade down the hatch and slammed it shut. It was all over in a second or two.

The 'whanngg' of the grenade inside the tank stopped it dead. There was no movement, and cautiously they lifted their heads.

The last burst of fighting took place round what had once been the mayor's office but, with the tanks hammering at it and the Brens chipping away at the window frames, the place began to dissolve into brick dust and fragmented stone. Eventually, a white sheet on the end of a pole appeared and wagged furiously.

'Cease fire!' Warley yelled.

As the firing stopped, a man stumbled out with his hands above his head and stood against the wall, cowering, obviously awaiting the blast of weaponry. When nothing happened, more men began to appear, dazed-looking but glad to be alive.

The last man out was Reis. Tall and straight-backed, his heart in his mouth because men in the heat of battle were sometimes too excited to check, he lifted his hands and prayed he'd survive to go home to his wife; something he could never have expected to do on the Russian front where you fought to the death like animals. As he stepped forward, McWatters knocked him to his knees with a blow between the shoulders from his rifle butt.

'Ye geikit Fascist bastarrd,' he snarled.

As his finger reached for the trigger, Warley knocked up the gun and shoved him aside.

'Yon's a Nazi hoor!'

'He looks uncommonly like the chap who let us fetch in our wounded,' Warley said calmly. 'Push off, McWatters. I'm running this show, not you.'

They grouped together again, their eyes flickering warily over the fronts of the houses. Apart from odd shots from the other side of the village, the fighting seemed to have ended and they were safe now because the spur of the escarpment behind the village protected them.

The dust settled slowly and the outlines of buildings emerged, then the ground beyond, scarred with craters and marked with smashed and splintered trees and the usual litter of war – German rifles, ammunition belts, old grenades, rags, paper – always paper – and here and there the grey flattened shapes of dead Germans. The village was a mass of rubble that stank of burning timber, explosives and the new dead.

The Germans were being rounded up in large numbers now. A sergeant-major with an Iron Cross, First Class, marched forward with his hands in the air, a starved-looking Italian boy of no more than fifteen walking behind him with a machine-pistol, a broad grin on his angelic face. Suddenly everything had gone quiet and all they could hear were voices – British voices – calling to each other.

As Warley drew a deep thankful breath, he saw Jago coming towards him.

'Tony! You okay?'

'Yes. You?'

'Yes. I think we've got the place.'

The captain of the Baluchis appeared shortly afterwards, followed by the colonel of the Punjabis.

'I think we'd better send a runner back to give them the gen,' the colonel said.

Warley saw Fletcher-Smith standing nearby. There was blood on his face but he was unhurt and it seemed that the blood belonged to someone else. Who better, he thought.

It was well into the afternoon when Fletcher-Smith appeared once more at Tallemach's headquarters. Tonge was there when he was brought in.

'You again?' Tallemach said. 'How did you do it this time?'

'Same as when I went back, sir,' Fletcher-Smith said. 'Down the ditch and across the stone bridge. It was nothing like as bad as last time.'

Tallemach smiled. 'This is getting to be a habit,' he said. He drew Tonge to one side. 'I think this chap deserves something, sir,' he said. 'This is the third time he's crossed the river under fire.'

When Fletcher-Smith had finished his report, Tonge moved forward. 'You'd better go and get some food,' he advised. 'Then find yourself a snug corner to wait for your people to be relieved.'

Fletcher-Smith stiffened. 'With your permission, sir, I'll rejoin my battalion.'

Tonge studied him carefully. There was no suggestion of false heroism about him.

'Crossing that bridge again?'

'They're getting jeeps and lorries across now, sir. They won't worry about me. And I was there when it started, so I'd like to be there when it finishes.'

'Why?'

Fletcher-Smith considered. There appeared to be only one answer. 'We're rather a good battalion, sir,' he said.

As Fletcher-Smith vanished, Tallemach smiled. 'I think this must be the beginning of the end for Jerry, sir,' he said. 'Funny we should think we were going to fail.'

Which raised quite a point, Tonge decided. He'd already made up his mind that Heathfield must go and had been working out the ways and means of doing it when he realised he'd have to be rather more circumspect about it than he'd intended.

Even before success had begun to appear from the fog of defeat, Heathfield had been curiously defiant.

'If I'm to be accused, sir,' he'd said, 'thank the Lord I'm being accused of attacking, not retreating.'

Now, with success snatched out of chaos by the ordinary fighting man, Tonge imagined that Heathfield's budding political instinct might even incline him to expect praise. Because, consider it how he might, Heathfield's plan *had* come off and, in the end, he'd been shown to be right; ironically because he'd stubbornly persisted when the others had been inclined to throw in the sponge. The fact that his rightness had only been proved by better men of lesser rank was nothing to do with it, and Tonge could hardly chuck out someone whose ideas had worked, whose pertinacity had paid dividends – even if, by all the rules, they ought not to have done. He'd have to wait and give him enough rope to hang himself. He had a suspicion it wouldn't take long.

'Another case,' he observed to Tallemach, 'of the private soldier saving his senior officer's reputation.'

'Yes, sir,' Tallemach said. 'I suppose I've a lot to be grateful for.'

Tonge lit a cigarette and turned towards his car. 'I wasn't thinking of you, Tom,' he said.

nine

They were relieved two nights later.

The wounded had all been evacuated by this time and the dead buried; the British first, laid under the stony soil just outside the cemetery where some of them had died. They'd been brought up from the river and from Deacon's Dip, from the machine-gun positions they'd rushed, from the wire, and from among the ruins of San Eusebio, their bodies not in the tidy attitudes you saw in Errol Flynn films but twisted bundles of flesh, blood and bones often blackened by high explosives. Major Peddy, the letter to his wife still in his pocket, was among them, along with Second-Lieutenant Taylor, Corporal Wymark, 766 Bawden, Martindale and a few more. They lay in neat rows. Army dead were like army living, always regimental. Crosses marked where they lay, neat white wooden markers made by the battalion carpenter of the Yellowjackets – because the carpenter of the North Yorkshires was under a cross himself – and they'd been painted by Lofty Duff who was a signwriter in civilian life.

The burial service had been conducted by O'Mara since the Anglican chaplain had still not appeared. Nobody minded the Latin. They wouldn't have minded if he'd done it in Swahili because O'Mara had been there with them. In fact, the service was a mixture of all denominations and perhaps his last words, spoken in English, touched them more closely than all the rest.

'In the hands of God the omniscient,' he said as he turned away, 'may the tears of Paradise fall upon them.'

After the British dead had come the Germans, but they made the prisoners do most of that because by this time, in the growing heat, the bodies had swelled and their skin had stretched so that their features had disappeared. Then, since they had to live in the place, they had started to tidy it up. A few dazed Italians had appeared from the ruins, hanging out white sheets as indications that they were on the side of the Allies and chanting repeatedly, *'Vivano i nostri liberatori!'*

Discarded weapons had been collected. A troop of Engineers had appeared with mine detectors, picket posts and tape to clear the minefields and to lay markings. Here and there, an occasional body was still being found; and a column of prisoners was moving rearwards under escort, passing the stretcher-bearers carrying their loads.

Warley reflected on what they'd achieved. He was saddened by their losses, though he knew casualties were not supposed to depress you because battles weren't won at the cost of a few black eyes. Jago was relieved it was over. He couldn't shake off the feeling that he was different. The violence of the night had jerked him out of his brooding, but he had decided he'd taken one chance too many and that from now on he was going to be more careful. Suddenly, he desperately wanted to survive the war.

They all reacted differently. Fletcher-Smith, now a corporal to fill one of the gaps that had been left by the dead, found himself pleased to be attached to HQ Company and told to keep his wits about him because, if he did, there was more promotion in the offing. Duff became a lance-corporal in his place. 'They're going to give 'im command of the war babies' platoon,' Parkin said, patting his head. 'All little fellers.' 000 Bawden, still lost without 766 Bawden, supposed that eventually he'd get over it because they'd never really had much in common beyond their names and the fact that they came from the same town. McWatters, who had fought his way from the river in his usual dour fashion, conducting his own little hate-filled war, expecting no mercy and giving none, considered the battle a victory for World Socialism. Henry White, looking like Mr Punch without his teeth, joined him in the view that the Germans were bastards. After all, they'd lost him a good set of dentures, hadn't they? Parkin's reaction to this disaster was as predictable as it had been to Duff's promotion. 'Always did say you'd lose them teeth, 'Enry,' he insisted. 'You shoulda changed 'em at the time of the Boer War.'

Lieutenant Deacon was proud that he'd added his name to the history books – because when the war was over and the history of the Italian Campaign was written, somebody would refer to Deacon's Dip just as they already referred to other such bumps and hollows on the world's surface as Fig Orchard, Aberdeen, Snipe and Kidney Ridge. He was still euphoric about Syzling who, scruffy as ever, was growing worried that his success might prove a dangerous thing, because Deacon now seemed to be expecting all sorts of things from him – even smartness.

Not a few of them were writing letters. Tallemach was trying to express to his wife his feelings about his son. 'I suppose we must be proud,' he was saying, unhappily conscious that his words were meaningless, 'and, since there are now only the two of us, we must learn to lean on each other more.' Gask, apparently unmoved by his destruction of a tank with a grenade, for which he'd been awarded an immediate Military Medal, was writing to his mother to tell her he'd been promoted sergeant. He was now aiming for company sergeant-major, he said, and was also increasing her allowance. He didn't mention the Military Medal in case she worried he'd been in danger.

CSM Farnsworth, aware that he would inevitably step into the dead Mr Zeal's shoes, wrote to his wife calmly, avoiding all talk of shells and machine-gunning, as he always had, making the battle sound like nothing much worse than a rough game of football. 'We've just been in action,' he said, 'but we came out of it not too badly. How's Jean's school report showing up, by the way? You didn't mention it in the last letter.' Just like a father away on business.

It was clear to them all now that the battle for Cassino had clarified. As they'd hung on grimly in front of San Eusebio the New Zealanders' attack on the town had finally succeeded, and they were now on Castle Hill, while the Gurkhas had got their entire battalion atop Hangman's. Slowly, gradually, the Monastery was being pinched out and they must now surely be in a position to throw the final punch. Next time, the Teds would not merely be pushed back a few miles. Next time the battle would be a masterpiece, a major operation with full orchestra and chorus. And, with clear indications that the winter weather was ending at last, they'd be able to mount it, not by companies and battalions, but by massed divisions.

It was barely dawn when Warley's men prepared to troop down the winding road from San Eusebio to the river. It still didn't pay to linger, because although San Eusebio was now in Allied hands, the Germans on the upper slopes could still drop shells in the flat fields along the riverside.

The Punjabis had taken over the town now. They were virtually untouched and were due to be supported by the King's Own from the 11th Indian Brigade. The bridges were still intact and the RAF was already seeking out the German guns higher up.

With that quaint custom of doing honours so beloved of the British Army, the captain of the Baluchis had conceded the privilege of leading the remnants of both battalions out of the town to Warley, and Farnsworth's iron voice was subdued as they formed up in the square.

'You will march out like the soldiers you never were,' he announced. 'Your own mothers won't recognise you. You're not scruffs. You're soldiers. So get those heads up. We said we'd lick these Ted bastards and we did. So look as if we have. When you get to the other side, they're going to be watching to see what we look like. So give 'em a good eyeful. You can be as mucky as you like, because you've been in a battle, but you'll move like soldiers. Get it?'

They got it. They looked like men who'd been through a whirlwind, buried and dug up again, and they were careful not to spoil the effect by shaving and washing too much. So they lined up in their torn and bloody uniforms – as they had earlier in the day for the war correspondents and photographers – several of them wearing bandages and carrying weapons which had been cleaned until they were spotless, fully prepared to create awe in the breasts of the onlookers.

Still Farnsworth wasn't satisfied. 'You wouldn't do credit to a whorehouse,' he said. 'Tighten that belt, that man! It's hanging off you like something hanging off a feller's boot. Adjust that strap, you! Up with that rifle! If I know him, the colonel's going to be across the other side waiting, and he's going to be proud of you or I'll know the reason why. You may not realise it, but you've just won a great victory. I've had it from Mr Warley, who got it from the colonel of the Punjabis, who got it from the general himself, brought back by our own special hero, Corporal Fletcher-Smith. The New Zealanders are into Cassino and we – you lot! – are in San Eusebio where we defeated the whole bloody Nazi nation. When everybody else was licked, the North Yorkshires were *not* licked. And that's the most important thing in a battle to any man. It's the question we always ask afterwards. Did we win? Well, let me inform you, we did. So look like it.'

They all knew what he was getting at – regimental spirit, that curious mystique which enabled soldiers to do things that ought to have been impossible, pride in themselves and their history. It wouldn't really matter to the people at the other side of the river what they looked like as they marched out. But it mattered to the North Yorkshires and that was the point Farnsworth was trying to make.

There was only one discordant note. Lieutenant Deacon's dulcet obbligato came through the darkness.

'Where's that bloody Piat, Syzling?' he was demanding.

'I lost it,' Syzling muttered.

'You can't lose something as big as a Piat, for God's sake!'

'Well, I did. I put it down.'

'Where?'

'I forgot.'

'I expect the bloody Punjabis collared it,' Deacon wailed. 'Good God, Syzling, that god-damned Piat ought to be framed and hung up in the regimental museum, the things we did with it! Didn't you realise?'

'No.'

'Sir!'

'Sir! No, I didn't, sir!'

Unity and amity seemed to have been forgotten. Things were back to normal.

Warley was occupied with his thoughts as he headed down the slope. The rain seemed to have gone for good because the sky was still clear and it felt warmer. Soon they'd be able to clean themselves up and wash and scrape off the mud without shivering. Mail would arrive and he intended to luxuriate in a bath in an avalanche of lather. They even knew where they were going – back to Trepiazze – and Warley fully intended to be billeted in Graziella Vanvitelli's home again.

It was another battle behind them, another step nearer home. It hadn't been a big battle compared with Alamein or Dunkirk, but, like Snipe and Kidney Ridge in the desert, it would be remembered. There'd be reports to write, more men to promote. There would probably even be a new colonel if Yuell's wound proved bad enough. In the meantime, as senior surviving officer, he supposed he'd be in command, and it would be pleasant to be running the show especially in Trepiazze, under the gaze of Graziella. He could remember every line and curve of her face, and her habit – half grave, half amused – of wrinkling her eyes at the corners as she explained something for him or sought a difficult English word. Then it struck him that, as commanding officer, he didn't have to share his billet with anyone and could have the whole house to himself if he wished, able to enjoy Graziella's company without Deacon bursting in, loud in his complaints about Syzling. He found he was looking forward to it enormously.

Yuell was sitting in a jeep in San Bartolomeo as they arrived. He looked pale and his leg was swathed in bandages. But he'd insisted on waiting for them to appear before he would allow himself to be taken away. Warley called for an eyes right and they gave him one that made their eyes click, while Warley threw him up a salute which would have done credit to the Brigade of Guards. Yuell returned it gravely. There was nothing more he asked for than this gesture from these men. His leg was agonisingly painful, he was full of dope, but he knew there was nothing now for him to do. He could rely on Warley to look after things. He'd arrived under Yuell's command four years before, a wide-eyed youngster still wet behind the ears and with a tendency to refer to the regimental colours hanging in Ripon Cathedral as 'those flags'. Now, he was capable of running the battalion and running it well, and Yuell intended to see that he was promoted into Peddy's place – and further if possible.

'Thank you,' he said to the jeep driver. 'That's all I wanted. To see them safe back. We can go now.'

There was hot food waiting for them in San Bartolomeo, and this time there was no shelling. And at long last there was dry straw to lie on, dry rooms to sit in, no longer the smell of damp and the chill of running water. Soon every bush and wall would be festooned with washed and drying clothing.

Several officers he knew came in to speak to Warley and congratulate him on what they'd done. He took it all as it came. They'd been told to take San Eusebio and they'd taken it. It was as simple as that. But now, before the quartermaster arrived with his new issues and they were still wearing the dirt of battle, there was a quiet happiness about him that was reflected in the faces of Jago, Deacon, Farnsworth, Gask, Fletcher-Smith and every single man who'd conducted himself with honour in the fight. *They'd* been there and these others had not. Only *they* knew what it had been like.

The thought ran through Warley's mind again and again. It produced a sort of contempt for other men, an unfair contempt, he knew, because their turn would come – very likely while he was sitting safely in Trepiazze holding Graziella Vanvitelli's hand. But it existed nevertheless. Henry of Navarre had summed it up exactly in a reply to one of his boastful generals.

'Go hang yourself, brave Crillon. We fought at Arques, and you were not there.'

That was the whole point of the thing. All that was left after you'd sifted through the rubbish dump of heroism and ineptitude, good will and jealousy, life and death – what soldiers lived on when they were too old to do anything else but remember. *They'd* been at San Eusebio and the others had not. Despite everything, it was curiously satisfying.

JOHN HARRIS

CHINA SEAS

In this action-packed adventure, Willie Sarth becomes a survivor. Forced to fight pirates on the East China Seas, wrestle for his life on the South China Seas and cross the Sea of Japan ravaged by typhus, Sarth is determined to come out alive. Dealing with human tragedy, war and revolution, Harris presents a novel which packs an awesome punch.

A FUNNY PLACE TO HOLD A WAR

Ginger Donnelly is on the trail of Nazi saboteurs in Sierra Leone. Whilst taking a midnight paddle, with a willing woman, in a canoe cajoled from a local fisherman, Donnelly sees an enormous seaplane thunder across the sky only to crash in a ball of brilliant flame. It seems like an accident... at least until a second plane explodes in a blistering shower along the same flight path.

JOHN HARRIS

LIVE FREE OR DIE!

Charles Walter Scully, cut off from his unit and running on empty, is trapped. It's 1944 and, though the Allied invasion of France has finally begun, for Scully the war isn't going well. That is, until he meets a French boy trying to get home to Paris. What begins is a hair-raising journey into the heart of France, an involvement with the French Liberation Front and one of the most monumental events of the war. Harris vividly portrays wartime France in a panorama of scenes that enthral and entertain the reader.

THE OLD TRADE OF KILLING

Harris' exciting adventure is set against the backdrop of the Western Desert and scene of the Eighth Army battles. The men who fought together in the Second World War return twenty years later in search of treasure. But twenty years can change a man. Young ideals have been replaced by greed. Comradeship has vanished along with innocence. And treachery and murder make for a breathtaking read.

JOHN HARRIS

THE SEA SHALL NOT HAVE THEM

This is John Harris' classic war novel of espionage in the most extreme of situations. An essential flight from France leaves the crew of RAF *Hudson* missing, and somewhere in the North Sea four men cling to a dinghy, praying for rescue before exposure kills them or the enemy finds them. One man is critically injured; another (a rocket expert) is carrying a briefcase stuffed with vital secrets. As time begins to run out each man yearns to evade capture. This story charts the daring and courage of these men, and the men who rescued them, in a breathtaking mission with the most awesome of consequences.

TAKE OR DESTROY!

Lieutenant-Colonel George Hockold must destroy Rommel's vast fuel reserves stored at the port of Qaba if the Eighth Army is to succeed in the Alamein offensive. Time is desperately running out, resources are scant and the commando unit Hockold must lead is a ragtag band of misfits scraped from the dregs of the British Army. They must attack Qaba. The orders? Take or destroy.

'One of the finest war novels of the year'
– *Evening News*

TITLES BY JOHN HARRIS AVAILABLE DIRECT
FROM HOUSE OF STRATUS

Quantity		£	$(US)	$(CAN)	€
	ARMY OF SHADOWS	6.99	12.95	19.95	13.50
	CHINA SEAS	6.99	12.95	19.95	13.50
	THE CLAWS OF MERCY	6.99	12.95	19.95	13.50
	CORPORAL COTTON'S LITTLE WAR	6.99	12.95	19.95	13.50
	THE CROSS OF LAZZARO	6.99	12.95	19.95	13.50
	FLAWED BANNER	6.99	12.95	19.95	13.50
	THE FOX FROM HIS LAIR	6.99	12.95	19.95	13.50
	A FUNNY PLACE TO HOLD A WAR	6.99	12.95	19.95	13.50
	GETAWAY	6.99	12.95	19.95	13.50
	HARKAWAY'S SIXTH COLUMN	6.99	12.95	19.95	13.50
	A KIND OF COURAGE	6.99	12.95	19.95	13.50
	LIVE FREE OR DIE!	6.99	12.95	19.95	13.50
	THE LONELY VOYAGE	6.99	12.95	19.95	13.50
	THE MERCENARIES	6.99	12.95	19.95	13.50
	NORTH STRIKE	6.99	12.95	19.95	13.50

ALL HOUSE OF STRATUS BOOKS ARE AVAILABLE FROM GOOD BOOKSHOPS
OR DIRECT FROM THE PUBLISHER:

Internet: www.houseofstratus.com including synopses and features.
Email: sales@houseofstratus.com
info@houseofstratus.com
(please quote author, title and credit card details.)